THE GREMLIN PRINCE

THE EMPOWERED SERIES
BOOK 1

USA TODAY BESTSELLING AUTHOR

HEATHER YOUNG-NICHOLS

The Gremlin Prince
The Empowered Series Book 1
USA Today Bestselling Author
Heather Young-Nichols

heatheryoungnichols.com

Also by Heather Young-Nichols

Shadow Coven

Haunted Magic

Cursed Magic

Stolen Magic

Fated Magic

Forever 18

Forever Grayson

Forever London

Forever Lennox

Heavy Hitter

Pushing Daisies

Daisy

Van

Bonham

Daltrey

Mack

Courting Chaos
Cross
Ransom
Booker
Dixon

Finding Love
Making Her Mine
Making Him Hers

Harbor Point
Love by the Slice
Love by the Mile
Love by the Rules

Gambling on Love
Highest Bidder
Highest Stakes
Highest Reward

Holiday Bites

All I Want

All of Me

The Fallout Series

Last Good Thing

Last First Kiss

Last Chance Love

With J.A. Hardt

Bound by Magic

With Amelia J. Matthews

Dirt on the Diamond

After Office Hours: Seducing the Professor

Chapter One

THE SOUND of the door slamming on its hinges chased me down the hallway as my shoes slapped quickly against the imported tile.

I needed to get to my room before they caught me. Even as quick as I was, they were quicker. The people who'd created, raised, and trained me were hot on my heels. Maybe if I'd worn tennis shoes instead of super cute wedge sandals, I could've made it.

"Alyssum Bracken, stop right there," he demanded in his official voice.

Three more steps would've gotten me out of the bright hallway and safely into the softness of my sanctuary. So close.

His official voice was the boom he used to control

The Assembly room and occasionally me. The voice that said he wasn't messing around and I'd regret it if I didn't do as he said. I stopped, although I wasn't going down without a fight.

"What?" I spat, crossing my arms under my breasts as I looked up at him.

His size intimidated most people, sometimes even Mom, but not me. With light-brown hair and gentle, brown eyes, even the solid muscles that bulged from under his shirt and his six-feet-plus height didn't scare me. He just looked like the big teddy bear who used to toss me around when I'd been a kid. No one agreed with me on the teddy bear part.

"The Assembly made their decision," he said, his jaw tense. "You must respect that."

"But he could—"

"There's no proof, and it's a waste of time to run off chasing ghosts." His face changed from the official mask to that of my dad and when he spoke again, it was back to a normal level. "Not to mention dangerous."

"I've done so much—"

He cut me off again by holding his hand up while shaking his head. "This is not a discussion. The decision is final."

"Ash," Mom intervened. She placed a hand on his arm and gave an almost imperceptible squeeze. "At least hear her out. This is not The Assembly room."

He took a deep breath and nodded without taking his glare off me. I looked a lot like my mother, which was part of what scared him. She was also small with blonde hair and blue eyes, the most beautiful thing he'd ever seen until I'd come along, according to him. And apparently, at my age, she could wrap a boy around her little finger without even trying. I was more likely to knock a guy over the head with a tree branch. Dad had no reason to worry about me in that area.

He worried anyway.

"I've done a lot of research, Dad. He's out there. I know he is." Relaxing a little when his jaw lost some of its tension, I continued. *Convince him or die trying.* "If I get the chance, I can bring him back."

"And what good do you think bringing Heath Sorrel back here will do? If he's still alive—and that's a huge *if*—we don't know that he'll be useful."

He asked the same question I hadn't been allowed to answer in the gallery, where our assembly was discussing the recent increase in tension with the Gobel community. They didn't want to hear anything I had to say. In the case of The Assembly, their questions were mostly rhetorical.

"You told me that the Sorrels were super powerful. Well, wouldn't that have been passed down to their child?"

"They *were* very powerful when they were alive." His deep, booming voice took on a different tone on the rare occasions he talked about his best friend. A sound that said he still missed the guy.

Glen Sorrel and my father had grown up together and it had been a heavy blow to my dad when Glen died. That was when my father took over as head of The Assembly. I'd been born a few years later, so I'd never had the chance to know them at all.

"This issue has been decided," he said more gently. "We will prepare for war and be ready if it should come."

He stalked away, his footsteps driving his point home with each heavy thud. My mother followed him closely. I took off into my room and slammed the large door behind me, hoping they heard it. Hoping I rattled the rafters throughout the stupid house.

To my father, I was still that little girl he'd fallen in love with the moment she'd been born. I often wondered if he'd ever see me as a grown-up. Someone who could contribute to our society. He'd trained me himself. He knew how strong I was yet remained content to let me waste my talent by sitting around the house.

Staying in my room for hours didn't help. I started going stir-crazy and looking for an outlet. My options were limited. The sun was setting and my ass would be in a world of trouble if I headed out to the copper mines alone after dark.

Instead, I fumed.

Leaving was dangerous with everything going on, but I knew I could make a difference. I just had to figure out how. If I'd been born a son, Dad would've let me go, no questions asked, but if he thought I'd let something like gender stand in my way, he was sadly mistaken.

With a little money, a car, and a credit card, I was all set. There were a few perks to being the daughter of your people's leader.

The only thing holding me back was me.

I'd never taken off on my own before and wasn't sure I wanted to push my parents that hard. Being Gremalian gave me a certain amount of freedom. I'd never had to deal with curfews or many rules, but to just leave without telling anyone would be a few steps too far.

Three soft raps on the door, Mom's signature

knock, brought me outside of myself. The door moved as she let herself in. I figured she'd come to me once my dad had calmed down since that was the way it always went with her.

Him first, then me.

"Alyssum, your father only wants what's best for you." She walked to the window looking out over the Delaware countryside.

Only Gremalians remained in Delaware, a small town on the Keweenaw Peninsula in very northern Michigan, miles from the nearest human city. Humans had abandoned it long ago. They hadn't been able to tough it through the harsh winters and had thought the copper supply had dwindled. In reality, Gremalians had chased the humans out as soon as someone had realized what the copper could do for us.

Our little town was remote enough that humans didn't venture up here too often anymore, which was nice. Gave us the opportunity to live our lives without having to worry about being discovered. Plus, we wouldn't have to share the copper. We also went to great lengths to guard against any human who might decide to go exploring.

Besides the "High Voltage" signs a few miles from town, our constant energy hummed in the air, which made humans uneasy. And if one happened to slip through, security did a mind zap thing—that was never fully explained to me—to make them forget. Or turned them into a vegetable. Luckily, that situation hardly ever arose.

"That's what he wants me to believe." I lay on my bed and stared at the ceiling, my hands behind my head, legs crossed at the ankles.

"He loves you very much and you know it." She paused the way she did when choosing her words carefully. "Saffron Sorrel was my best friend."

That got my attention. I bolted upright to get a look at her. She still had her back to me, her voice calm and even. The Sorrels were mentioned so rarely that I couldn't *not* pay very close attention.

"We knew each other a little before we all got married. But once we were, Ash and Glen were inseparable, so Saffron and I were too. For five years, your father and Glen made names for themselves within The Assembly, and eventually, Glen was elected and your father was by his side. Glen had big dreams for our people. He wanted..." Her memories were in a far-off place. "It doesn't matter." She sighed. "I was there when Heath was born and, I admit, I was a little jealous because we hadn't been blessed yet." She finally looked over with a tired little smile. "Losing the baby along with our friends was almost more than we could handle, but, Alyssum, losing you is something we could not bear. You understand what I'm saying?"

I knew what she was going to say. I'd heard it many times growing up and could recite the speech from memory. "Be careful... Don't goad anyone into any fights..."

I stopped talking as soon as I realized why my mom had come into my room in the first place. By telling me that she and my dad couldn't bear to lose me, she was warning me to behave. To be careful. If Mom was warning me and not outright telling me I couldn't go, then she was giving me permission to leave Delaware to see if I could find the Sorrels' son.

My eyes grew wide as my mother tossed a roll of cash my way. I snatched it right out of the air as she shoved a copper necklace in my hand, a small token to most people, but Mom was giving it to me because she knew it was important to send me out into the world with something that could help me heal. Copper was that for us.

"I love you, Mom."

She gave me a quick squeeze and left the room.

I yanked open the closet and pulled out a small, brown, leather satchel, tattered from years of use.

Even though I was jumping on the inside, I still took the time to neatly fold every article of clothing. No way would I be ironing anything when I got there. A few of my must-haves went into a red backpack: a couple of books and a laptop. I double-checked to make sure all the appropriate chargers made it in too. The only thing left to grab was my purse, which I found hidden half under the bed.

After one last look around, I grabbed the neck-lace—a teardrop charm hanging from a delicate chain—Mom had given me and shoved my phone into my back pocket. Power tingled across my skin as soon as I'd touched it. While I knew most of us carried copper when leaving Delaware, I hadn't given it much thought. It made sense that my mom would give me extra protection. Besides the healing capability, copper also enhanced our powers, some-thing I might need on the outside.

I pushed open the window on the south side and dropped the brown bag to the ground, then flung the backpack over my shoulders. The other window on the west wall overlooked the roof of our sunroom. Although I'd snuck out many times starting when I turned thirteen, this seemed different.

I was nineteen years old now and no longer sneaking off to meet Sage, former friend and first boyfriend to climb through the mines and revel in the surge we Gremalians got by being close to copper. Nor was I leaving to kiss that same boy for hours at a time on the banks of Lake Superior like I had the summer after I'd turned fifteen. I was running away to search for Heath, the son of our dead ex-leader, a boy I'd never seen and who may not have survived the car accident that had taken his parents' lives.

The first drop to the sunroom roof was only two feet, after which I used an old chimney pipe to shimmy to the ground before running and grabbing the first bag without stopping. Within minutes, I was on the road in the car my parents had bought me when I'd graduated high school.

Leaving after sunset worked to my advantage. I made it to Mackinaw City in good time, just over five hours. After another three on the road, I had to stop near Saginaw to sleep. My eyes had been sagging until, finally, it had become too dangerous to continue. I slept a bit, then took some time during breakfast at a Denny's to go over all the research again just to make sure I hadn't missed anything.

I double-checked the map for the exact location of the fiery car accident and the nearest hospital Heath would've likely been taken to, using my finger to trace the path from accident to hospital on the map to make sure my theory made sense. Then I was back on the road.

Although it would've been quicker to go through Canada, I went south, through Ohio, since I didn't have a passport or the time to get one. Twelve long hours later, every meal eaten with one hand on the wheel, I stopped at the first motel I'd crossed paths with in Putnam Valley, New York.

Since I'd arrived so late, I wasn't about to search for and compare motels. My room fit the appearance of an old-style, roadside type of accommodation to a T. I'd slept in worse places; at least it was clean. After a hot shower, the bed could've been made of nails and I wouldn't have noticed.

Tomorrow could've changed everything.

Chapter Two

Putnam Valley was small, but it was still much bigger than Delaware. With just over eleven thousand people, it looked exactly like I'd imagined it would. The feel of the tree-lined streets, how the pedestrians walked almost lazily down the street, and most of the shops being small mom-and-pop types instantly made me feel at home. There wasn't a big box store in sight.

When I walked into the diner-style restaurant—a place that looked like it hadn't been updated much since opening, all the way down to the crooked, worn sign that read "Frost's"—I found the table I wanted, in the corner away from everyone else. It was a perfect spot to watch the door as well as the street outside.

The black-haired, emo-goth high schooler with a nose ring to show her rebellion and more perk than her ensemble would have suggested didn't seem to mind when I asked if I could have the table in the corner. She returned right away with black coffee, or what my mother called *a bad habit.* I'd drink it hot or cold, with or without flavoring. It didn't matter to me as long as I got my fix.

Nervous energy set in once I had time to think. The internet had turned up a little information—a news article about the car accident and a follow up about the fact that the family that had been killed were still unidentified—meant that I might's had thousands of people to go through to find Heath. The articles mentioned, the family—a man, woman, and baby—and that they'd been taken to a hospital. I never found anything saying they died.

We knew that Glen and Saffron were dead. Our security team that had been sent saw them with their own eyes. They however did not see the baby. That was where the confusion was. It was determined that no baby could've survived the crash yet the security team left Putnam Valley before confirming.

The whole thing was daunting now that I was there but it was why I'd came.

Then he just walked right in, making my job that

much easier.

I felt it before ever laying eyes on him.

A blanket of warmth covered my body from head to toe, like a warm cocoon of safety telling me one of my own was nearby. He strolled in casually, wearing well-worn jeans and a dark-blue T-shirt. He had brown hair, short with a just-out-of-bed look that I knew had taken at least twenty minutes to perfect. He rested his elbows on the take-out counter, giving the plump, forty-something waitress a flirty smile, and dropped some money on the counter, which was rewarded with two large bags of food. Then he left.

It was *him. How did I get so lucky?*

It didn't seem like he'd sensed me but I'd sure sensed him, though, and man, was it intense.

His parents had been headed to New York City to blend in and protect their son from everything going on back home. Years ago, I'd found a news article with a photo of what had been left of their car after the firemen had put the flames out. My mom had ripped it from my hands as quickly as she could, but I'd already read enough details to start my journey. Once I'd narrowed down which hospital the Sorrels' six-month-old baby most likely would've been taken to had he survived, it wasn't too hard to connect the dots.

The internet was a wonderful thing because it had enabled me to find out that Alice, a nurse in the pediatric intensive care unit, and her husband had adopted a baby boy soon after. An orphan who had spent some time in the pediatric ICU where she'd worked, which made it a huge feel-good story. It had taken me months of research both in The Assembly's library and online to find Heath, but it had totally been worth it.

Even if no one would listen to me that the orphan was Heath Sorrel. Hell, they'd barely listen to me at all.

I followed him for two days after first seeing him in the diner, getting to know Putnam Valley and his routine, all the while trying to figure out how to insert myself into his life. He worked in an auto shop and seemed to enjoy his motorcycle. I should have figured he'd be doing something mechanical. We were extremely good with mechanics and technology. He took long rides in the evening and rode to work, even though he lived less than a mile away, so I decided work would be the easiest place to approach him. At the very least, meeting him at his job gave me a non-suspicious reason to be where he was.

Once I'd gotten a feel for Heath's schedule, I let a lot of antifreeze out of my copper-colored Mini

Cooper and drove around until steam billowed out from under the hood. The outfit I'd picked that morning—a dark-blue, flowing skirt that just brushed my knees with a pink tank top and a pair of strappy wedges—accentuated all the girliness I had to offer. Since I was short, extra height never hurt, and honestly, I liked the *skirt and tank top* look as much as the look I usually rocked with jeans, T-shirts, and workout clothes.

I walked past the open garage doors a couple of times, trying to determine if he was already working on a car. I didn't see or feel him anywhere. I took a deep breath and went around front, through the main door, and found him standing behind the counter, in the middle of a conversation with an older man.

That lovely warmth covered me again, maybe even more than before. The boy looked good. Standing six feet tall, if not slightly taller, with broad shoulders, a narrow waist, and hard muscles, along with a prominent vein running down his arms from the manual labor in the shop, made him much more imposing than the more rounded older man leaning on the counter. So hot as well.

They were clearly debating something, yet both of their faces were relaxed—playful, even. Apparently, I'd been really quiet because it took a full two minutes for either of them to notice me. Maybe a bell on the front door would have done them some good. I didn't usually fade into the background, but I could have been a drink cooler in the corner for the way they ignored me.

"Hey, young lady. What can we do for you?" The older one asked.

"My car is steaming." I pointed out the window at my pretty baby spewing white mist. "I was just driving around when it started." The old guy gave me friendly smile. My eyes went to Heath, although I shouldn't have assumed that was still his name, then quickly back. "I was hoping someone could look at it for me."

The older man put his hand on the younger one's shoulder and said, "I think my son here can handle that." Ah, so he was Heath's dad, Alice's husband, and seemed quite nice. I quickly went through all the information in my head, trying to remember his name. I came up with a big fat nothing.

"Sure," Heath said, running his fingers through his hair. "Can I have your keys?"

I handed them over and watched as walked out front and folded his large frame into my tiny car to pull it into one of the bays. He came back within a few minutes. I expected that. Gremalians and our way with mechanics. Should've been easy for him.

"Your radiator's bone dry," he said.

"Is that bad?" I asked, even though I knew it was. He smiled a beautiful smile as his light, cerulean eyes danced at my apparent cluelessness.

"Yeah, that's bad, but easy to fix. I don't think you were driving with it steaming long enough to do any serious damage," he explained. His dad came out of the office, so he added, "Tyler's bringing back more antifreeze. It'll be about twenty minutes. I'm going to check the radiator for a leak while we wait."

"How do you do that? Is there an instrument you use or something?"

A curl of hair fell over my shoulder and I twirled it around my index finger absently. I knew it would be considered flirting and I was okay with that. Twirling my hair really was a habit. But a habit that happened to help me out when I needed it to.

His brows furrowed like he was either trying to figure me out or hold back other words he didn't want to say. "Just water."

"You can go back and watch if you want," his dad said after I'd sort of forgotten he was there.

"Oh, I wouldn't want to get in the way."

"You won't. Go on back with Jensen."

His dad reacted as I'd hoped, but Jensen didn't seem to care either way.

Jensen Burkhardt waved me along, although it looked as though he did it grudgingly.

We passed two other cars and a few mechanics hard at work before getting to my Cooper. I stood back and watched him get started. It wasn't going as smoothly as I'd planned since, for whatever reason, perhaps too much time around humans, he wasn't picking up on anything.

A prickle started up my spine and covered my entire body. The hair on my arms stood on end. I frantically searched the room with my eyes, trying not to look out of place. A man with a curly mop of dark hair and a matching tuft on his chin came out from under the hood next to us. He asked Jensen a question. I wasn't paying enough attention to the words to know what he'd asked.

Jensen said something about grabbing a part for him and then said to me, "Oh, this is Aric."

I had a feeling that Aric was new to the shop because there was no way a Gobel had been around long and Jensen hadn't noticed or had a reaction. Aric and I stared each other down. His dark eyes, the same color of his hair, remained calm. Mine didn't.

"What are you doing here, Gobel?" My tone was

threatening, but I kept a polite smile on my face while taking a step toward him.

"The name's Aric Bramble and I suspect we're here for the same reason."

"How did you find him?" I seethed. No way should he be here with the Sorrels' son.

"That's not important. I'm not your enemy," he insisted. I scoffed. "Really. I'm trying to prevent a war. No biggie."

"What?"

I didn't believe him, and the muscles coming out of his grease-stained T-shirt were distracting me.

"Look, he's coming back," he said. "We should talk. I've got an apartment on Fifth." I raised an eyebrow, wondering if he was trying to set me up. "I'm sure your Spidey-sense can find me there tomorrow, after five," he added quickly just as Jensen rejoined us.

After a long bout of silence that made me uncomfortable, I asked, "So, what's that?"

Jensen looked at me like I was the dumbest blonde he'd ever seen, but I couldn't squander this chance with him. He drew his words out as if he were talking to a toddler. "The engine."

I had to giggle at the look on his face. "I know.

Figured I should ask a question. I feel stupid just standing here trying not to get dirty."

Aric went back to work on his side of the garage while I tried to forget he was there. I'd deal with him later.

Laughing a little, Jensen continued working until a kid who looked more like the tall, lanky, awkward boys I'd gone to school with showed up with the antifreeze. With the radiator filled, Jensen said he'd meet me inside after pulling around, so that was where I headed. His dad was pretty funny in those few minutes we had alone. He had the same easy-going manner I'd noticed in Jensen.

"So, how much do I owe you?" I started to open my pink crossover purse as my eyes fell back on him.

"No charge," Mr. Burkhardt answered, waving his hand in front of him.

"Oh, I can't do that."

"I insist. Just write down your name and phone number." He slid an invoice across the counter and my eyebrows went up. "For customer records and inventory of the antifreeze."

I nodded. I was going to do it either way, but I didn't want him to think I would give in too easily. Now that my information was there, I hoped Jensen would use it.

"Are you new to town or just passing through?" Mr. Burkhardt asked.

Jensen leaned against the back counter and crossed his arms over his chest while staring, annoyingly, at the back of his father's head. Even annoyed, he looked pretty sexy. Though I didn't think I wanted him to look at me the way he was glaring at his dad.

"Just exploring." I smiled. "I drove until somewhere looked like a good place to stop."

"Well, it was nice to meet you. Hey, if you've got nothing to do, there's a town picnic and fireworks display for Memorial Day." He turned the paper to read my name. "Alyssum Bracken. That's unique."

"It's a flower," Jensen and I answered at the same time, which brought a smile to my face.

"Most people don't know that." After another minute of awkwardness, I added, "Thanks again."

After glancing back at Jensen and his dad one more time, I left the shop.

Now I had two missions in Putnam Valley.

Convince Jensen to come back to Michigan and help us in the coming war.

And kill a Gobel.

Chapter Three

WALKING past each door of the only apartment complex on Fifth slowly, it didn't take long for the familiar prickling crept up my neck and the hair on my arms stood up the way it did whenever a Gobel came around. I pounded hard just below the cheap, gold 3B hanging above a peephole and heard, or rather felt, him coming to the door.

Aric didn't look surprised to see me; actually, he was unnervingly relaxed in a worn pair of cargo shorts and a black T-shirt.

Before he could get a word out, I grabbed his neck, shoving him inside against the far wall. It felt good to exert some energy.

"What are you up to?" I spat through clenched

teeth, giving my fingers an extra squeeze against his trachea, feeling his heart pound at the pulse point.

"Jesus, Alyssum." The words came out hoarse enough that I decided to loosen my grip just a couple of notches so I could hear him. "I'm here for the same reason as you are. To stop the war."

I smirked. "I don't want to stop the war. I just want to make sure we win it." After a little hesitation, I relaxed my hand and released his throat but backed up to put some distance between us. I folded my arms under my breasts the way I always did when I was giving my parents a hard time. Usually, though, with guys, it just made them look at my chest.

He was definitely a guy.

"Wouldn't it be even better if we could stop it from happening in the first place? I think he can do that. You do too, right?"

"I'm not telling you what I do or do not know, Gobel." I wasn't entirely certain what Heath— Jensen—could do, if anything.

"I've heard of you... strong, fierce," Aric started. A cocky smile spread across my face. Then he continued with, "Pigheaded, rule breaker."

"Yeah, yeah. Flattery isn't going to help you today. Gobel."

Aric cleared his throat before speaking again. I must've been squeezing even harder than I'd thought. "I want to get Jensen back to Delaware. If he's as powerful as my people fear, the Gobel Assembly might back down. I have people I don't want hurt."

The legend of Glen Sorrel went deeper than I'd thought if the mere *thought* of what Jensen possessed could be enough to make the Gobel back down. I saw the flaws in his plan. The chances he'd be taking assumed Jensen packed the punch we both hoped he did. It was the same chance I was taking, even though Jensen's return might not have been enough. A fight might still happen. My muscles relaxed. I agreed with him about one thing, though.

Jensen had to come home.

"Okay, Gob—Aric." I rolled my eyes. "I'm going out on a limb here and giving you the benefit of the doubt on this one." My wedged heels thudded against the linoleum as I stalked toward him. "But if you're up to something, *your* throat isn't the only one I'll rip out."

His eyes widened. "Damn. What's that supposed to mean?"

"I mean"—another step closer—"your mother, your father, and, honestly, since you're Gobel, you must have like a dozen or so brothers and sisters. I'll hunt each one down and end your entire family's existence. Got it?"

"Yeah, yeah." He waved his hands as if what I'd just said to him hadn't had the effect I'd intended. "Christ, Alyssum, you need to calm down. We're on the same side here."

I didn't trust him.

Turning on my heels, I left the kitchen to sit on the tired couch in his living room. I swung a leg over my knee, thinking about how I loved it when I got to be badass, but even I had to admit I probably looked pretty silly. I was five-foot-three. Him, more than six feet. I hardly looked threatening in comparison, but I could follow through on every threat I ever made.

I knew it. I was sure he knew it, too.

We sat in the sparsely furnished room for two hours, discussing our options.

I didn't give him much information about what I thought should happen after we got Jensen on board. That would be up to *my* assembly, not his. Then something occurred to me. Aric was risking his life just by being here. If his people found out, they'd kill him for fraternizing with the enemy or some other stupid code-of-conduct violation.

With that in mind, I began to consider that I just might be able to trust him, at least a little.

My entire body unclenched. I hadn't even realized I'd been holding myself so rigid until my muscles released. We were raised to fear Gobel, to want to end them, and to never, ever allow them into our lives. I always did have a hard time following the rules.

When I was all planned out, I jumped up from the couch and headed out.

After returning to the motel, I sat on the bed with my dinner next to me while using my laptop, even though the Wi-Fi connection was spotty at best. There were a few new emails from Dahlia, my best friend. With increasing capital letters, she asked where the hell I was. I guess she decided that since I wasn't answering text messages this was the way to go.

I hadn't turned my phone on since getting here so my father couldn't track me.

There was also one strongly worded message from my dad indicating he knew what I was up to. In no uncertain terms, he told me that I should turn the car around and head home. My saving grace was that he'd never taken the time to listen to details and therefore had no idea where I actually was, unlike my mom. She listened to everything.

Cheeseburger gone, email sent to my mom assuring her I'd arrived safe and sound, leaving out where I was in case Dad read it, I shut the laptop to head into town. I couldn't send Dahlia anything just in case someone else got a hold of it. She must've been pissed that I'd left without saying anything or worse... not taking her with me.

I parked my car at one end of Main Street to walk and window shop. The town blended as much small-town charm as it could with the big city, whose shadow it lived in, and the air felt so much better than the stagnant condition of my room. The elderly air conditioner humming in the corner was doing its best.

A quaint fabric shop was nestled next to McDonald's. I, myself, preferred the independent bookstore on the corner. None of the cities close to my town had a bookstore that size. I loved going through the stacks instead of ordering books off the internet to be picked up at a post office twenty miles away in Eagle River. Getting my paranormal romance required a lot of effort.

The eReader Mom got me for Christmas this past year still sat unopened because I was stubbornly sticking to hard copy only. However this trip told me that I should rethink that. Our town was too small to have a library, and too far for two days shipping.

I rounded the back corner of the bookstore, five books in my arms, and found Aric sitting on the floor, legs stretched out and crossed at the ankles with a book on his lap. Instead of saying anything, I gave his foot a hard but playful kick. His eyes popped open, like he was about to give someone a piece of his mind, but instead, he smiled when he saw it was me.

Apparently, I'd made friends with a Gobel in a day. Nineteen years of ingrained hate be damned.

"Looking for something to do?" he asked, pushing himself up to his full height. He stood close, as if we'd known each other for years.

"Yeah, they have actual stuff here, you know. It's kind of weird." I leaned a shoulder against one of the black shelves.

"You don't get out of Delaware much, do you?"

"Not really. I mean, I've gone away with my parents a little, but I mostly just go to the Eagle River post office," I admitted. He burst out with a laugh. My town was sparse. It only had the post office, a small grocery, and a bar. You never had to go far for a bar in rural Michigan. "I know. Exciting."

"Hey, want some coffee?" he asked.

I nodded and after I paid for my selections, we headed down two blocks to the coffee shop.

"So, where have you been so far?" he asked once we were settled at a tall table in front of the biggest window.

After a large gulp of the piping-hot tea I'd ordered, I said, "Just a few places. Detroit, Grand Rapids, places like that. My mom and I did go to Florida twice and a few other states for assembly business on those rare occasions when my dad decided to take us with him."

Aric's face dropped. "That's right. Your dad is the head of The Assembly." I nodded. The words came with a hint of fear, like he'd just remembered that fact. "Shit."

I knew what he was thinking. It was what I would've been thinking if I were him. It was bad enough that he'd put himself in bed with the Gremalians—so to speak—but working directly with the head of The Assembly through me would be seen as high treason by his people.

"Don't worry. If you help me, I won't let anything happen to you. From either side. My dad's a big teddy bear," I assured him. He almost spit his coffee out, then coughed hard three times trying to clear his throat and get some air. "Really. I know how to handle him."

"Yeah. I'm sure the leader of the Gremalians is all squishy inside."

I shrugged. "He is with me... most of the time."

We talked a while longer about his childhood and mine. I learned our upbringing had been pretty similar, although he hadn't had to deal with the added crap I'd had to deal with as the daughter of an assembly leader. We both ordered a second cup, which I didn't finish, then called it a night. It was nice to have someone to talk to in this strange town, even if I didn't fully trust him yet.

In the morning, I decided to do some shopping. Because of how quickly I'd left, my packing had been so minimal, even going to a laundromat twice a week wouldn't stop me from having to re-wear an outfit every couple of days, which I wasn't willing to do. I hadn't even packed enough underwear.

I found a couple of cute shops and bought a few skirts, shorts, shirts, and some shoes. I even found a small lingerie shop to take care of my lack of underwear.

On my second trip back to the car, my hands were overflowing with bags. Yet I'd only spent a couple hundred dollars. Thanks to sales and a pretty cool thrift shop, I'd gotten everything I'd needed on the cheap. Didn't want to use my credit card unless I absolutely had to. Mom would be the one to see the charges and she already knew where I was. I figured I should give Dad as few chances to find me as possible.

So focused on trying not to drop my bags, I wasn't watching where I was going and hit what felt like a brick wall. Stumbling back, I lost my footing and the pavement rapidly approached as I fell. A hand on each arm grabbed me just before my face hit the cement. Apparently, the wall I'd hit was a wall of muscle.

"Sorry," I said.

I looked up to find Aric's hand wrapped around my left arm and Jensen's wrapped around my right. Once I was balanced, they let go. I had to take two small steps to actually see their faces. Aric and Jensen were almost the same height, but Aric looked to be about an extra quarter of an inch taller.

"Hey, this is Alyssum," Aric started. He looked over at Jensen. "She came into the shop yesterday."

"I remember." He flashed a sexy smile. I don't think he was even trying to be overtly sexy, but it worked. "How are you?"

"Good." I returned the smile, hoping it was a good one. "The car's good, too. No more issues."

"Good to hear." He looked me over quickly but thoroughly. The way his eyes searched my body warmed every inch of my skin.

"Doing a little shopping there, Alyssum?" Aric asked, pointing to my excessive baggage.

"Yeah, well, a girl's got needs, right?" Then I realized I was flashing them the lingerie bag. Neither of them reacted but I could only shake my head and end the conversation. "Anyway, I better get going before these end up all over the sidewalk."

I moved to go around them.

"Do you need some help?" Jensen asked.

"That would be great." Not only because I had a lot of bags, but no way in hell would I pass up an interaction with Jensen. I needed to insert myself into his life if I was ever going to convince him to come with me and I'd been about to turn back and ask him for help myself.

I handed everything to the guys and we headed to my car, parked just across the street. After loading it all in, I slammed my trunk closed.

"Thanks, guys," I said.

"No problem," Jensen said, then they were back off to wherever they'd been headed.

Before getting in my car, I glanced over my shoulder and caught Jensen doing the same. I smiled shyly, turned around, and hopped into the car.

Over the next few days, I ran into Jensen several times. Sometimes I orchestrated our meetings; other times, they were just accidents. He'd stop to talk to me, just the random neighborly small talk, and every time, we'd chat a little longer. I started to hope that maybe he liked me or, at the very least, was getting used to me.

Me being me, I wanted to jump right in, tell him who he was and insist he come back to Delaware with me. But the practical side told me that going to fast with this guy would mean losing the chance. He'd run. There'd been something in his face when I came into the shop that first time that gave me the impression that I should earn his trust first. Make sure he knew I wouldn't try to hurt him or mess with his head. That way, he'd know everything I said was true.

Our conversations were all so sterile and cordial that I almost wanted to give up. I'd already found myself thinking about him when he wasn't around in ways that had nothing to do with saving our people. I hated that, but we needed Jensen. He was like Obi-Wan Kenobi to my Princess Leia. He was my only hope. If he had the type of power his parents supposedly had, there'd be no losing.

Though he didn't show any signs of knowing he had power or know what he was.

"We have to stop running into each other like this," Jensen said. He'd caught me by surprise as I'd rounded a corner on the way to freaking nowhere. While in New York, when I got bored, I tended to just walk off all the extra energy I had. Sometimes it worked; sometimes it didn't.

"Jesus." I held my chest. He really had startled me.

"Sorry," he replied, laughing. "Where you headed?" There was something warmer and more relaxed about him.

"Nowhere, just walking. Probably to get my billionth cup of coffee of the day."

"I'll walk with you."

He turned around and fell in step beside me, close yet not close enough for us to be touching. Damn it. He held the door open at the coffee shop I went to so often, the staff was beginning to know my order before I even said it, which was extra impressive since what I ordered changed with my mood. I was in a caramel macchiato mood.

He held his cup of straight black like it was going out of style. "How are you liking Putnam Valley?"

"I like it. It's nice to be in a city for a change."

"City?" He smirked. "I take it Delaware is pretty small then?"

He remembered where I lived? Interesting. I'd only told him in passing one of the times we'd run into each other. "I'd be surprised if it's on a regular map."

"Have you been to the city yet?" I shook my head

"New York City? How close are we?"

"'Bout an hour away. I make the trip every couple of weeks for the shop. Just a quick run." He paused to take another swig.

"I haven't but maybe I'll add it to the list." I told him this knowing I'd never make it there. All I wanted to do was get him back home.

He nodded, said he had to get back to work, and left me sitting in the coffee shop with a smile on my face and a hankering for another cup.

At least now I thought he'd gotten to know me enough that the time was coming soon to tell him who he really was.

And what he really was.

Chapter Four

Between my run-ins with Jensen, Aric and I got together pretty often, running and climbing anything and everything we could find to stay in shape. He pushed me, teased that he could run three laps in the time it took me to run one, but come on; the dude had almost a foot on me, making his strides much larger.

After finishing dinner at Frost's, another place where they were starting to know me by name, we walked back to his apartment. I loved that I could walk just about anywhere in town without a problem. Since the motel was farther out, I usually drove into town whenever the mood struck, parked my car in the first parking lot I saw upon entering Putnam

Valley, and walked everywhere until I was ready to go back to the motel.

The summer night was quiet and crisp when we stopped at the corner, waiting for the light to change. Aric cupped my face and leaned in until his lips touched mine.

This man was an enemy of my people. I was supposed to hate him for the sheer reason of what he was. Except I was letting him kiss me on the corner under the light. My father would explode with anger while my mother would try to convince me it was a bad idea.

It was a bad idea. I already knew that but oh did it feel so good at that moment.

"Sorry," he said quietly after he pulled back, not looking like he meant it. "I probably shouldn't have done that."

"No. You shouldn't have." Being with a Gobel was against everything I stood for. Even this kiss would've gotten me punishment that I couldn't imagine. For sure, The Assembly would never trust me again. "But why do you think that?" My racing heart made my voice breathy.

"I have a list of reasons not to kiss you, actually."

I laughed. If I thought about it, I could come up

with one, too. Mine would probably be longer than his.

"Okay." I faced him, crossing the street without looking to keep him right beside me, never missing a beat. "What's number one?"

"You're Gremalian." He paused. "Oh, wait, not just that. You're the Gremalian daughter of the *head* of the Gremalian Assembly."

"Oh, please." I brushed him off as if that meant nothing, though we both knew better. "Number two?"

"You came here for him."

I rolled my eyes. "I came here for him to save my people."

"We work together," he continued.

"That's true."

"You're very young."

Now I stopped and scoffed. "I'm nineteen. You're only

"I am two years older than you but you're very young, Alyssum. I can see it in your face." He was talking about experience not years and that meant I couldn't counter that reasoning because he wasn't wrong. Finally he sighed. "You like him."

"Who?" Playing dumb was much easier than fessing up. Walking ahead of hm helped a little, too. I knew exactly who he was talking about, and he was right.

"Jensen."

We turned one more corner and ended up back at his apartment. I'd already decided not to go in. Since I'd parked my car outside of his apartment, I stopped there. When I didn't say anything, he started talking again.

"It's okay, Alyssum. He's a likable guy."

"What makes you say that? About me?"

"I'm quite perceptive. Plus, you blush every time you see him. I wasn't going to kiss you. I didn't want to confuse things. We're talking war and have loved ones on opposite sides, but apparently, somewhere along the way, I decided to throw my hat in the ring."

I cocked my head to the side and scrunched my face. "It's a good hat." I had another question that couldn't wait. I took a deep breath because the answer might not be what I wanted to hear. "Does it bother you that I like him?"

Aric swallowed and thought about that. "It bothers me that you like him. It bothers me more that he likes you, but I'm an adult. I can deal with that for now. It's not like I have a claim on you and we are a terrible idea."

That answer was part of what I'd wanted to hear

and part of what I hadn't. It made sense, but I wasn't ready to say that I wanted to be with either of them. Like them? Yes. Date them? Absolutely. But push one away? Definitely not.

"He doesn't look at me twice," I told him which at the time I thought was true.

He snorted and shook his head. "I told you. You're very young."

Although I wanted to know exactly what he meant by that, I hopped in my car and went home— or, in my case, a small motel room over a thousand miles away from home. My room felt empty and much too quiet. I didn't even have a book to hunker down with because I'd already read the ones I'd bought in town.

I didn't sleep much on a good day, but ever since I'd arrived in New York, I'd slept even less. Since it was still kind of early, even for Small Town, USA, I drove to the bookstore to feed my habit and ended up with a few magazines that I couldn't normally get back home. I overheard some people talking about the holiday celebration the next day and remem-bered Mr. Burkhardt inviting me to the Memorial Day Festival. Sounded like something the whole town would be attending.

I needed to be there too.

. . .

The next day at the park, throngs of kids chased wildly after each other. Melted popsicles ran down their arms, mixing sticky with sweat. It reminded me of home, that the human and Gremalian worlds weren't so different after all. I walked around, looking for Jensen or Mr. Burkhardt, trying not to *appear* like I was looking for them.

I stopped at a vendor cart and ordered a cherry snow cone to give me something to do. Also, it was hot. The scorching temps from earlier had tapered off, making the weather a bit more bearable, and the ice felt good going down my throat. I wished I'd pulled my hair into a ponytail when I felt a drop of sweat run down the back of my neck.

"Fancy meeting you here." Jensen came up behind me while I watched some girls playing hopscotch.

"It sounded fun and I haven't seen fireworks in a while," I replied.

"'Round here, it's like Christmas. So is the Fourth of July. Basically, we like to watch things explode into pretty colors. Our stuff is set up over that way." He jutted his thumb behind him. "Come on."

"Are you sure? I don't want to intrude."

"Please, there are tons of people. My parents take in all the strays," he said. My eyebrows shot up. Was he comparing me to a dog? "I didn't mean—"

I giggled and decided to give him a break. "Don't worry about it."

We walked back slowly, making conversation like every other time we'd run into each other. It was a lot easier to get comfortable with him than I'd thought it'd be. Talking to him was almost natural, as if we'd known each other all along. I was afraid he'd be wary of me, but he was laid-back enough that it hadn't been an issue.

He asked about my family, but I couldn't really tell the whole truth. That would come in time. As with every time we were together, I constantly tried to figure him out.

Was he laid-back? Yes. Confident? Mostly. Once in a while, he seemed less sure of himself than his normal mannerisms would have me believe.

None of that should have even mattered. Not to me. All I was supposed to care about was getting him home, but I cared about his feelings. Damn it, I cared about *him*.

"You done?" he asked, pointing to the empty snow cone cup I was still carrying.

I handed it to him and he tossed it in the trash can we passed just before I saw his group. It looked more like a house party than a picnic. There were portable tents everywhere. A couple of picnic tables were already full of people. Others were either sitting on blankets in the grass or standing with drinks in their hands, laughing, talking, and seemingly having a very good time. One guy, about fifty years old, had clearly enjoyed a few too many drinks, as represented by his loud voice, swaying footsteps, and slurred words. Somehow, they all noticed me, the newcomer, right away.

"I send you for ice and you bring back a girl?" a woman, presumably his mother, asked as she walked over to us.

Of course, she looked nothing like him. The gray was starting to creep into her short, manageable mom-cut that human women tended to get by the time they reached forty-five.

Her eyes slid over me and her assessing me seeped into my pours. I just didn't know if I passed or failed.

"Forgot the ice." His eyes jumped from her to me, then to nothing. "This is Alyssum," he said to her. Then he turned to me and said, "And this is my mom."

"Don't worry, Alice. I've got an extra bag in the cooler," called another woman around his mom's age.

"That's okay, Mrs. Hancock. I'll go back." Jensen turned to me. "Feel like another walk?"

"Sure."

We headed out the way we'd come just as slowly as before. There was no rush. Everywhere I looked, people were enjoying food and their time with friends. Nobody seemed to care about anything else.

"How long are you in town?" he asked.

"Not sure. It's kind of indefinite."

"Hmmm..." It was the sound of someone thinking. "No job? School to get back to?"

"Nothing too pressing." If you didn't count the tensions that had been amping up when I left Delaware.

War was coming but it'd be a little while before talks completely broke down. I hoped.

After getting some ice from the vendor, on our way back to the group, Jensen reached up as we passed under a tree and pulled off a handful of leaves. He let a few trail in the breeze. The rest crunched in his hand, which gave him a distraction to focus on even though he was carrying a ten-pound bag of ice in his other hand.

"Are you staying with friends?"

"No. I'm at a hotel."

"Oh god!" He rolled his eyes.

"It's not that bad."

"I'm sure it isn't." His tone was playful which said he knew exactly what that motel was like.

At the rate we were walking, I started to worry the ice would be water by the time we got back. Still, I wasn't complaining. It felt natural being with him, comfortable.

After giving his mom the ice, we sat on a couple of swings nearby and continued to talk. There was something about talking to Jensen. Something that put me right at ease and made me feel... connected. Grounded.

Once the sky had darkened enough, some of the kids took out sparklers. Soon, the only light around the group were some lanterns his dad had lit, and the shimmering snaps off the ends of the sparklers. I watched Jensen straighten a blanket, then come back to me.

"The show's going to start soon," he said.

"Wouldn't miss it."

We sat down, side by side, not even a foot apart. I'd come to Putnam Valley to convince him his people needed him. I hadn't entertained the idea I'd actually like him so much. Even with the warm air, I liked the feeling of his body heat covering the right side of me. He felt relaxing and familiar, as if my body already knew his on a subconscious level.

The first warning boom got everyone quiet and situated. Then the show started. Small pops of color against the night sky brought a smile to my face. As the flares climbed higher and higher, everyone else started lying back on the ground to get a better view, so I laid down too. Jensen did the same beside me.

The fireworks were perfect, even more beautiful than they'd been the few times my mom had taken me to Marquette to watch the display over Lake Superior on the Fourth of July. Our shoulders almost touched and, a few booms later, his pinky finger looped around mine, waking my body up. That was when I had to look over. I needed to see if that small touch had the same effect on him that it'd had on me.

He wasn't watching the show. He was watching me. I held his gaze for a full minute. The dropping and clenching in my stomach became too much and I had to move my eyes from his. What I was feeling right then had nothing to do with us being Gremalian. Intertwining the rest of our fingers, we lay there like that until it was over.

Before I had a chance to sit up, he pulled his hand back and jumped to his feet. The party went back to full swing like there'd never been any interruption. Music started, drinks got poured, and people resumed eating. It was like someone had pushed the *pause* button during the show and then hit *play*.

"Hey." I tapped his bicep, which was rock-hard under my finger. I felt a spark. Not one of those 'Love at First Sight' type sparks, but an actual spark of static electricity. It was frustrating that he didn't seem to feel anything. "I think I'm going to go."

"Really?" He looked disappointed, which sent the butterflies in my stomach wild. I wanted him to be disappointed, wanted him to ask me to stay, propose marriage—anything to keep me there. Okay, a proposal would be premature. Anything else would be good.

"Yeah, I'm kinda tired."

Really, I needed some space and perspective. Two guys in two days had shown some interest in me, which I wasn't used to. Sure, I'd had a semi-serious boyfriend until the year before, but Sage was now only part of my life because he was part of my father's security team. I hadn't let our relationship go very far. The realization that I found him heinous had kind of squashed all romance. It was hip being my father's lap dog that turned me off.

"How long does this whole thing last?" I twirled my finger in the air to indicate the party.

"Oh, some of these people will end up sleeping here"—he laughed—"so possibly all night."

"Thanks for inviting me. I had a lot of fun."

He nodded, eyeing me for a few seconds. "Where are you parked?"

"Way out. But it's a nice night. I don't mind the walk."

He brushed his hands off on his khaki shorts. "I'll walk with you."

"That'd be great." With a goodbye to the new people I'd met and a "Don't be a stranger" from Jensen's dad, we headed out in the general direction of my car.

We didn't talk much, just a random comment here or there. Instead, we let grasshoppers chirp us a soundtrack. He trusted me. I could *feel* it. My purpose in coming had been to gain his trust, but my plan had taken an unexpected turn somewhere along the way. I had a whole new batch of feelings for Jensen.

"Here I am," I said, hitting the button on my keychain to unlock the doors.

I leaned casually against the front panel on the driver's side, palms resting against the hood. He stopped just before his knees could brush my thighs, so close, I couldn't help looking up at him. The girl in me wanted him to dive in for our first kiss. I was pretty sure it'd be a good one.

"I'd like to see you again," he said softly. A smile played with his lips. "On purpose."

"You have my number. Or rather, your dad does."

I could already read his next move, which, on the one hand, made me feel like he had yanked an imaginary cord attached to my belly button, drawing me closer to him. On the other, it let me know that I was as good at reading people as I thought I was. His hands cupped the sides of my face as he moved in slowly.

When our lips met, I closed my eyes, allowing myself to get lost in his softness and the burnt sparkler smell that coated his skin from helping the smaller kids ignite theirs. His mouth was gentle against mine, but the electricity we shared was palpable. Given that Gremalians had the power to draw on electricity, it didn't surprise me. Though I'd never felt it quite like this with Sage.

His mouth moved against mine. His thumbs caressed my cheeks as his tongue touched mine. This kiss left my knees shaking and it ended too quickly.

"I swear I didn't plan that," he said, resting his forehead on mine, just a touch out of breath.

"I wouldn't care if you had."

Another quick peck and I was on my way. I drove up the dirt road slowly so I could watch him in the rearview.

He disappeared into the night and I knew... This was now about more than just wanting him to stop a war.

Chapter Five

THE LONGER I stayed in Putnam Valley, the less I wanted to go home.

Disappointment, possible punishment, and a society on the brink of war waiting for me wasn't exactly drawing me back. Here, I had two hot guys to occupy my time.

With Jensen, I got to see what it was like to be human, an experience I'd never thought I wanted, or even considered to be potentially enjoyable, until I'd met him.

Unfortunately, being with Aric didn't automatically mean I got to be myself. I wasn't ready for him to know everything about me, my powers, and what my people could do if he didn't know already.

To be fair, I hadn't given Jensen the opportunity to know all of me, either. I was always myself with him, minus all the Gremalian stuff. Though I worried this wasn't going to end well.

Jensen and Aric were friends. Real friends, which was unusual for a Gobel. They didn't make friends easily, which was why their society was as contained as it was and their only interaction with outsiders, for the most part, came in the form of war.

That weekend, the three of us decided to go to Putnam Lake. Together. As if it were totally normal for two Gremalians to hang out with a Gobel.

The old rust bucket Aric had bought once he'd gotten to Putnam Valley rambled over the dirt road that led to the swimming side of the lake.

The beach had already gotten pretty crowded, which wasn't surprising, considering the day had turned from warm to almost scorching before noon. Young women working on their tans in some of the skimpiest bikinis I'd ever seen covered the sand. The guys watching said women created a barrier between us and them.

We set ourselves up far away from the others. Jensen dropped the cooler full of drinks and snacks, then made himself at home right next to me. When they took their shirts off, it was more than the sun scorching my skin. They were all hard abs and muscles. I'd worn a two-piece swimsuit, not a bikini. I'd always preferred the more classic styles of bathing suits. Those from the 1940s were my favorite.

Aric ran into the water, disappearing into the lake before I'd even turned around. I took a seat on the blanket and started putting on sunscreen. I definitely didn't want to bake myself golden like most of the women around me probably intended to. I liked a tan only through sunscreen.

"Want help with your back?" Jensen asked, handing me a bottle of water.

I nodded. His strong hands were on my skin before I'd had the chance to prepare myself. He rubbed the lotion in slow circles. I had to close my eyes to contain the warm, fuzzy feelings spreading through my body. After covering my back, he went to my shoulders and then down my arms. I'd already taken care of my arms, but I certainly wasn't going to tell him that. I wanted to feel the warmth everywhere, forgetting, for a second, that we were in public and not alone.

"You're hanging out with him too. I'm right, aren't I?" he said quietly as he continued to rub the sunscreen on my skin. When I didn't answer, he continued. "We don't talk about you, but I see things."

"Does that bother you? That I'm dating two people at the same time?" I asked him.

"Well, I don't love it, but we don't own you and I have a feeling either of us acting like we do would be a bad thing."

I narrowed my eyes at him over my shoulder. "It would be a very bad thing."

"You know you can't do this forever, right?"

"I know," I said quietly. I knew that, eventually, somebody's feelings would get hurt or this blossoming alliance between the three of us would crumble. Neither outcome made me feel good.

"What are you guys up to?" Aric broke into my very pleasurable moment and Jensen's hands were gone in an instant.

"Just making sure my bases are covered. I'd hate to miss a spot and get a sunburn."

I smiled up into Aric's shadow. I couldn't see him at all because he was blocking the light, like an eclipse.

The lazy afternoon went by far too quickly. Just past dinner time, I was ready to go. We'd snacked the day away, so I needed some proper food. A dull ache had started in my forehead, the first sign I'd spent too much time in the sun.

I didn't think it was a coincidence that Aric went out of his way to drop Jensen off first. Logically, I should've been first, but he'd gone around the back way, which had taken ten minutes longer, to magically pull in front of Jensen's apartment.

With a quick good-bye and a second look at me, Jensen made a quiet sound of frustration at the back of his throat before he jumped out, grabbed his bag and cooler from the back, and headed in. I didn't move over, though I probably should have. I was becoming addicted to the warm prickling that Aric gave me. I had no idea what the hell I was doing.

"So, you're taking another shortcut?" I asked as he turned in the complete opposite direction of the motel.

"Yup. Hey, you two had some alone time at the beach. I figure it's only fair."

I gave him a smile and shook my head.

"You know we've got to act soon." He said it as if it was a foregone conclusion which I'd been thinking the same thing. I hadn't been here long but the time was coming. Jensen clearly trusted us to some extent.

At this point, I was the only one delaying the inevitable.

"I know. It's just so..."

"Normal here," he finished for me. I nodded. "I know. It's almost like the world we live in doesn't exist anymore but the longer we wait..."

"The worse it's going to get. Are you in touch with your family?" I wasn't. I couldn't be because my dad would haul my ass back without another thought.

Aric shook his head. "I can't contact them. For all I know, the war has already begun. The only reason I hadn't already told Jensen about everything before you got here is I can't prove to him what he should be able to do. I... don't even know how to start to explain it. Then you showed up and I thought you'd do it. You and him are the same so you should be able to explain how to tap into it."

"It's probably the same as you." I furrowed my brows. "I don't think a war has started. When I left, they were still in talks and I think both sides want the war to be a last resort. My mom knows where I am and I think she would've have sent a message. What do you mean you can't contact them?"

His gaze settled on me for longer than I was comfortable with given that he was driving.

"Alyssum. Being here isn't just treason for me. I've turned my back on my entire family just by talking to you. A couple of my brothers know what I'm doing and will help but they're all in danger."

Oh shit. That was true. Friendships were forbidden and him defying that edict could've put his whole family in jeopardy.

It was time. I had to tell Jensen what he was and why I'd come to Putnam Valley.

The next day, Aric asked me to go for a run with him. His energy must've been bouncing around his body the way mine was. We took off and it became a race of who was faster than who.

I was lighter which meant my steps were quicker but his stride was twice mine. It evened out somewhat but he never ran out of breath and I had a sneaking suspicion that he wasn't running his fastest.

OK. So Gobel were fast.

After six miles, we stopped, stretching our muscles and shaking our appendages out. Aric didn't sound winded while I probably sounded like a dehydrated mule begging for water.

"So why is Jensen so important?" he asked before

offering me a drink of his water bottle. Mine had already been drained.

I took a second drink then handed the bottle back to him. "Jensen's father was the head of The Assembly and he was powerful. Like off the charts powerful." I'd keep back that Glen had been more powerful than my own father because he didn't need to know that. "Hopefully, Jensen has those powers. Enough to scare the Gobel into not acting."

Aric snorted. "We'll see about that."

"We won't know until we get him back home but he could be the most powerful that we've ever seen. I think there's more to all of this but no one tells me anything and I'm not allowed in the room when The Assembly meets. Not until the public portion."

"A more powerful Gremalian than most of us have ever seen? That's something we wouldn't be expecting," Aric said.

"I know. What did you think your people were worried about?"

He shook his head. "All I knew was that The Assembly has always feared someone returning on your side. That's why I started to dig and how I found out about your former leader, but I couldn't find anything about the leader's kid, which I thought was weird. If I had to guess, I'd say I got here the same way you did. I just did it first."

Of course, he'd gotten here first. I groaned to let him know I didn't appreciate him pointing that out, but he most likely didn't have an overbearing father holding him back.

We walked the rest of the way, curving around, completing a circle of the town, and went back to his apartment to rest. I went inside for a drink. Neither of us looked like we'd just run miles; we'd barely broken a sweat. After chugging down more cold water, we both got very quiet. The small room closed in on us. I could smell the musk he'd been emitting since we'd started the run, a deliciously sweet aroma that I'd struggled to ignore. We dropped our bottles and met in the middle of the room.

When our lips met, Aric lifted me off the floor. The prickling that accompanied being near a Gobel made everything more intense, causing me to shudder. He took me to the couch in the living room. His mouth never left mine, his tongue brushing my lips, asking for permission that I willingly gave, an assault of knee-weakening kisses.

I tried really hard not to compare him to Jensen and keep my head in the moment. No matter how hard I tried, Jensen was always somewhere lurking in the corner.

His hands started up my shirt, stopping to squeeze the sides of my ribcage. His skin on mine felt warm enough to melt my insides. When I pulled back, his lips moved to my neck, making a trail to my collarbone, then over to my shoulder, not missing a spot. It felt good, but if he was kissing me and I was thinking of Jensen, that meant something. I didn't think about Aric when Jensen kissed me.

"Aric..." I wasn't sure he'd heard me. "Aric!" I said louder. I pushed against his chest.

"What's wrong?" His face was so close, I had to sit up to put some distance between us.

"We need to stop."

"Why?" His eyes narrowed. I dropped mine as an answer, hoping he'd figure it out and I wouldn't have to say it out loud.

"Ah..." He sat up as well. "Jensen?" I nodded.

He scooted to the right, farther away from me. Instead of trying to deny anything regarding Jensen, I got up and headed to the door to leave.

"You had to choose eventually, Alyssum." He was suddenly right next to me, his breath warming the side of my face, sweet and hot. "I just wanted to make sure you knew that I was one of the choices but it's seems you've made your decision but it doesn't change anything about what we need to do."

My eyes met his, chocolate and kind.

He wasn't wrong. Stopping him because Jensen was on my mind was a choice though I hadn't made it intentionally.

Besides we had bigger things to worry about than my stupid heart.

Chapter Six

THE KNOCK on my hotel door took me by surprise and put me immediately on edge.

I tiptoed over to peek out the window in case it was Dad or his pit bull Sage or just some random murderer. Standing there in the moonlight, Jensen couldn't have been hotter. He was wearing jeans and black T-shirt that was just tight enough to outline the muscles underneath. A hard chest that I'd gotten a good look at when we were at the beach.

I took a deep breath before opening the door.

"Hey." I answered with a smile.

"Hi." He looked me up and down and I was suddenly thankful that I'd kept the cute shorts and lacy, pink cami on instead of changing into a pair of ratty, old pajamas.

"Sorry to just drop by."

"That's okay." I gave him a flirty smile. "But if you think you can just come to my hotel for a—"

He shook his head quickly, cutting me off. "I wasn't thinking that." He was almost too easy to tease and I loved that about him.

"I'm just messing with you. What's up? Do you want to come in?"

I moved aside and swung my arm as further invitation.

"Now I don't." He scowled and it made me smile. "I came to see if you want to go for a ride." I dropped my jaw and widened my eyes, pretending to be shocked. "I mean on my motorcycle. Geez, you make things hard."

I smirked and it took him a few seconds to get why. A smile played on his lips, then the rest of his face dropped. "I think I'm just going to leave now."

"Wait, Jensen, wait," I said through fits of laughter. I shoved the room key in my back pocket and grabbed the pink sweater that went with the cami to run after him. It wasn't a particularly cool night, but I thought the sweater might come in handy when speeding down the highway on the back of a motorcycle. When I caught him, he was already sitting on his bike, about to take off.

"I'm sorry, I'm sorry. I'd love to go for a ride. I'll be good, I promise."

That time, he smirked. "No one said you had to be good."

Before I knew what I was doing, I leaned in and pressed my lips against his. Though I'd clearly taken him by surprise, he responded. His lips were soft but demanding. His hand grabbed my hips and pulled me to him. I braced myself with my palms on the sides of his neck as I melted into him basking in the warmth of his mouth.

After pulling back, I held his gaze for as long as I could before he handed me a helmet. Once I had it buckled, I hopped on the back of his bike and we roared off into the night.

I didn't know how long he drove with my arms wrapped tightly around him, my body pushing against his back. It wasn't long enough, as far as I was concerned. I rode with my eyes closed. *Stupid girl.*

At some point, we stopped. He didn't move at first and I didn't notice that the bike was no longer running. I finally realized he was waiting for me to get off first, so I did. I pulled the helmet off and saw we were at a park with a small pond. The swings moved in the breeze like they carried the ghosts of the children who'd played there. The moon reflecting in the rippling water was peaceful and beautiful.

"Is this a play date?" I handed him the helmet and he swung a leg over to stand up. "I mean it's beautiful, but—"

"It's quiet." I felt his eyes on me. "We can go somewhere else."

I started to slowly walk toward the swings. They'd always been my favorite when I was a kid, back when I could swing higher than any of my friends.

"I'm just kidding," I said over my shoulder so he'd follow.

"Do you always do that?" I threw him a questioning look. "Joke about everything?"

"Not always." *Honesty, Alyssum.* "But when I feel awkward I tend to. Defense mechanism and all that."

"You, awkward? Please."

I smiled at that. It was nice to know that my tough, confident exterior wasn't a figment of my imagination.

We slowly swung next to each other much like we had on Memorial Day, talking over the sound of lapping waves. Aric was right. Jensen was a great guy. I started to feel guilty, like I was manipulating him or something, but I wasn't. I'd liked him from the start, and it just so happened he could help save my life and our people. He just didn't know it yet. How I was able to argue with myself, listen to him, and make witty conversation was beyond even me.

After a while, we made our way back to his bike. He looked over at me after getting on first. It was the only time we were roughly the same height, and something took over. I pounced, smashing my lips to his. *Real subtle, Alyssum.*

I climbed on his bike and straddled him.

When his hands cautiously slid up my thighs to rest on my hips, his tongue slid over mine at the same pace. I pulled at his shirt enough to allow me to get under it and have access to the silky, hard skin beneath. I hadn't even noticed I was crushing our bodies together until his chest was almost against mine.

It was a flurry of lips and tongue as he squeezed me so hard I hoped there'd be finger marks left but doubted there would be.

"Wow," I said, pulling away, with a breathlessness he'd probably intended. "Moms are right. You can't trust a guy on a motorcycle."

His eyes sparkled. His voice got low and husky. "*You* attacked *me*."

"But you didn't stop me."

"Now, why would I do that?" He kissed me again, soft and chaste, yet his eyes were intoxicating. I couldn't bring myself to close mine.

Damn it. I was falling... hard.

"Get on." He nodded his head behind him.

On the way home, I hugged him as he drove. It was more than just hanging on and I was suddenly reminded of what Aric said when I was last with him.

I'd already made my choice. I'd dated both of them casually but what I felt for Jensen was more than casual.

As he drove, I pushed my hands under his shirt, just above the waistband on his jeans. A pinky finger may have slipped underneath enough to brush the tip of his now hardening cock. It was just one finger and just one touch, but the motorcycle left the road quickly and skidded to a hard stop in the gravel. He turned to me without getting off the motorcycle.

"Yeah, you can't do that." His face was totally serious and I couldn't figure out what he was referring to.

I cocked my head to the side and fought a grin. "What?"

"Your hands." He looked me pointedly in the eyes.

"Oh... sorry?" My apology came out as a question because I wasn't really sorry. I liked that my touch distracted him, liked how he felt on my skin, but maybe I shouldn't distract him while he was driving. Yeah, that might not be such a stellar idea. "Got it. Hands to myself."

I held on to the side of the seat, leaning away from him and sunk my teeth into my lower lip.

"No, no. I want you to hold on to me, but on top of my clothes so I don't kill the both of us."

"You and your rules." As soon as he'd sat back down, I wrapped my arms around him and intended to abided by all of his rules as I laid my head on his back.

For a quick second, he folded one of his hands over mine, then returned it to the handlebar.

By midweek, the heat kicked in full force, adding enough humidity to make being outside truly uncomfortable.

Instead of sitting around the small motel room,

its antiquated air conditioner humming loudly in the corner, I went to a movie. I hadn't seen one in quite a while so I picked the newest rom-com with the intent to enjoy the air conditioning.

After paying admission and getting a cold diet pop, I went in and found a seat. Then I saw Jensen. He stood there with a sort of surprised look on his face, which I didn't understand at first, so I put on my best smile and went over to his end of the aisle on the other side of the theater.

"Hi."

"Hey." Jensen shoved his hands in his pockets, shifting his weight nervously, which confused me even more. "So, you found the theater."

"Yeah, I haven't seen a movie in forever and didn't have any other plans tonight," I said.

I definitely wouldn't mind having him next to me in a dark theater. He didn't get the hint I was throwing, the one that said, *"Hey, drop whatever dud friends you came with and sit with me."* My whole body tingled with anticipation, but...nothing. *Damn.*

"Yeah..." His voice trailed off while he looked around, avoiding my face.

Just then, a woman about his age with legs as long as I was tall, chestnut hair, and deep-set eyes bounced up beside him, threading her arm through his.

"There you are," she said in a child-like voice with a singsong quality, the kind that made you want to stab someone with a fork. Her voice sounded as fake as the smile she threw once she'd taken the time to notice me standing there.

"I'm Ashley."

"Alyssum," I answered.

I already didn't like her and really hated what I was feeling. I could eviscerate her before anyone knew what was happening. I wouldn't. Sometimes I wished I was more violent. That feeling had a name. Jealousy. I was jealous of some mousy woman for no other reason than she was with him. I'd never been jealous of another woman in my whole life. It just wasn't me.

The men like Sage that my father had lead the fight or at least participate were another story.

"Um, anyway," I said, somehow managing to keep the smile on my face, "I'm gonna go find a seat."

"Enjoy the movie," she chirped.

"You too." Then I gave him a hard look, steeling myself against his blue eyes and the way they made my insides liquefy.

I moved through a group of people who'd sat in

my row while I'd had my back turned until I collapsed into a red-cushioned seat on an aisle all the way on the other side, halfway to the screen, which wasn't actually very far from where Jensen was sitting with Ashley. The theater wasn't large enough to offer me the distance I craved. Partway through, I felt eyes on me.

At first, I brushed it off as "new girl in a small town" curiosity since the feeling waxed and waned. Then I caught the person paying me too much attention.

Jensen was with his date in the row in front of mine, off to my right. When he looked at her, he could see me in his peripheral and even look at me full-on without her noticing. I caught him once and our eyes locked. I knew I should look away immediately, but, for whatever reason, I didn't.

Ashley leaned in to whisper something in his ear, which finally broke our connection. The fun of watching the movie that I couldn't focus on and soaking up some free air wore off and I had to get out of there. Right as I was about to go through the door to the street, he called my name. While instinct told me to keep walking, my feet didn't listen. I halted where I stood.

"Alyssum, hey. Where ya going?"

"Home... The motel," I said. He nodded and didn't say anything else. "You do realize you're on a date, right?"

Jensen smiled that great smile he broke out every now and then probably due to the bitchy tone I'd used.

"Yeah."

"So, what are you doing out here?" I asked.

"Officially? Using the restroom."

He leaned his shoulder on the wall next to me, which just happened to keep us out of sight. We were blocked by a red, velvet curtain. He was hiding me. Back home, most guys would have announced to the world that they were close to me just because that meant they might be in good with Dad. Though I hated to admit it, it felt good not having to worry about the intentions of the people I was interacting with. I could get used to that.

"So, if you're 'officially' using the restroom, what are you doing here with me in a dark nook of the movie theater lobby?"

"I have no idea." He sighed. "Ashley—"

"You left a woman in there to come out here to talk to me about her? Wow. I guess I seriously misjudged a few things."

I needed to get out of there before I did something drastic, like cry or punch him in the face. The latter was more likely, so I headed for the door. I had no right to be saying these things to him. It was such a double standard and I wasn't really mad at him anyway. I was mad at myself for feeling this way about him being on a date.

I wanted to stay near him longer, yet I needed to get away. The burn of the green-eyed monster rose from my stomach again after I'd worked so hard to beat it down with an imaginary club. I absolutely could not see that woman with him again. If I did, I knew I wouldn't be able to keep my emotions in check. She hadn't done anything wrong, but I hated her. I'd never hated someone I didn't know unless he or she was a Gobel.

When I pulled back into the little motel, a large, black SUV was in the spot next to where I normally parked. It was too familiar. After I'd shifted into park and turned my Mini off, I took a deep breath, then dropped my head back against the headrest to close my eyes for a few seconds. Anyone could be inside that black monster, but since there was no way for me to get inside my room without the driver seeing me, I had to face the music.

The SUV's driver's door opened the same time mine did. When I came around to the front, one of the guys on Dad's security team was leaning against the vehicle with an arm on the hood. I sighed in relief. If he were my dad, it would've been much worse.

"Flint, what are you doing here?"

Flint wasn't just on the security team; he was the head of it. He organized everything, made sure our family was safe and trained recruits. He was good at his job and looked the part with bulky muscles, a military cut, black cargo pants, a black T-shirt, and black boots. As if that wouldn't stand out in Putnam Valley.

"Your mother sent me."

"She told you I'm here? What's wrong?" I asked. He nodded. If she'd sent him, something had to be wrong. "I'm not ready to come back yet." Unless it was dire but I left that part out.

He could make me if he really wanted to, but I hoped he didn't really want to. His orders came from Mom and she'd been okay with me coming here. Actually, she'd encouraged it.

"It's been too long, Alyssum. Your dad is about to send the cavalry for you."

Obviously, there was a conversation that needed

to take place. I waved my hand to indicate that he should follow me. We went inside the motel room so no one was likely to overhear.

"Does he know where I am?" I asked once he'd shut the door behind him. If Dad knew where I was, this mission was likely over and I hadn't even told Jensen about Gremalians yet.

"He doesn't. He doesn't know I'm here. Your mother assures him that she knows where you are and that you're safe, but his patience is wearing thin and I can't guarantee that I won't be ordered to disclose your location when I get back. If he finds out where I've gone."

Flint crossed his arms over his chest. He wasn't quite old enough to be my father, but sometimes, when he was showing his disappointment in me, it felt like he could be.

"She hasn't told him?" I asked. That was unlike Mom. Usually, she told him everything.

"She hasn't. And let's just say that isn't something that goes over well with your father."

"I can imagine." I snorted.

"Alyssum, things have been happening. It's getting dangerous and everyone would feel better if you were where we could protect you. While your mother hasn't told me much, I do know you're on this mission to bring home the prodigal son, but again, it's been too long. Time to throw in the towel and come home with me."

He'd spoken with such authority that I almost agreed out of reflex. Almost.

"What's happened?"

Flint sighed but didn't change his stance. "There was a big fire at the copper mines. We didn't start it, obviously. I'll give you one guess who did." *Gobel.* "The mines are okay, but some people got hurt. We have intel that the Gobel are training for something big and there have been a few skirmishes. There was a pretty big security breach at the house as well."

The last part got my attention the most. There was always danger lurking, but I couldn't remember a time when something had happened at our house, the place where The Assembly met.

"What happened, Flint?" I didn't actually think he'd tell me, but it was worth a try. I wasn't part of The Assembly or part of security. Breaches were usually need-to-know and it'd been made clear that I never needed to know.

"Everyone is fine," he assured me and that was as much information as I was going to get out of him.

"Good," I said, nodding absently. "I can't go yet. Can I trust you to keep a secret?" He thought a few seconds, then gave a quick nod. "I found him. I found the Sorrels' son. He's alive. He made it out of the car the night of the crash. Someone got him out." I swallowed hard. "But I haven't told him yet. I will, soon. But I need just a little more time. Please." I hated begging, but Jensen was worth it. "Is there anything you can do to give me just a little more time? I'll head home as soon as I can."

Flint took a deep breath, then blew it out of his nose slowly. It was a habit of his when he was thinking things over. I didn't even think he realized he was doing it.

"I'll do what I can," he said. I started to speak, but he put a hand up. "I'll tell your mother I saw you and that you are fine. I'll also tell her you're on your way home soon, but I will leave everything else out because I'm not sure I understand what you're trying to do here." He shuffled slightly closer to me. "But, Alyssum, I'm warning you, you don't have much time before an entire security force shows up here for you. Your mother can't keep Ash in the dark forever."

"Okay." I nodded. "Okay, I promise."

Flint turned to leave and I ran to the window so I could see him disappear for myself. One thing I'd learned a long time ago was that Flint was a man of his word. If he said he wouldn't tell anyone what I told him, he wouldn't. But I also knew he wouldn't give me much leeway. He'd put an end to what I was trying to do if I took too long.

It was time to tell Jensen the truth even though he would think I'm crazy.

Chapter Seven

MY ROOM FELT EVEN SMALLER after Flint left.

I was wired. Sleep was out of the question. Instead of bothering to try to nod off, I called Aric, hoping he wasn't busy. He answered on the second ring and sounded genuinely happy to hear from me. We talked for an hour before he asked me to dinner the next night. Even though I really, really liked Aric, even I had to admit it wasn't my stomach that tingled when I talked to him but an entirely different part of my body. Our conversations was easier than any Gremalian would've thought it could be with a Gobel.

Plus, it was kind of nice not to have to tweak any of my stories to sound normal. His stories would sound just as crazy to the humans as mine.

I felt better after talking to him. I was able to slip into my pajamas and lie down. I felt like I might actually get some rest. Then my phone rang and the ID flashed Jensen's name. I'd only recently turned it on but ignored anything from someone back home.

I didn't know if I should answer it or ignore it. I wanted to because I need him for the whole "saving our people" thing, but part of me wanted to make him sweat after seeing him out on a date. In the end, I answered because he hadn't done anything wrong to begin with. We weren't dating exclusively, and I couldn't let my more jealous feelings get the better of me.

"What'd you do? Dump the poor woman off as soon as the movie was over?" Harassing him was the byproduct of me wanting to know how the date had gone.

"Something like that." His voice sounded husky and fluid, like I could bathe in it.

"Did you at least stop the car or just slow down and push her out?" Though I was trying to sound playful, I kind of hoped he'd just pushed her out and kept driving. Yeah, that wasn't a side of me I appreciated.

"I came to a complete stop," he joked back.

"How nice of you." I waited for him to continue

and when he didn't, I said, "Was there a reason for this 'not-so-late' night call?"

My fingers strummed against my cotton-covered leg. I've talked to him a hundred times, yet nervous energy flowed through me.

"Yeah, to see if you'd go out with me tomorrow?"

I let the silence hang in the air before answering to picture him on the other end, not knowing what was going on in my head. "I already have plans for tomorrow."

"With Aric?" Bam. He sighed, sounding a little defeated. "Okay, how about the day after?"

"I'm not sure."

"Come on, Alyssum. Are you mad at me? I mean, we never said—"

"No. Really, I don't know. I need to get the oil changed in my car, so I have to find a car place. My dad will kill me if I burn up the motor, especially after the antifreeze issue, and I've put it off too long already."

"Really? An oil change?" The sound of him both wanting to believe my excuse and not really believing it made me smile. The oil change wasn't an excuse. My car needed the attention. "Just bring it in, I'll do it."

"That's okay." I giggled, which had to put him at

ease a little. "You guys are always busy; that's why I didn't ask. And I don't want it to be weird."

"Alyssum, seriously. Just bring the fucking thing in and it'll get done. Come in late afternoon. I'll change the oil and then go home and change my clothes so we can go out. Okay?"

"If you're sure." I twirled a lock of hair around my finger until it cut off the circulation and the tip started to throb.

"Hey, if it's the only way I can make sure you're available to go out, I'll rebuild the motor if I have to."

"I don't think that will be necessary."

After we hung up, the green eyed monster started to wane. After all, he called me after dropping her off. My feelings for Aric and Jensen weren't equal. Obviously. I needed to make it clear to both of them.

I passed the time the next day by watching TV. It'd been forever since I'd gotten to just lie around and watch TV. I found I wasn't really missing much. Reality TV pretty much sucked and that seemed to be the only thing ever on. Who wanted reality when they lived it every day?

After getting my hair fixed how I liked it into

loose curls and putting on the little bit of makeup that I did like to wear, I headed over to the shop for my oil change.

The first person I saw when cool air from the reception area hit me was Jensen's dad.

"Hey, young lady. Haven't seen you in a while. How are you?"

He gave me a bear hug, lifting me a good foot off the floor. That was his small-town charm, something we didn't have in our small town. Of course, our small town was more like a military barracks in a lot of ways.

"Good. You?" My voice was strained since he was squeezing the air out of my lungs. He put me back on the ground.

"Yup. So..." He went back around and leaned on his elbows on top of the counter, an unabashedly large grin on his face. "Been keeping our boy busy?"

The old guy's face was so bright with hope that it just about killed me, but I was also reminded that Jensen had plenty of people to occupy his time.

"Not just me," I muttered under my breath. Mr. Burkhardt heard me and his face changed to one of a proud dad. Men.

"*Dad!*" Jensen came in just then. He must have heard that last bit. His white shirt was smudged with oil stains and a fine sheen of sweat covered his skin just enough that the fabric clung to the well-sculpted muscles rippling down his abdomen. I dropped my keys in his hand, lightly grazing his palm. Even that small gesture sent sparks through my body.

In all the times we'd touched, Jensen hadn't acknowledged a single spark.

Once Jensen brought my car inside and got started, I went through the door into the garage area and found a stool by the toolboxes. Jensen noticed me almost immediately and glanced over his shoulder often to catch my eye.

When he rolled out from underneath, I watched his eyes crawl up my calves until they met my skirt, then jump to my face. His gaze was a like a caress that flooded my body with warmth.

"Shit, shit, shit," a voice boomed from my right. A wrench landed not far from my feet. "Alyssum." Aric ran over, clearly shocked to see how close the tool had come to hitting me. "Did that hit you?"

"No." I laughed quietly. "What's wrong?"

"I can't fix this damn car. It's an electrical issue, but..."

"Stand back," I whispered just to him. He hopped behind the steering wheel and, once Jensen had slid back under my car, I casually looked around to make sure no one was watching, then twirled my index finger in the air, picking up some static electricity. A small spark shot out, hitting the car's engine. Aric turned the key and the engine fired immediately. Aric gave me a small nod of thanks; it felt good to use my power and it was one that Aric didn't have.

My attention went back to Jensen, who'd not only finished the oil but also checked everything under the hood to make sure all the fluids were topped off. Apparently, I'd also neglected the windshield wiper fluid because it was bone dry.

Oops.

He dropped the hood and turned to me while wiping the grease on his hands onto a rag.

"All set," Jensen said. He tossed the blue cloth onto a tall, silver box and waved his fingers, letting me know to follow him. We went back to the reception area. I think Jensen just wanted to get away from Aric since, once the door closed behind us, he turned to continue the conversation.

"So, I'll go get cleaned up and we can head out."

"Do you want a ride?" I scrunched my face because the dude was covered in dirt, oil, and sweat, and having him in my car was less-than-appealing.

Luckily, he shook his head. "I rode my bike in. If

you want to come to my place to wait, I'll be quick. I promise."

"Wow, just what every woman wants to hear," I said. That got a laugh out of him as every muscle in his body relaxed.

We would be alone at his apartment. Was this the perfect time to tell him what he is?

Chapter Eight

Jensen lived moderately close to the garage and I followed him the whole way. Not because I'd never been there but I'd never gone there from the garage. It wasn't a big town but that didn't mean I couldn't have taken a wrong turn.

When the door to his apartment swung open, we entered the living room first. With a quick look around, I noted a feminine touch. His mom must have fixed the place up. Alice didn't seem like the type of woman who'd let her son fester in a rat hole or frat house. That wasn't to say there were flowered curtains all around; everything was very manly, from the dark couch down to the much-too-large television and bare walls, aside from a clock.

"I'll just be a few minutes."

And he was off. Within thirty seconds, the shower rained down in the bathroom. I gave myself a private tour of the rest of his place. He had quite a bit of square footage, more than I'd first thought. An attached dining room held a small, four-person table. There was a galley kitchen that ran the width on the far end with an opening that allowed anyone in the kitchen to talk to anyone who wasn't. I even let myself wander the other direction, into his bedroom. A large, unmade bed sat under a row of windows.

The mass of tangled blankets and sheets brought other thoughts to mind.

"Whoa." Jensen's voice startled me. I turned quickly at the sound of his voice and found him in the doorway with just a towel wrapped around his waist and small drops of water glistening from his chest and abs. "I didn't expect..."

"Sorry." I might have actually started to blush. I swore I could feel his body heat two feet away and wanted to feel it closer. "I was just wandering... I don't even know how I ended up in here. I wasn't snooping, I swear."

His smile looked even more delicious when he was all clean and wet. It took just about all I had not to pounce on him. Given that he was naked under that towel, it would have gotten super weird, super quick.

"You just surprised me." An awkward silence fell over us for what felt like ages. "I, uh, need to get dressed."

"Right." I snapped back to reality. "I'll be in the living room."

I'm such an idiot. Caught in his bedroom? Why did I go in there?

Being a guy must be far too easy because in less time than it took me to do my hair, he was completely put-together. He looked like he'd stepped out of a movie. I couldn't focus on anything but him when he came out in jeans and a white T-shirt that had a slight V-neck, just enough to tease me with his collarbones. Though I'd never heard a blow dryer, his hair looked perfect.

First, we ate at this small pizza place up the road from the theater. Just a quick bite before the movie he planned on taking me to. I discovered I was pretty good at getting on and off his bike in a skirt without flashing all my goodies to anyone watching. I liked riding with him, liked being that close and being able to wrap my arms around his waist. It was comfortable.

"I'm pretty sure you've already seen this one," I said, nudging his arm as we stood in line to get tickets. It was the same movie I'd gone to when I saw him with Ashley.

"Like I could concentrate."

After purchasing our tickets, he offered to buy snacks, but I was completely full. I asked for a diet pop and was teased, yet again, for calling it "pop

"What did you mean, you couldn't concentrate?" I asked as we took our seats in a completely different section than the one he'd sat in with Ashley. I wanted to know, but if he told me he'd spent the time making out with that woman, I might throw up.

"I watched you more than the movie," he said, making me smile. "Then, after you left, I just wanted to get out of here. I literally remember nothing about the movie."

"Aww." I pushed up out of my seat to kiss his cheek.

He turned to me, looking very serious. "Alyssum, I want to explain that."

"You don't have to. We never said we weren't seeing other people."

"I know." The words came out flat and jealousy quickly crossed over his face again.

"Ashley asked me out just after I met you. I didn't want to go; she's boring and far too perky," he said. "But her mom works with mine and our dads are kind of friends. It would've been weird if I'd turned her down."

"And now is the poor woman waiting for date number two?"

"Lord no. She, ah… 'doesn't think my head was in the game.' Her words."

The lights dimmed. After previews, the movie went by quickly as I sat, very comfortably, with my head on his shoulder and my hand in his. I didn't want the date to end. Every time he kissed the top of my head or tickled my arm with his fingertips, my entire body tingled like I'd just licked the end of a nine-volt battery. For the second time, I couldn't concentrate on this movie and decided that I'd prob-ably never actually see it.

When we headed back to his place, I thought I'd just get in my car and go, but I couldn't say *no* when he invited me in.

Once we were through the door, his lips crashed into mine.

He cupped my face and rested the other hand on

my hip, squeezing as he licked at my lips. There was an explosion of electricity rippling through my body and I hoped he felt it too. This wasn't just because we were Gremalian. It couldn't be. I'd kissed other Gremalians and it'd never felt like this.

Jensen tilted my head back to take the kiss deeper as he walked me toward his couch. I didn't worry about falling. He wouldn't let anything happen to me. It was something I knew as well as I knew my own name.

The backs of my legs hit the couch but instead of falling back, Jensen's strong arms slowly lowered me to the cushion. The pressure of his body had me spread my legs so that he could settle between them.

I suddenly wanted one of those T-shirts that read *My perfect weight is Jensen Burkhardt on top of me.*

It would've been easy to let it go from there. Thin cotton was the only thing standing between us. His hand inched up my side, under my shirt; he cupped my breast through my bra. Every muscle in my body tightened as sense crept back into my brain.

I pushed gently against his chest.

"Sorry." He brought the kiss to an end but didn't move though there was no doubt he would have if I'd wanted him to. "I, uh..."

"No, no."

I pulled myself up to a sitting position, which forced him up as well. We faced each other, and our eyes locked as our breathing came back to normal and our pulses slowed.

"I just... I can't really..." Words were not my friend at that moment. *Okay, time to talk like grown-ups.* Taking a deep breath, calming my nerves, I dove right in. "Jensen, I can't let this"—I waved my finger between the two of us—"go any further right now."

He nodded as he ran his tongue over his bottom lip as if he was savoring the taste of me still left that. "I wasn't trying to pressure you. It just felt right."

"It totally feels right." Nothing had ever felt righter. More right? "It's just that there is something I need to make cleat before we go there." His brows furrowed. "Not with you."

"Ah." He sized me up, like he was trying to figure out how to say or ask something. "Aric?" I couldn't bring myself to confirm.

"I don't... I'm pretty sure he already knows but I'd feel better talking to him. If I don't... I'll feel like a shitty person. A shitty friend."

"I understand." He fell quiet for only a moment. "I saw you two together."

I physically felt the blood drain from my face. "You saw... what?"

Jensen eyed my reaction and his voice came out ragged, either from our previous activity or anger. I wasn't sure which. "Yeah, uh, coming and going from his place a couple of times. I've passed you running, stuff like that. I didn't think it was a big deal, but judging from the look on your face, I'm a little more worried now." He let out a nervous laugh.

"Nothing's happened. I just... It's just I know how I felt seeing you with Ashley." I turned to the side, slipped my shoes on, and found my purse. I took my keys out and held them tightly in my hand. The metal digging into my skin brought me back to Earth. I knew what I had to do. "So, I'm gonna go."

He walked me to my car, which was parked around the corner from his apartment. That spot had been the closest to his place at that time. Once we'd made it to my car, I was reminded of our first kiss after the fireworks. He'd walked me to my car then too.

"We'll talk soon?" he asked when our eyes locked again as he played with the ends of my hair.

"Definitely."

He kissed me again, softer and a lot less intensely but with all the same feeling as before.

"I have to tell you, Alyssum. I don't want there to be any confusion." His face wasn't more than a couple of inches from mine as his breath feathered against my skin. "I want to be with you. I don't want you seeing anyone else and I don't want to see anyone else. That said... If it's him, just tell me, because I can't let it be both of us anymore." His eyes dropped to my lips, then found their way back to mine. "I'm selfish like that."

My breath stumbled in my throat before I said, "I like selfish." Yet I couldn't explain that it wasn't both of them. I'd make sure that Aric understood he and I were only going to be friends but it wasn't both of them.

The motel room had never felt more like home than it did that night. Small and familiar, a place where I could put on my comfies and sink down into the lumpy mattress. I wished for sleep. My mind raced over details of what I had to do next.

Talk to Aric.

Tell Jensen he's a Gremalian.

The next morning, a Saturday, I knew Jensen wasn't working and Aric would be, so I headed to Burkhardt's Garage. There was no one inside to greet me and I didn't see anyone working, but I waited.

"Oh, Alyssum, Jensen's not here." Mr. Burkhardt's booming voice caused me to jump. He'd entered the reception room from the office, which I had my back turned to.

"I'm actually looking for Aric."

His face dropped but he recovered quickly. I had to suppress a grin. He waved his hand in the direction of the shop, which was where I found Aric leaning over the motor of a bright-red convertible.

"Hey," he said when he saw me coming.

I took extra caution getting to his bay, stepping over air hoses and tools, thankful that I hadn't worn my signature wedges, instead opting for shorts and flat sandals. Otherwise, I'd have probably fallen flat on my face

"So, what's up?" Aric leaned against the car, folding his arms over his chest and crossing his legs at the ankle. "You came to tell me you want to be with him, right?"

"Aric…"

"It's fine Alyssum. I knew that's how this whole thing would end up and we've been more friends than anything."

"I wanted to make sure you knew what was happening before…" I took a deep breath. "I didn't want to hurt your feelings."

"You're not. Don't worry about it. Besides it's not like you can take a Gobel home to Mom."

I snorted. No. That wouldn't have been optimal but I would've done it and my mother would've accepted it. My father on the other hand...

"He might not want me," I told him though shouldn't have been talking to him about this at all. "He might not when he finds out why I'm here."

"He will. He's going to be pissed for sure and probably think you've lost your mind but he'll get over it." He shrugged. "He has to."

"You know you've become one of my best friends, right?" I'd chosen those words carefully. I had Delilah back home who'd been my best friend for a long time. With Aric, I needed him to know how important he was to me and I knew what his reaction would be. I didn't want to hurt him but I needed this.

His head snapped to the side, jaw tensing with words he wouldn't say.

The friendship card.

It was a big one among the Gobel, the one that trumped all others once they cared about someone. He couldn't betray a friend very easily, even if he wanted to, and whatever that friendship button inside his people was, I needed to use it to my advantage.

"So, we're good then?" It was the last question I wanted to ask. If he said *no*, that he never wanted to see me again, I was sure I'd cry on the spot. I cared about Aric a lot, but, when I looked deeper, it was as a friend. Our friendship would help us through this awkward situation. It had to.

"You know us goblins... can't get rid of us that easily." He said those words to put me at ease, I was sure, because that was the kind of thing a Gobel would do for their friend, but the tone told me a lot more.

I laughed, which put me at ease. Even if he'd developed feelings for me and I for him, though it wasn't what I felt for Jensen, he made me laugh.

"I'd hug you, but you're gross. So, I owe you one." I smirked, testing the waters of our new friendship.

"Yeah, I don't like IOUs." He pulled me into a big, greasy bear hug, ignoring all my protests and wiping his hands up and down my back, leaving his mark. "Now that that's settled," he said as he let me go, "we need to head back soon. He needs to know what's really going on no matter how pissed he's going to be."

"I know." I nodded as I spoke.

"I can—"

"No, I'll do it."

That way if Jensen pushes me away, it won't be with an audience.

As I headed back out through the main lobby, Mr. Burkhardt said, "Jensen's out at our place."

I turned slowly to face him. "Your place?"

"Yeah." He scratched the back of his head. "He's helping get some things cleaned up. You can head out there if you need to."

He couldn't have overheard my conversation with Aric. I didn't think but I did need to talk to Jensen so I asked for the address then headed back to the motel.

Though now the anxiety of actually having to tell him was setting in and I wished we could just stay in this safe place where there was no coming war.

But that wasn't my reality.

My reality included a war against the people of one of my new best friends.

Chapter Nine

BEFORE GOING out to find Jensen, I changed my clothes *again* because of all the grease Aric had gotten on me with that hug. I even had a smear of grease across my cheek. At least I didn't need a whole shower. Wiping away the grease on my face and touching up my makeup was good enough.

The Burkhardts lived just a few miles out on what used to be a large farm but his grandparents sold most of the land years ago.

I pulled into the horseshoe driveway and stopped in the middle. His mom stepped out onto the front porch that wrapped all the way around the white house. She immediately looked disappointed, throwing a tense, not-*quite*-rude greeting that told me where Jensen was and made me wonder what he'd them about us.

Jensen was out back, behind the garage, moving wood to make room for another delivery, I'd guess with his radio so loud he couldn't have heard me coming.

Leaning against the corner of the garage, I watched him work. His muscles strained when he picked up more than he should have for each load, and with his shirt off, his body glistening in the summer sun, who could blame my Peeping Tom routine? The longer I watched him, the more I didn't want to just *watch* him.

The man was beautiful sweat and all.

"I always wondered how you stay in shape," I called out over the sound of the radio.

He spun in surprise, dropping two logs in the process. "Hey." He smiled wide. "What are you doing here?"

"Just a little stalking."

"Well, that's always welcome."

I grinned and tucked a piece of hair behind my ear. "Your dad told me you were here."

Jensen tossed the armload to the ground and grabbed the T-shirt that hung off the side of the truck to give his chest and arms a wipe-down before coming over to me.

"Something wrong?" he asked.

He led me by the hand over to the big, black truck where the music was coming from. After dropping the tailgate and going around to lower the volume, he came back to sit beside me. Even with all the physical activity and the perspiration, he still smelled sweet. It was like a musky, earthy smell that drew me in.

"I went to the shop first—"

"I told you I wasn't working today, right?" He eyed me curiously, those beautiful, blue eyes narrowing on mine.

"I went to talk to Aric."

His jaw tensed. "And?"

"We talked. I made things clear. We're friends." I shrugged because that was the best I had. "I just didn't want there to be any confusion if we..." I let my voice trail off because getting ahead of myself wasn't going to help.

Hell. I'd already set myself up for heartbreak by not telling Jensen what he is.

Jensen leaned over, stroking my bottom lip, then cheek, with a thumb before bringing his soft lips to mine. His mouth pressed against mine, demanding that I submit and I was more than ready to.

His other arm wrapped around my back then tugged me toward him. As his tongue licked at my lips, coaxing me to open for him, I didn't care that he'd been doing sweaty work outside or that we were at his parent's house.

All I cared about was his mouth on mine.

Until someone cleared their throat.

My spine straightened, ending the kiss, but Jensen chuckled. He could see who was there over my shoulder but I didn't want to turn to look.

"What's up?" he asked.

"I brought you some lemonade," his mother said making my stomach clench in an entirely different way.

My reaction was ridiculous. I was a grown woman. Jensen was a grown man. His mother *catching* us shouldn't have affected me. It certainly didn't him.

Jensen hopped off the tailgate then went over to take the glasses from his mother before bringing one back to me.

"Thank you," I said quietly.

Mrs. Burkhardt glanced at me but didn't

respond. Instead, she focused back on Jensen. "Don't forget the Dittmans are coming for dinner tonight. You said you'd be here."

I raised my brows.

"Ashley's family," he whispered, even though his mom was right there and would hear either way.

"Ah, I see. The future wife's coming over. I guess the girlfriend should leave."

Jensen laughed loudly, though his mother didn't seem to appreciate the comment.

She looked like she'd been sucking on too many of those lemons anyway. I made a mental note to ask later if that was her normal disposition or something only I brought out.

After assuring his mother he'd be there, Jensen walked me slowly to my car, a sticky arm around my shoulder.

"It was the motorcycle, right?" Jensen's hip nudged mine.

"'Course. Because I couldn't find any other douche on a bike who'd have me." I gave him a sharp elbow to the solar plexus, just hard enough for him to feel it. "Hey, since you have plans tonight, could I borrow you for lunch tomorrow? Or breakfast if that's better for you."

"I think I can make time for lunch with my girlfriend."

I rolled my eyes. "Just don't think this means I'm open for business or anything."

He smirked back at me. "Wouldn't dream of it." I raised an eyebrow. "Okay, maybe I *would* dream of it, but I assume nothing."

Another elbow to his ribs got more laughter out of him. I could only shake my head.

Though I didn't think it'd be long before we did actually get naked.

The thing I loved about Putnam Valley was that, compared to home, it was huge. I had actual options as to where I could eat. Back home, my only choice was the one family-run restaurant. Putnam Valley even had a Chinese restaurant, something you'd have to drive miles for in the Upper Peninsula and likely it wouldn't be good Chinese food.

I chose the deli for Jensen's and my lunch on Monday because they made the best sandwiches I'd ever eaten and Jensen ended up not being able to make it yesterday. His dad wasn't feeling good and he needed to take care of admin things at the shop.

"Hey," he said when he arrived before pinching my chin between his thumb and forefinger to tilt my head for a kiss.

No. Can't get distracted.

As he slid into the opposite side of the booth, he said, "I don't usually leave the shop for lunch unless I'm getting everyone's takeout. This is a nice change."

"I got your order," I told him sliding his sandwich across from him then slowly unwrapped my own.

He dove in like a starving badger but my stomach was roiling with acid so I didn't take a single bite.

I had fallen for this man so quickly and the prospect of him pushing me away once he finds out everything was more than I thought I could handle.

"I have to tell you something," I blurted out.

Our gazes locked for a moment before I glanced away. I'd never been this uncomfortable in my life.

I'd thought it would be easy. No sweat. I'd roll into town, make him take notice, get him alone and tell him who he really was. Instead, I'd fallen for the guy. Now, not only was his return on the line, but a relationship was, too. I hadn't seen that coming.

"Why do I not like the sound of that?" he replied. The booth creaked as he sat back, folding his arms across the muscles in his chest. I tried not to notice.

"It's no big deal. I mean, it is, but it's not, you know?"

I couldn't have made less sense if I were actually speaking Mandarin. What the hell was wrong with me?

I'd once fought a six-pack of evil fairies—really, just a bunch of overzealous high school boys—on my own when I was fifteen, which had impressed even our most experienced fighters since I'd kicked their asses.

Yet the minute I had to tell a man I liked something important, I could barely put a coherent sentence together.

"Okay, well, I know you're not pregnant." He snorted at his joke. "So, out with it."

With one deep breath, I used all that air to spit it out. "I'm Gremalian, and so are you. We need you to come home to help save our people."

That was when I finally looked at him again. He either didn't believe me, or didn't understand, because I'd explained nothing and sounded psychotic. The entire sentence had come out as one word.

"Gremlin? Like Gizmo?" He cocked his head to the side and smirked.

A nervous laugh came out, but I rolled my eyes. "No, those gremlins are the bastardization of our people. I'm not small and green, am I?"

"You *are* pretty small," he teased.

"That's just a coincidence."

"I mean, I heard you say you're a gremlin."

"Jensen." I sighed. "I'm serious."

I was silently begging him to believe me but he stood up to leave instead.

"I can see that you think you are, but you're also making no sense. I've got work to do. An old carburetor is calling my name. We can talk later."

Then he was gone.

When I saw his motorcycle pass the front window, I had to act.

Shit. I tore out of there like my pants were on fire and curried to my car. I sped through town, trying to beat him back to the shop.

I failed.

His head start was too much for me to overcome. So, instead of busting in there to haul Aric out, I loitered at the corner until I caught his eye and waved him over.

"Some kind of lunch, I guess," Aric called out to

me before getting all the way into the parking lot. I shushed him with a finger over my mouth and gestured for him to hurry.

"I told him."

"What?" Aric's voice dropped the way it should have.

"I told him. He didn't believe me and he left. Of course, I really explained nothing, which I'm thinking was the wrong way to go." *Deflect with humor; that's the Alyssum way.*

Pushing his shoulders back to stand tall, he said, "That explains his weirdness."

"What?" I pulled him by the arm to the other side of the building in the hopes Jensen wouldn't see us.

"He's been pissed since he's been back. Slamming drawers, cursing under his breath. Everyone's kind of keeping their distance. They think he's had a stroke or something because that's not like him. I mean, me, they expect it from. Not him." He paused to look at me. I tried to envision a pissed-off Aric tearing apart the garage. "Do you think he thinks he got stuck with the crazy chick?"

"Probably," I muttered. "I mean, there are a number of ways I thought he might react but this wasn't one of them. What do we do?"

I still couldn't believe I was asking a Gobel for advice. My father would roll over in his grave and he wasn't even dead yet.

"Okay, I'm supposed to go to his dad's tonight with him to watch the baseball game—"

"I never understood the appeal of that game."

"Not really the point here, Alyssum." A look of bemusement crossed his face. "It starts at seven. We'll have to lay it all out for him. You probably shouldn't have tried to do it at lunch anyway. And in public?" He tisked.

"I wanted to do it at the motel yesterday but he couldn't come."

Aric snorted. "There are so many things I could say about that sentence."

I slapped his arm, though once I'd said the words, I'd thought it too. "Aric."

"OK. Seven?"

I agreed.

Aric had become one of the most trusted people in my life. Jensen too, of course. I trusted both of them more than my own parents. It didn't help that I thought my parents would feed me to wolves if it suited our people. Our people came first. I came last.

Well, maybe with my mom I came second. Or tied for second. She loved me. She supported me coming here but my dad was the priority and his priority was the people.

Aric went back to work, pretending he knew nothing, and I went around the other side to sneak back to my car two blocks away.

Just hours from now, the fate of my people would be decided.

Chapter Ten

Waiting for the guys to get to Jensen's parent's house was like waiting for a jury of my peers to decide my fate.

Maybe I was being a little dramatic but the hours dragged.

If I were home, I'd walk the shores of Lake Superior or journey into the depths of the copper mine until I just couldn't contain the power coursing my body and had to tear ass out of there before I exploded.

I could practice my power, although I didn't need the extra practice, or train with some of the guys, which was always fun. I could usually find something to do at home. I could just be me.

It hit me that I was actually homesick. *Yikes.* That was a cold slap of reality. I'd wanted to leave home for almost as long as I could remember. Now I was gone and I wanted to head back.

I glanced at the clock and it was finally after seven. I could meet up with them.

When I got to the house, Jensen's mother was a little nicer to me than she had been before. Which was good. He was close to his parents. Her not hating me would come in handy.

She invited me in then said to follow her which I did.

"Jensen," she said once we were in the archway to the living room. "Alyssum's here."

His gaze popped up full of surprise when he saw me in his parent's living room. The he pushed himself out of the chair.

"Hey." But there was no kiss hello for me this time.

"Can we talk?" I asked as I nervously glanced at Aric who was sitting on the couch, hoping Jensen wouldn't want to do it here. That would be a huge problem.

He waved his hand, indicating that I should follow him. We climbed a single flight of stairs. The stairs creaked behind me so I glanced back and found Aric coming too.

We stopped at the first room on the right.

"In here," Jensen said then waited for the two of us to get inside before following.

"Your room?" I asked while Aric shut the door gently. Jensen didn't have any siblings, so this was most likely his room, but it was little more than a shrine to the teenage boy he had been. Posters of football players on the wall. Some trophies on a shelf across from the closet.

It didn't reflect the man I'd grown to care for.

"It was," he said.

"Right, sorry." I took a breath. "Okay, I shouldn't have sprung anything on you at lunch and I'm sorry for that. I did it wrong a little warning might've been appropriate" I was starting to ramble so I took a deep breath and blew it out slowly. "Whatever. Look, what I said is true." He sat back on the edge of the desk and crossed his arms over his chest. "Let me start over."

"Are you trying to prank me or something?" he asked as Aric moved closer to us. "Are you two in on some sort of gag? I'm not falling for whatever this is."

"Just listen to her, Jensen." Aric spoke for the

first time. He was leaning a shoulder against the wall in a very relaxed position. "We aren't trying to trick you. What she's trying to tell you is true and she can prove it. It's important."

"'We'? What the fuck, Alyssum?"

"Just give me a minute, please."

Jensen sighed heavily and tensed his jaw but then nodded.

"I'm part of a race of people called Gremalians. So are you. And yes, humans bastardized us into tiny, green troublemakers who had a lot of rules most of which are false." Aric cleared his throat. "Although yes, the eating after midnight thing is true but it's only until five in the morning or you'll get a hellish case of debilitating heartburn."

Aric snickered this time so I lifted a middle finger and pushed it as close to him as I could get without moving away from Jensen.

"We're not all that different from humans. We just want to live our lives in peace." I'd leave out the coming war part for now. It was all a lot to take in.

"Let's say this is true," Jensen started, though I thought he was beginning to think there was a tiny chance I was telling the truth. Then he pointed at Aric. "Why does he know about this?"

"He's a Gobel." Like that would mean anything to him.

"A goblin?" He clawed his hands down the front of his face.

I giggled, more from nerves than anything else, but it *did* strike me as funny. Aric laughed too. "No, Gobel. It's basically the same as Gremalian, but different. I know that doesn't make sense."

"*None* of this makes any sense. Do you expect me to believe this?"

Jensen's heavy footsteps clunked against the floor as he went to the door and yanked it open.

"You just let him leave?" I gave Aric a little push.

"It looks like he needs some air. If this is sinking in at all, he'd need to do something. What'd you expect? You'd come in and say, 'Hey, you're a gremlin,' and he'd be all, 'That's cool.' Don't think so, Alyssum."

Before I left the room, I gave Aric my best death glare, mostly because I didn't want to admit that he'd hit the nail on the head. I'd thought if he got to know me before I told him, that with some convincing, he'd believe me.

Aric was right behind me again as we went after Jensen. The front door banged shut so I took a gamble and followed. Finally, we found him behind the garage.

"Maybe you two should stop following me," he said angrily.

"We can't. Jensen, we're normal people, just not completely... human," I said. His shoulders tensed even more. "I know that sounds terrible, but it doesn't change who you are or who I am or that when you woke up this morning, I was your girlfriend. You work in a garage. All of these things are exactly the same as the fact that you were Gremalian when you woke up this morning. The only difference is that now you know it and I can prove it."

Silence hung in the air, thick and stagnant, like an uncomfortable corset squeezing my lungs. It seemed like forever before he spoke again.

"Why do you need to save your people?" His tone was full of skepticism.

"*Our* people," I corrected. "We're natural enemies. Us and the Gobel. Usually." I glanced at Aric. "Control of power, control of the land where the copper mines are... I don't know." I sighed.

"It's all of that," Aric said from his spot against the garage.

"Think of it like this. We're the Hatfields and they're the McCoys." Since he wasn't running away,

I continued but moved a bit closer to place my hand on his shoulder. The muscle there jumped. "If you concentrate, Jensen, you'll know I'm telling the truth. You have to know it." I thought for a minute. "Don't you feel it whenever Aric's around? A prickling up your neck and your hair stands on end? Anything unusual at all?"

The tension in his muscles eased a tiny bit. "Here I thought I was just bi-curious."

"What?" I smiled back. At least he was talking to us. That was something. He turned to face us. I hoped it was a sign that he was starting to understand what we were trying to tell him.

"There was a time, a *very short time*, that I thought I might be... *attractedtohim*." He said the last three words very quickly so that they came out as one crunched together word. Aric and I had still heard it and we both howled with laughter, Aric louder than me.

"I *am* pretty sexy," Aric said through his laughter.

"Asshole," Jensen said while shaking his head.

"I know things. I can convince you. I can prove all of this if you give me the chance." I promised. Showing him my power would've been easy and actually was something I'd planned to from the start but he seemed to need a little more easing into this whole thing.

"Like what? What do you know?"

"You're adopted—"

"I could have told you that."

"But you didn't. You showed up at the hospital your mom works at, right? After your parents were killed in a car accident." I left out that they were being chased by a group of Gobel. That was for later. He remained silent. "Your birth parents' names were Glen and Saffron Sorrel."

Jensen thought about that for a minute, biting his bottom lip the way he did whenever he was really trying to figure something out.

"How much of this was real?" He waved his finger between us. I took his face in my hands, which made it nearly impossible for him to look anywhere but at me.

"All of it, Jensen. I swear, all of it." Jensen's eyes slowly searched the landscape of my face to see if I was telling the truth. I wasn't hiding anything anymore. "And I'm going to have to leave soon. A war is about to break out and we need everyone we can get."

"How does he fit into this?" Jensen pointed at

Aric as if I wouldn't know whom he was talking about without the gesture.

"Like I said he's a Gobel."

He blew out a breath, like he didn't understand. "I'm so confused. I thought you are at war with them."

"We are, but Aric wants to help stop it from happening."

"How is he going to do that?"

"You, or the threat of you, might be able to stop it. With my help, of course."

"You?" He shook his head.

"Yeah, I know I don't look like much, but I'm pretty badass." I gave his shoulder a playful hit.

He smiled at me the way he had before I'd told him all of the stuff about Gremalians and Gobel. "Somehow, I can see that. But why don't you prove it?"

I smirked and Aric snorted from behind me. "All right, but you get to explain what happens to the lights."

His eyebrows shot up. Pulling his arm out in front of him, I took a deep breath and lightly touched my fingertips to the sensitive skin on the underside of his forearm. The lights in the house dimmed as I drew the power to me. Flashes sparked across his skin.

I kept the flashes small. I didn't want to hurt him but Jensen started to squirm anyway. His eyes widened and, little by little, I increased the voltage just enough to create a warm, tingling sensation that would drive him nuts. The house came back to full power when Jensen broke our connection. When he yanked back, we started to fall. His arm circled my waist, pulling me on top of him as we hit the ground.

"How did you do that?" His words came out slightly breathless.

"I promise I'll explain everything," I said, my face only inches from his, "but we don't have much time."

"And you need me to come with you?" His blue eyes met mine with an intensity that felt like he was looking into my soul.

"I need you to come with me."

"Because you could get hurt?"

I swallowed hard. "Because we could all get hurt."

His chest pressed against me as he took in air.

"OK," he said. "I'm not sure I believe all of this even with whatever you just did but I'll go. If you need me, I'll go."

A rush of relief flooded my body as I slid further up his body and kissed him.

It didn't matter if Aric was there or if anyone else was watching.

Jensen just agreed to help save our people. That deserved so much more than a kiss but for now this would have to do.

We had people to save and time was running out.

Chapter Eleven

Since Jensen agreed to go with us, I wanted to leave right away but because his mother's birthday was that weekend, Jensen insisted we stay at least until then. He said he needed to make some arrangements, but I think he also needed some time to process everything we'd told him and showed him, so Aric and I gave him as much space as we could for the rest of that week.

Even though I wanted to see him, Jensen was busy all day and called me later in the evening. It was the best he could do right now and I'd take it.

"Aric gave my dad his notice," he told me as I laid on the lumpy motel mattress.

"Yeah?"

"Yeah and Dad approved my vacation time off."

That was what we were telling his parents. That Jensen wanted to ride back home with me and meet my family. "I've never taken time off and he said he'd manage."

"I'm glad he's OK with it but sorry if it's going to put any strain on him." I liked Jensen's dad after all.

He snorted. "Please. He's pretty excited that we're going." I snickered. "I think he thinks meeting your family makes a statement and it's not like I'll be in Michigan forever."

My heart sunk. We hadn't talked about how long he'd be there just that he was coming. Yeah. It made sense that he'd come home eventually but where would that leave us? I'd never considered living outside of Delaware. I needed to be near the copper or my power would weaken. I didn't know how to feel about that.

"We'll figure that out," I told him but then added, "Right?"

"Yeah, Alyssum. We'll figure it out."

Though he didn't sound so sure, I'd have to believe him.

Mrs. Burkhardt's idea of heaven was the backyard, a BBQ, her two favorite guys, and a few friends, Aric included. I didn't think I fit into the equation, but she didn't bat an eye when I showed up at Jensen's insistence.

Truthfully, I couldn't imagine anything better.

With my family, there weren't any cookouts, not a lot of together time at all. That wasn't true of all Gremalian families, just mine specifically. Dad was always busy running our government while Mom acted like she didn't notice how busy he was. She spent time with me whenever Dad didn't need her.

While Jensen worked the grill, I leaned back in the nearest chair, raising my face to the sun, allowing the heat to warm my body. With sunglasses hiding my eyes, I figured Jensen couldn't see me looking at him. I was wrong.

"Stop watching me like that." He snapped the tongs in my face, jarring me out of the trance-like state I was in from thinking about him.

"How can you even tell?"

"I can feel it. And you're gonna make me burn the steaks."

He leaned over me, a hand on each armrest, slowly lowering himself to kiss me. It was quick, and he pulled back like he'd just realized there were twenty people around us.

"I don't like lying to them," he said low enough that I'd be the only one to hear him.

"You're parents?" I asked. He nodded.

When Jensen told his parents that he was going home with me to meet my parents, it wasn't technically a lie but it wasn't the full truth either.

"My mom's not exactly happy about us going."

"You mean you going."

"I'm not," Mrs. Burkhardt said from nowhere. "But he's a grown man and can do as he like."

"Don't worry, Mrs. Burkhardt," Aric said as he dropped his arm around her. "I'm going with them. I'll make sure these two don't get into any trouble."

She looked up at with more kindness than she'd been looking at me. "You're going? All right. I guess I don't have to worry."

Aric laughed loudly as Jensen tried not to.

She liked me just enough to not hate me, but I think she was worried that I might get Jensen in trouble somehow. All I could do was shake my head and wait out the time until we left.

Which was today. After the birthday party.

Jense's mood turned grumpy as we packed my car up outside his apartment that evening.

"I can't believe we're taking this fucking thing,"

he said as he put my back in the back. "It's too small. There's not even enough space for everything."

I cringed knowing that I was the one with the most things. I'd only brought one back with me when I came to New York but was taking much more back. The guys each only had one duffle bag and Aric wasn't even here yet.

"Why can't we take my bike?" It sounded more like a complaint than a question. "Let Aric take all this shit in his car."

"It's a long drive and I wouldn't be able to walk once we got there. My thighs would be mush from squeezing you." I heard the sexual innuendo as soon as I'd said it and a raised eyebrow from Jensen told me he'd heard it too. "Plus, you know he"—I jutted my thumb behind me to an approaching Aric—"has to go with us. And we have a stop to make for someone else. I think that would be a pretty tight squeeze."

Jenssen raised an eyebrow. He didn't know there would be four people in the car.

"I'm sure he wouldn't mind," Jensen mumbled. I shoved his shoulder playfully.

After giggling at the two giants squishing themselves into my tiny car, I drove the first leg of the trip until we were an hour across the state line. I hadn't been sleeping well all week, and my lids started drooping from the monotony of the road. While we all had some special talents, none of us were immune to dying in an accident, so it was time for a break.

I pulled into a rest stop and, after stretching my legs, went in to splash some cold water on my face. It felt good, but it wasn't enough for me to keep driving.

When I came out of the restroom, I headed for the car but saw that Aric and Jensen were no longer inside. To wait for them, I walked around to stretch out my legs a little more and stopped at the large map of Pennsylvania behind a Plexiglas window. I stared at it so long that I wasn't really seeing it anymore until a voice beside me brought me out.

"Hey," a tall, blond man about my age said. He was right next to me with another guy, a dark-haired one, a few steps away.

"Hi." I smiled back but quickly returned to focusing on the map, willing these guys to leave me alone. I wasn't scared. I could handle them easily but it'd be better for them if they just went away.

"I'm Andy. Where ya headed?"

Okay, in another world or another time, that Andy kid might have been cute. But seeing as how I'd been hanging with possibly two of the finest men to walk the Earth, Andy... He just looked young. Who tried to pick up women at a rest area anyway?

I didn't answer his question, didn't introduce myself, or tell him I was headed home. Even Gremalians were well versed in stranger danger.

"See ya," I said and I started to walk away, but he followed making me roll my eyes though he wouldn't see it.

"Did I say something wrong? Because, girl, you're hot, and I'm just looking for some fun."

Scratch the "in another world, he'd be cute" crap. He was heinous.

Spinning on my heels, I faced him. "Look, leave me alone or you won't like the consequences."

A slimy smile spread across his face. "That's hot. Threaten me again."

His smirk set me off and I started to throw a punch, but he reached out and grabbed my wrist, squeezing just tight enough to hurt. I was about to unleash some serious electric violence and a torrent of threats and words he most likely wouldn't understand when his eyes widened and his body tightened.

Suddenly, he let go and walked away.

What the hell?

As I turned back toward the car, Aric and Jensen stood just three feet away, both arms crossed, causing

their muscles to bulge. Their glares were so dangerous, I was surprised the kid hadn't pissed himself.

My jaw clenched and released. "I could've
handled that myself," I said as I passed them.

"Oh, we know you could," Jensen said.

"Just having some fun, Alyssum." Aric chuckled.

"Whatever," I said, coming back to the car with
them trailing behind. "I need a break. Someone else
is going to have to drive."

"I'll do it," they said together.

I rolled my eyes. *Men.* "Whatever. I'm resting in
the back seat either way." I climbed in and waited for
them to decide.

Aric got behind the wheel and slid the seat all
the way back until it slammed into my knees, making
me growl at him.

"Christ, Aric, thanks for leaving me a little
room," I told him as Jensen climbed into the backseat
with me.

He snorted. "You're little. I think there's plenty
of leg space."

I hit the headrest in frustration, which only made
him chuckle louder. Jensen rested his hand on the
inside of my thigh; my head fell onto his shoulder.
With my eyes closed, I still felt like someone was
watching me. When I opened my eyes up, I saw Aric

glance in the rearview mirror, then back to the road. Our eyes locked for seconds at a time before I reclosed my lids.

When I woke up, it was dark. It took a few minutes for me to get acclimated to my surroundings. Jensen was driving, Aric riding shotgun, which left me the whole backseat to myself. I took advantage, stretching my arms and legs to their fullest.

Cars didn't make the most comfortable beds. As de facto decision-maker, I declared it was time to stop for the night. We'd made it all the way to Akron. Solid sleep sounded very good.

"They only had one room available." I dangled the key in front of them. It was a mom-and-pop road-side motel that had old-fashioned keys instead of the card swipey things. I saw the looks on their faces, though, and neither was too happy about sharing a room.

"Seriously?" Jensen scoffed.

"Yeah, I think they're cleaning blood from the others," I said. Neither laughed. "Look, we're all friends here. It'll be a little cozy, but we'll manage."

Not waiting for them to comment, I popped the hatch and grabbed my overnight bag, then opened the door to the room. I was extremely happy to see a bed. They could sleep outside, for all I cared. Instead, they followed.

We found very little, just two full beds and a TV, but at least it was clean. I checked the time and sent Aric out for food. If we waited too long, I wouldn't be able to eat—Jensen, either, whether he believed it or not. I didn't know about him, but I was starving, so waiting till morning was out of the question.

"So, what's the sleeping arrangement here?" Jensen asked as soon as Aric had left. I dug for some pajamas in the brown leather bag I'd brought with me.

"What do you want it to be?" I turned to face him and decided to break some of the tension I'd felt hanging around since we'd left New York. "If you want to share a bed with Aric, test out that whole bi-curious thing, I'm okay with that."

He shook my comment off. "He still has feelings for you, Alyssum."

"And what do *you* have for me?" I crossed the bed between us on my knees, coming to rest only inches in front him. His body heat radiated across me, warming me from head to toe. He warmed parts of my body the sun couldn't reach.

"I have all kinds of feelings for you." He sighed,

watching me intently. "Maybe I'll just sleep out in the car."

"Really?" I smirked. "You're going to sleep out there and leave me in here alone with him? I doubt that."

We locked eyes. His were hard; mine were soft, hopefully flirty.

"No." He sighed again. "So, I'll sleep…"

"You can sleep with me. I mean, if you want to." My stomach dropped at the thought. "It's not like we're going to have sex with Aric right freaking there."

And I'd never had a man in my bed for the whole night before. Ah, never had a man in my bed, period. What was I getting myself into? Yet the thought of having Jensen beside me was an attractive one.

"Not the first time, anyway."

I smiled big. "Was that a joke, Jensen Burkhardt? I do believe I'm rubbing off on you."

Balling his shirt in my fists, I pulled him in for a kiss. It was only meant to be a reassuring kiss, but I got carried away and it lasted longer than expected. All that desire and need left me flushed and both of us out of breath.

"He knows, don't worry about it. But I can't have a bunch of jealousy mucking everything up."

Jensen relented, nodding as if he understood.

In the end, I got one bed alone. After a bunch of macho bravado over which of them would sleep on the floor, Jensen "won." Apparently, neither would admit they wanted the comfort of a mattress and, at that point, I just didn't care.

The room was set up in such a way that Jensen could use the maroon-flowered bedspread from my bed to make the carpet between me and the wall as comfortable as possible. That was where there was the most room, so that was where Jensen slept.

Aric passed out as soon as his head hit the pillow, his light snore the only sound in the room. Of course, my ever-present insomnia didn't disappoint. I tossed around so much that I started to worry I'd keep Jensen up since his head was near the squeaking springs.

After using the bathroom and getting a drink of water, I tiptoed back to bed and stopped short just to look Jensen over. He seemed comfortable enough; the blanket I'd folded in half draped over his waist, leaving his bare chest free and one hand lying heavily on perfectly etched abs. He might have been even cuter asleep than he was awake. Even when his muscles were relaxed, he looked strong.

Quietly, I scooted into the crook of his arm and

laid my head on his shoulder. I wanted to be close to him but not close enough to disturb his sleep. When an arm tightened around my waist, I knew I had.

"Sorry," I whispered. "I didn't mean to wake you."

"It's a great way to be awakened." The parking lot lights peeked in through the curtains, creating a glow in the room. He had to cast his eyes down to see me.

"Couldn't sleep?" he asked. I shook my head. "Something wrong? Not that I mind having you in my bed... or floor, rather."

"No. I've always had trouble sleeping. Used to drive my parents nuts." The muscles in my body started to relax up against his body. He relaxed muscles I hadn't even realized were tight. "But this feels pretty comfortable."

"Come on, you don't want to fall asleep on the floor. Let's get in bed." He tried pushing me off, but either he wasn't trying very hard or I was stronger than even I thought.

"I don't want him"—my thumb jutted in Aric's direction—"to wake up to that, you know. I just don't want to throw it in his face. Wasn't that your point earlier?"

Jensen thought for a moment. "I'll stay just until

you fall asleep, then come back to the floor. How's that sound?"

"Like a plan." I smiled up at him.

Before we moved, I listened to make sure the light sound of Aric's sleep remained rhythmic and even. Jensen spooned against my back, holding me to his chest with his arm, and kissed me behind my ear twice. His breath on my neck sent a shiver to my toes right before I nodded off.

It was the best sleep I'd had possibly ever.

Every muscle in my body called out to be stretched or used when I woke the next morning. True to his word, Jensen wasn't beside me and actually wasn't on the floor, either but the shower in the bathroom raged. Aric sat on his bed, pajama bottoms only, looking over a map I didn't remember him having and didn't understand the purpose. We had GPS on our phones.

After a quick breakfast, we were back on the road.

The closer to Delaware we got, the more determined I became not only to train Jensen but to keep a war from happening.

Chapter Twelve

We made better time driving during the day. I figured there wouldn't be as many cars at night and that the lack of cars would make driving easier, but during the day, everyone was rushing to get somewhere. We were going just as fast during the day as we were during the night, but with the added benefit of being wide awake.

I'd decided that it'd be best to get home after most of the town had gone to sleep. That way I could get to my parents about Aric and Jensen before the entire community was awake. Plus we had Aric's stop to make.

"Why are we stopping in Mackinaw?" I asked him as we got ready for the next day driving.

"Have to go to the Island." That didn't answer the question as to why.

"We don't have time to be tourists, Aric."

"I don't want to be a tourist," he countered.

"Then why are we going to an island?" Jensen asked, reminding me that he probably didn't even know what Mackinac Island was.

"Have to pick up my brother."

I stuttered to a stop next to the car. "Your brother? You didn't say we were picking up your brother." One Gobel was tricky. Two were dangerous. At least going into Delaware. "You need to explain."

Aric let out a long sigh then leaned against my Mini Cooper.

"My older brother, Kale," he began. "He married a human and moved away a few years ago. He didn't want the constant battles between us and you. Especially after he fell in love with a human. She's human. Easily hurt. She doesn't even have a way to heal herself and he could lose her." He took a breath. "He didn't want to risk it."

"And you're still in contact with him?" Usually when a Gremalian left the community, there was very little to no contact. I assumed the Gobel were the same.

"Of course. He's my brother. Though I'm the only one that has been. I told him how I planned to stop the war and he wants to help. If we can cool things between our people, Kale could come home."

As I nodded, I grabbed the door handle and yanked it open. "Let's go get Kale then."

We were on the road ten minutes—me driving, Jensen next to me, and Aric in the backseat—when Jensen asked, "Explain the Assembly. I'm not sure I understand."

After unintentionally glancing at Aric in the back, I told him, "It's like any form of government. My father is basically the president. The Assembly is like congress, I guess. But it's... I don't know mixed. Like part monarch, part democracy."

He furrowed his brows. "That makes no sense."

"Well, my dad—the president king—was chosen to succeed by your father. It's not an elected position. The leader gets to choose his successor."

"His?" he countered. "Hasn't there been a woman leader?"

After rolling my eyes, I said, "No. So your grandfather chose your dad who then chose mine to succeed him or before that run things when he wasn't there. I assume your dad would've chosen you when you were old enough."

"But the Sorrels left town?" Jensen asked and it didn't evade me that he only referred to them by their last name. Made sense given that Jensen had grown up with loving parents and they were his parents.

"Right. They left to protect you but Glen drew up the papers officially placing my father before he left. If a successor screws up enough, The Assembly could theoretically remove him and choose a new one. That's never happened that I know of."

"Does that mean you're next in line?" Jensen asked.

I chuckled. "No, my dad would never name me. First of all, we've never had a female leader. Secondly, with you coming back, I'm sure it would revert back to you."

"What if I don't want it?"

"Then you say you don't want it, but I'd wait to make that decision."

We took quite a few breaks, mainly at rest areas and a restaurant to eat lunch, yet we still made it to Mackinaw City early. That was where we decided to take the longest break and have dinner. Aric and I introduced Jensen to pasties, chicken, and vegetables baked in a pie-like crust. Then walked around the outdoor mall which had me drooling over all the homemade fudge in multiple shop windows. Mackinaw City was famous for its fudge. "Fudgies," also known as tourists, came from all over to buy some. The fudge shops had just about any flavor combination a girl could dream of. I was surprised I didn't fall into a fudge coma just from browsing.

"So, let's go get Kale," Aric said out of the blue.

"Right. Is he here?" Jensen asked, walking along the path by the Old Mackinac Point Lighthouse.

"Not quite. We have to take the ferry."

I started jumping and clapping like a kid. "I can't believe we get to go to Mackinac Island?"

Aric gave me a half-smile.

I loved the island, had been there several times with my parents. It was Jensen's first time to Michigan and taking a newbie was almost as exciting.

It was basically my favorite place on Earth; I was happy that I would be the one to introduce him to the island.

After getting the tickets, I practically skipped down the platform to the boat. The front open area was already full, so we found seats inside, by a window. The ride was always too short for me. At least I got to enjoy it with my favorite people.

Once we were docked and off the ferry, the first

smell to hit was manure. It was never pleasant but by the time we got to Main Street, you didn't notice it anymore.

Aric headed off in one direction to go after his brother and we went the opposite way. Apparently, Kale wasn't totally comfortable working with us and didn't like us knowing he lived on the island, let alone exactly where. That was fine with me. It would be hours before the last ferry returned to the mainland and I wasn't about to waste a minute of it.

As soon as Aric headed off on his own, I took Jensen's hand and dragged him to Fort Mackinac. Because it was later in the day, we didn't go in but sat in the grass looking up at the imposing white wall built for protection hundreds of years ago.

"Sorry we can't go in," I told him. "We'll come back."

Then we strolled down Market Street to make our way to the beach right as the sunset cast yellow-and-red ripples across the water.

Being back in Michigan felt more like home than I'd remembered. I toed off my shoes and stood where the sand met the water to allow small waves to barely touch my toes.

Hey the water was beautiful but Lake Huron was cold.

Jensen wrapped his arms around my waist, leaning down to put his chin on my shoulder, and held me tightly.

"This is one of my favorite places," I told him as I stared out across the lake. "My dad brings us here once in a while. Being here at night is magical."

I kept talking, even after he'd pushed my long hair aside and run his lips up and down the side of my neck, doing his best to distract me. I closed my eyes, thoroughly enjoying the sensations rippling to my toes.

"We'll have to come back and stay some time," he whispered against my skin.

"Mmm, I'd like that."

"Hey, there you are." Aric called before he hit the beach.

Jensen dropped his arms and took a step back.

"You don't have to do that, you know," Aric said once he'd gotten closer.

"Do what?" Jensen asked.

"Pretend like you're not together whenever I'm around." He came to a stop right beside us. "I'm a big boy."

"We just—" I had no idea what I was going to say to explain it. It didn't matter because he cut me off anyway.

"I appreciate the gesture, but this friendship thing is only going to work if we're all normal. I mean, as normal as goblins and gremlins can be." He smiled big and the two of us laughed. Only Jensen called us that. "Besides, Alyssum, you know how hard it would be for me to break a friendship."

"Why is that?" Jensen asked, taking my hand in his as we headed back to the boat.

"I have no idea. Some inbred, innate, intolerable trait from however long ago we came to exist." Aric smiled big again.

"It's a Gobel thing," I offered as an easier explanation.

"It's a pain in the freaking ass, is what it is."

As I slipped my sandals back on, I asked, "Where's your brother?"

"Coming. He wanted to say goodbye to his wife alone." Aric let out a full—but fake—full body shutter.

The three of us made our way back to the ferry and waited for the tall, strong looking Gobel with slightly lighter hair than Aric to join us. Introductions were made but it was clear that Kale might have promised to help but that didn't mean he was totally comfortable with us Gremalians.

I leaned into Jensen as the beautiful colors

reflected off the waves on the lake as the ferry glided across. We were alone... Or as alone as you can be in a half full ferry. But while Aric and Kale were riding on the top of the ferry, we could enjoy this moment in our own little bubble.

I wanted to soak up every moment of this because I knew it couldn't last.

We arrived in Delaware late enough that the town was mostly asleep or at least in for the night. A few nightlights peeked out of the windows of my house but otherwise, the town was quiet.

"This place his huge," Jensen muttered.

Turning to the house I'd grown up in, trying to see it as he did, I had to agree. It was large, *huge* for a house.

"Only part of it is actually ours," I told him. "The main area is like our capital building and houses all The Assembly functions."

"Like?"

"Meetings, dinners, there are some training rooms. My father's office. There's a small building out back where official visitor sleep but that rarely happens."

"You're sure we should stay here?" Aric asked as

we walked around to the back of the house, each of us carrying a bag.

"You need to be here," I said once we were standing under my bedroom window. I flung my back onto my back to prepare to climb in the way I'd left.

"Yeah, but what happens when they find us?" Aric whispered loudly.

"I got your back. Don't worry. So, you guys just do what I do and don't fall."

"Why aren't we going in the front door?" Kale asked. "We're here to see your dad, right?"

"Yes. But I'd rather we all get a decent night sleep and start with all that in the morning. It's why I wanted to get here late."

We climbed up the chimney to get onto the sunroom roof then walked carefully over to the window, hoping that Mom hadn't let anyone lock it. When I slid open smoothly, I silently thanked her. It was only two feet from the sunroom, an easy climb. Aric sent Jensen up first, then Kale, and brought up the rear.

As soon as I got inside, I dropped the backpack, ran to my dark, four-poster bed, and belly-flopped onto the deep-blue comforter.

"Oh, I've missed you," I said into the mattress,

my voice muffled as I made imaginary blanket angels. The guys snickered quietly.

"Wow, nice room," Aric said. "Mine's not nearly as big and I had to share."

Kale shoved his shoulder playfully.

"Had? Past tense?" I asked.

"Yeah, I moved out the minute I could. We do have apartment buildings and houses."

"Not to mention," Kale said, "more than three guys to a room will chase you away pretty quick."

"Well, there's only three of you. I should be good."

"How many brothers and sisters do you have?" Jensen asked.

"Five brothers, five sisters," Kale answered.

Jensen's eyes widened with disbelief, so I replied, "Oh, you have a small Gobel family."

Both Kale and Aric laughed at that one, but it was true. Some families had fifteen kids. To an only child, like Jensen and me, it was hard to imagine.

I retrieved some blankets and extra pillows from the closet, the ones I kept on hand for when deep winter set in and it got cold so that they could make a bed on my floor. Even though Aric was comfortable with us all sleeping in a room together, I wasn't comfortable having Jensen in my bed with the possibility of someone coming in before we woke up.

"Hey," Aric said, throwing his brother a pillow. "You have to sleep between us."

"Why?" Kale asked, looking to his brother, then Jensen.

"Because he may or may not have unholy feelings for me and I don't want him 'accidentally' spooning me in the middle of the night or something," Aric said. Kale and I were already tearing up from laughing so hard while trying to stay quiet. My room was pretty far from the others. I'd chosen it for that reason alone. But still, there was no reason to chance someone hearing us. "I'm not down with the dude cuddle."

"Fuck off," Jensen said dryly.

"Aww, poor baby," I teased. I gave him a quick kiss goodnight after promising they'd get beds of their own the next day, although I did threaten that the brothers would have to share.

We were all exhausted. Yes, the next day could be bad. I knew my dad would freak out when he discovered I'd brought Kale and Aric into our house. Just the fact that I'd let three guys sleep in my room with me would be reason enough for him to get pissed. I had my work cut out for me. Not only would I have to keep everyone in the house calm the next day, but I also had to get Dad to listen to me. He didn't have the greatest track record of giving me the benefit of the doubt, but I was going to have to rely on Mom to help me out there.

"Hey, Jensen?" Kale said in the dark, once all the rumbling had settled down.

"Yeah," he mumbled.

"Just so we're clear. If you want any of this, you have to buy me dinner first."

Jensen's pillow hit Kale in the face hard enough to make Kale groan. Another round of muted thunder rolled through the room before we all fell silent.

I hoped they'd all get a decent night sleep while knowing that my brain would never shut off.

Tomorrow would determine if all of my efforts were worth the trouble.

Chapter Thirteen

"Alyssum's home!"

The voice was hidden behind the fog making it almost impossible to make the words our at first.

"You're back," the voice said again.

Something heavy hit me like a Mack truck.

The fourteen-year-old chatterbox that had just landed on my stomach had effectively knocked the wind out of me. What a rude awakening.

Blossom, the daughter of my mom's best friend, sometimes spent the night when her parents were out of town. She only weighed about eighty pounds, but the sharp bones she called "elbows" pretty much punctured my diaphragm.

"Get off me," I pled. She hopped off and that was when she saw them.

"You have *boys* in your room?"

She squealed, her expression so innocently bright that I could have smacked it off her. It was far too early for that kind of exuberance.

Blossom was almost my height, all skin and bones. She had dark brown hair that she always had braided and brown eyes that somehow always sparkled.

"Blossom, no." I threw my blankets off to chase her. Aric, Kale, and Jensen jumped up when the door hit the wall as I ran out of the room. It was too late. She was already in the main area talking at warp speed to anyone who would listen.

Chaos erupted. No one would listen to me but their own voice grew urgent.

"Wait. I can explain," I said loudly as six of my father's security force, dragged Jensen, Aric, and Kale from my room.

They be able to tell that Jensen was a Gremalian but they'd also know that Aric and Kale weren't.

The worst part was that Sage was the one calling out the orders above the noise. I could've done without him

"Hold on. Wait!" My pleas fell on deaf ears.

They tied Aric's hands together tightly as he protested. He couldn't use them even if he wanted to. It was an odd sight, seeing him cuffed with white zip ties while wearing nothing but pajama pants, his hair a mess. Kale threw a punch but he was outnumbered and his powers would've been a better choice. Though if he'd used them, we'd have no chance of getting my father to trust them.

It's probably why he didn't.

Kale was thrown to the ground with his face in ceramic tile and a foot on the back of his neck.

They stood guard next to Jensen, but he didn't get the same treatment because it was Gremalian. Unfamiliar but still one of us.

Damn it. It was an early security meeting and the house was full of people. There had been more than one embarrassing trek to the kitchen for breakfast during my teenage years only to find a bunch of grown men staring down at me.

Since no one was listening to me, I drew up whatever power in the room I could and threw a low-wattage energy ball directly at Sage. It hit his arm just hard enough to grab his attention and make him take a step back. I wanted to throw a more powerful one but thought better of it.

"What the hell, Alyssum?" Sage spat the words out. He was tall maybe five feel ten inches which put him just shorter than Jensen with dirty blonde hair and brown eyes that lacked any kind of sparkle. He also looked ready to retaliate but wouldn't in front of my father.

"Let them go," I demanded, grabbing Aric's arm to pull him behind me. Sage grabbed his other side, putting us in a tug of war. Sage wasn't that big, especially when standing next to Aric, though that wasn't to say he didn't have some strength. I threw another energy ball. It hit his side. Then another at the goon whose name I could never remember. I wasn't trying to hurt them, just get them to release the guys so I could explain.

"Enough," my father's voice boomed. Everyone got very still. No one, except me, ever disobeyed my father. "My office, Alyssum."

"Not without them." I folded my arms under my breasts and put all my weight on one hip, the stance I took whenever I wasn't going to budge.

I would never admit it to anyone, but in that moment, I was thankful for my father. He was many things and methodical was one of them. He would put a stop to the mob mentality taking over the security team because of Aric and Kale being inside the house. Since I was his daughter, he often shut me down without listening to my side of the story, but he wasn't likely to do that when others were involved.

Fortunately, there were many others involved this time around.

"Now," he boomed again, his eyes on fire.

"No way. The minute I leave, these jackasses are going to drag them out of here and do god-knows-what," I said. The vein in my father's neck started to bulge making me drop the stubborn act and try reason. "I can explain. I just don't want anything to happen while I do. Do you think I'd bring someone here who I thought was a danger?"

Finally, he relented. "Let them go," he ordered.

Sage reluctantly cut Aric's ties then gave a nod for his guys to get their foot off Kale's neck. I grabbed Aric's hand to pull him away, then followed my father and mother down the hall toward his office, waving for Jensen and Kale to come too. Once we were safely inside the office, I let go of his hand.

Our bare feet slapped against the marble floor of his very dark room. Finding your daughter with three half-naked guys in her bedroom would cause enough of a problem whether two were Gobel or not. But each of them were just in their pajama pants without a shirt so that wasn't helping my father's mood.

Cherrywood covered everything that leather didn't and Dad's imposing desk stood in the middle of the room. It was what anyone would call a "man cave," but with better lighting, you hardly noticed.

My dad sighed heavily. Before he could speak, my mom wrapped her arms around me tightly. "It's nice to have you home. Even if you brought... guests."

"Thanks, Mom. It's good to be back." Then I glanced back at my dad. "I think."

She let go, eying Jensen and Aric as she moved back near my dad. She barely gave Kale a glance.

"What kind of homecoming did you expect?" he railed. I sighed. "You leave in the middle of the night. No one knew where you'd gone, only that you were okay." I glanced at my mother, who kept her eyes on him. "You come back with three men, two of whom are Gobel. Do you care to explain any of this?"

"I left to find the Sorrels' son, Dad. You knew that. This"—I pointed to Jensen—"is him."

"You can't be sure of that." He eyed Jensen suspiciously. "Heath Sorrel died with his parents."

"Where was his body, then? Why was it always reported that he was presumed dead? Dad, I'm sure."

He scanned Jensen up and down, jaw clenched like he was trying to see something familiar. Maybe he was afraid he would.

"And the Gobel?" He pointed to the brothers

standing side by side.

"Well, that's a funny story."

I went on to tell them almost everything that had happened since leaving home. I explained that I found Aric already with Jensen and everything that had come after that.

"Aric and Kale will help us. I trust them and so should you. There are others who don't want war, on both sides."

"You know war is the last thing I want to happen. But—"

"Then let us help you," I said. He hadn't wanted me involved at all but now I was.

Dad thought about it for an eternity, then answered with only a small nod and swept past us out the door. He'd made his decision and this time, he was going to trust me.

Back in the entryway, an even bigger crowd had gathered. It never took long for word to spread throughout a small town. The guys leaned against a wall that put them away from the angry Gremalians that had gathered. I stood between them and the crowd as if I could hold back our entire community. I wouldn't be able to but I'd die trying.

My dad swept in and immediately took control of the situation, hushing the crowd by holding up his hands. He'd always said Glen had been the born leader, but watching him work made me doubt that anyone would have been better at it than my father.

As my father tried to quelch any fears, a shriek just loud enough for me and the guys to hear took my attention from the gathering. A body slammed into me, squeezing tightly so I couldn't breathe.

"The wayward daughter returns," Dahlia, my best friend, said.

She crushed me in her arms. When I pulled back, I wasn't surprised to find her perfectly put together. She was the exact opposite of me. I was short; she was tall. I had blonde hair, she brown. My eyes were blue, while hers were so dark, they looked black. She could do magic with a makeup brush while I could barely get a passing grade.

"Couldn't stay away forever." I caught Aric and Jensen eying our little interaction. "I'm sorry I couldn't reach out. I didn't want my father to know."

She scoffed. "I wouldn't have told him shit and you know it. But you left without a word to anyone. People worry, Alyssum. Not me, but people. It's not like I'm your best friend or anything." Dahlia glanced over to the guys again then back to the security team, who was still clearing out the area. "I suppose, though, since you came back with guys who look like them"—she indicated Aric, Kale, and Jensen with a wave of her hand—"You can be forgiven. Introductions will be necessary."

She bumped me with her hip as she walked away.

I shook my head while chuckling under my breath then with the flick of her wrist, she hit my shoulder with a spark that made me take a step back like someone had bumped into me in a crowd.

My eyes narrowed and I flicked my fingers at her, sending a small jolt at her butt. She yelped and jumped. All eyes in the room went to her. I put on my best innocent look and shrugged.

It felt good to be somewhere that I could use my power at will. Holding it back in New York had been hard.

My father cleared his throat, then went back to business.

Once everything had calmed down and the entryway had cleared mostly out, the four of us headed back to my room.

We each took turns in the bathroom, although what I thought we all could've really used was some more sleep. Our days of normalcy were over. The foreseeable future would be all about meeting with my father and then the rest of The Assembly. Decisions and training had become the priority the minute we'd stepped on the property.

The guys stayed in my room when I was summoned back to Dad's office.

"What were you thinking, Alyssum," he said after I slumped down into the chair across from him.

"I was thinking that we needed a big gun on our side. Jensen's the big gun."

"Alyssum," he said through a sigh. "The Gobel?"

"I know. I was ready to rip his throat out when I saw him in New York but Aric's a good guy, Dad. He wants to protect his family just like we do. I trust him and you should too."

"And the other one?"

"Kale?" Yeah, I didn't know him well so that was trickier. "Aric trusts him which means I do too. They're going to help us. What if we could live in a world where we aren't constantly on the verge of war with the Gobel?"

"You know that's what we all want."

"Then trust me a little. Trust them a little. What's the worst that can happen? We go to war anyway?"

Dad took his time mulling that over. He wasn't one to make rash decisions too often.

"So what's your plan?" he finally asked, though

he'd never asked me that before.

I sat up straighter and took a deep breath. "I want to train Jensen. Get him up to speed. He doesn't seem to know how to tap into his powers but if I can get him there, he might have everything his parents did." Which I'd been told the Sorrel family were legendary and that was why they were the leaders. "Kale wants to go see his family. See if he can convince any of them to join us in stopping the war but that has to be the objective. Stopping the war. Not winning it. Otherwise they'll have to fight with their side."

"Stopping the war is all I've ever wanted. War doesn't benefit anyone, Alyssum."

"Then we agree."

"OK." He sighed again then leaned his elbows on his desk. "You start training Jensen. Kale can go home to do his thing. They can all stay here and I'll make it very clear that they aren't to be touched. That they are all under my protection."

"Excellent."

"I really hope this works, Alyssum."

So did I.

Every day I was finding more people that I cared about and didn't want to see hurt. Even more than that, I didn't want to have to fight against them.

Chapter Fourteen

THE AFTERNOON, we gathered in the meeting room and were surrounded by a round of angry voices, each trying to yell over the other.

"Official" Ash slammed his meaty paw down on the desk where he sat, bringing them all to a hush.

"Whether or not you're comfortable," he said loudly, "This is what's happening. My daughter risked everything to give us a chance at peace and we aren't going to waste it."

"Man, I wish I could've gone with Kale," Aric mumbled under his breath.

Right then, *I* wished I could've gone with Kale. The Assembly room stuff was pretty boring even with all the yelling and animated gesticulating.

Aric, Jensen, and I were at the back of the room leaning against a wall since we weren't actually supposed to be in there all.

"He said it was best if one of you stay behind," I reminded him.

"I know, I know."

Everyone in the room began to disperse as Dad came stomping toward us. I'd hoped he hadn't noticed us here.

"You three shouldn't be in this room," he told us.

"I know. It was my idea."

He shook his head and sighed. "Of course it was." Aric and Jensen chuckled from beside me. Screw them all. I had the best ideas. "OK. You two —"he pointed at Aric and me—"Will start training Jensen immediately. Figure out how much of his parent's powers he has in him. The sooner the better."

"We'll start tomorrow."

"Today would be better."

"It would but they haven't gotten settled into rooms yet, we barely slept last night. We'll start tomorrow."

It was begrudgingly but he nodded in agreement.

Agreeing with me must've been tough for him.

The only upside to the day came when I got to show the guys which rooms they'd be staying in. If nothing else, our house was impressive. Both rooms were down a different hallway than mine, by design, I was sure. My mom had made the arrangements and who knew what she could sense. I guessed she wasn't taking any chances, so they were the only two down that way.

The large rooms were complete with anything a person could want, including a fully stocked mini-fridge. I didn't even have one of those. Really, it was just a small fridge with pop, water, and a few snacks under the plasma TVs hanging from the wall. It looked as if she'd had the rooms made up especially for them because, at one point, they'd been much more feminine with deep-purple duvets that were now dark green.

After Aric was settled with the bag he'd left in the car, I went in to help Jensen, which was code for spending time with him. Things had gotten so crazy and were about to get worse so I'd take any time I could get.

"This has been a crazy day," he said, putting his clothes in the dresser.

"The craziest." I flopped onto the bed and watched him work.

He shut the last drawer and lay beside me, our shoulders touching. "So, you *are* kind of badass."

I smiled over at him. "You haven't seen anything yet. Just wait until tomorrow."

He wanted to know about the energy balls I threw. I explained that I could pick up energy from the air. Lightning was best, but any would do, by controlling the voltage, I could use it as a weapon. He should have been able to, as well. I also told him how I'd zapped the car back to life for Aric at the garage. Not everyone could do that. Some of us had to have direct energy, like from a storm or manmade electricity. I didn't always form them into balls; actually, that was rare. I preferred sparks and bolts. He listened to me with wide, blue eyes, but he didn't seem too freaked out.

"That guy you hit... "

"Sage," I spat, knowing where that was going before he said anything.

"You seem to have a lot of hostility toward him."

"Sage had been holding Aric and his goons had had Kale. That's reason enough for hostility. Someone had to do something." I shrugged him off, flipping over.

"Is that it?"

His eyes were watching me carefully. "He and I

used to date. He's an ass." I hoped that would be enough.

"Did you and he…?"

I closed my eyes, trying to hold back my disgust at the thought of Sage touching me in such intimate ways. *Yuck.*

"No. Never. The last time he kissed me, I bit his tongue hard enough to make him bleed," I said. Jensen roared with laughter. "Yeah, that was fun, actually."

"Now I kinda feel bad for the poor guy."

"Trust me, you won't after you're here a while," I said. We fell quiet, his hand above my head, absently playing with my hair. "Make sure you call your parents every now and then just to keep grounded."

"I will." His eyes went from the ceiling to my face. "Do we get to go out while we're here?"

"Ha, better than that. Tomorrow, we get to start training. After that, you won't want to be around me as much." I wanted to keep things playful, at least as much as I could. "I might just scare you off."

"Unlikely."

"I'll make sure we get some time alone." I flipped over to my side, propping up on my elbow.

"And what are we telling your parents? About us?"

"Nothing." I slipped my hand under his shirt and caressed the sculpted plane hiding beneath, reminding myself of that time on his motorcycle where I'd slipped my finger into his pants and touched his cock. Neither of us had made a move like that since. He let out a ragged breath and closed his eyes. Maybe he was remembering that, too. "My mom probably already knows about us."

His eyelids opened just enough to see me. "How?"

"She can... sense things. Probably had a read on it before she'd even come in the room. It isn't a magical Gremalian thing. It's a normal psychic thing."

My hand jiggled on his stomach as he laughed. "Did you really just say 'normal psychic thing'?" he asked. I nodded with a grin. "I can't believe that doesn't weird me out."

Overall, he'd taken everything pretty much in stride. I kinda assumed at first, it was more because he wanted to be with me rather than believing it was all real. Now he couldn't deny anything.

Lightly trailing a path along his stomach, I leaned over and kissed him just because I wanted to. He moaned, but it came out like a growl as he pushed his hand into my hair, holding tightly as he deepened the kiss.

I braced my hands on the sides of his neck as I climbed on top of him. Even though he was surprised, he didn't miss a beat. I pulled him up, yanked his shirt above his head, and let him lie back down. His hands rested on my upper thighs and he kissed me like he really, really meant it, squeezing my legs softly. It turned me on to have him half-naked and flawless underneath me.

Then he did the same to me, pulling my shirt off in one movement. Thankfully, I was the type of woman who sometimes wore undergarments for their cuteness rather than solely for their function, so my bra had a wow factor. Pink and lacy, but not see-through. I watched as he took me in before suddenly rolling us causing me to squeal in surprise. My fingers were on the button of his pants but I had no idea what the hell I intended to do. I'd never done this before. Well, I'd done some of this but not sex. I was a virgin yet was very willing to stamp that card right that moment.

His hands inched up my sides and, but just when he was about to cup my breasts, there was a loud bang on his door.

My heart dropped and I started searching for the

shirt he'd thrown on the floor next to the bed. I fell off with a *thud*. We both giggled softly. Just as the door opened, Jensen got on all fours on his mattress and I rolled under the bed.

"Dude, I'm not sure I'm gonna be able to sleep in these big rooms. You?" I couldn't see Aric but heard the change in his voice when he must have finally looked at Jensen and realized what he'd walked in on. "I, uh... sorry. I didn't mean to... "

"It's okay," Jensen said. The springs squeaked just a bit in my face as Jensen presumably rolled back to sit up. "But you might want to wait to be invited in next time."

I slapped a hand over my mouth to keep from laughing. Apparently, I hadn't been as quiet as I'd intended.

"You can come out, Alyssum." Aric's tone remained light and full of humor like he was trying to hold back laughter as well.

"Um... actually, I kinda can't."

The fact that I only had a bra on must have in Jensen's brain because he jumped up and ushered Aric from the room, shutting the door and clicking the lock. I slid out and put my shirt back on before I was on my feet.

"I guess I should've locked that." He scraped his fingers on the back of his head. "I didn't expect… "

"Yeah, me, either," I said. We stood there awkwardly, staring at each other, and I felt heat rising in my face. "Okay, I'm gonna go, then."

He smiled widely. A little cocky, actually, but I liked it.

Chapter Fifteen

Jensen needed to acclimate himself with Delaware and his people so I decided to start our training with a tour. It wouldn't take long because there wasn't really much to show him. Still, he should see it.

As I was headed to his room, my mother stood outside one of the sitting rooms and called me over. She hadn't even called my name loudly yet I jumped and let out a yelp. No matter what I tried to get out of going in there, she insisted. Besides, asking me to come in wasn't really a question. It was an order.

The light-green room wasn't good for anything other than sitting, entertaining guests you didn't really want to stay long, or reading. It was really nice to curl up in front of the fireplace with a good book and a warm blanket on your legs in the middle of winter. Right now when we sat in those chairs, the air conditioning had to work overtime to keep the house cool.

"I'm very glad you're home," she said.

"Why didn't you tell Dad that I emailed you regularly?" I asked right away. He'd been extra mad that I'd stayed out of contact, but I'd assumed she'd at least mention some of my emails. "He was pissed." She gave that look of disapproval. *"Language, Alyssum,"* she usually said.

"If I had, he would have sent Sage and his men after you. Your emails were best kept between us, don't you think?" she said. I nodded. I would've been mortified and humiliated if I'd been stalked down and dragged back by Sage, as Flint had warned. "What I want to ask you has nothing to do with the political atmosphere out there," she said, pointing at the door. "I want to ask you about those boys."

Trying to stifle a smile at her tone, I shifted uncomfortably and asked, "What about them?"

"Are you really going to make me spell it out, Alyssum? I could read you the minute I saw you in the hallway."

I rolled my eyes and dropped my head back. It

kinda sucked to have a mother who could feel things like that. "Then I don't really need to explain, do I?"

"But I'm getting... conflicting information." She watched me intently. Even a couple of deep breaths couldn't calm my nerves under her motherly eyes.

I took a deep breath and looked out the window. There was no getting out of this conversation. "Well, don't be conflicted. Jensen and I are together. Aric and I are friends. Close friends, yet just friends."

Falling back in my seat, I folded my hands over my stomach, still not willing to look at her and still feeling her eyes all over me.

"How 'together' are you?" As she eyed me suspiciously, her face smoothed once she got her answer. I didn't say anything and hoped I was successful at keeping the blush from my face. She was satisfied nonetheless.

"Happy?" I snapped once I'd realized she was done reading me.

"If you are. Just... be careful."

"Yes, Mother. We've had that talk, thank you." I wanted out of the room, away from her so my feelings could be mine again.

"About the other matter, I feel you should know that your father has information he hasn't given you yet, in regard to Heath." She put her hand up to stop me from correcting her, as I'd already done several times. "Sorry, Jensen. I don't know that it's relevant, but if you hit a brick wall at some point, go to him."

She stood, smoothing her dress before heading to the door.

I hopped up after her. "What is it?"

"I don't actually know. I '*know*.'" Code for it was one of her feelings again. She never gave specifics. "We missed you."

My mom, unlike my dad, was always truthful. If she didn't want me to know something, she'd just say it. There were no lame excuses. So I believed her when she said she didn't know what the information was.

"I missed you, too. Even Dad with his booming 'do what I say' voice," I said. She raised an eyebrow at my admission to missing my dad. He and I butted heads pretty often. She probably suspected that I would have reveled in the time apart. "Trust me, I was as shocked as you are about missing him. I now know how it feels to be homesick. Satisfied?"

She didn't answer. By the smile playing at the corners of her lips, I knew she was. I got an image of her and Dad praying for me to be miserable in New York, or wherever he thought I'd gone.

"Hey," I said as she turned to go. "Do you think it'd be okay for me to show Jensen around?"

Mom thought about that question. "I think it would be. Security has been stepped up and other than that one breach while you were away, things have been quiet in town. The violence has been mainly out at the mines, so don't go there and don't leave Delaware. Otherwise, I think it's a good idea."

"I won't take him out to the mines, I promise," I said, but that wasn't good enough. She cocked her head at me, looking expectant. "And we won't leave Delaware."

She nodded and I let her leave after that.

"Wait," I called after her as I ran out into the hallway. "What breach?"

"Talk to your father." Her voice trailed down the hallway like a song.

Once I had Jensen, we walked, his arm around my shoulder, through the part of town where the little market sat nestled between a small library and a bar.

"We might not have much," I told him. "But we definitely have a bar that's mostly used by the men when they have to work out their manly energy. I'll know where to look for you if you ever come up missing."

"Please," he scoffed. "That wasn't my thing back home so I don't think it'd be my thing here."

The first break on our journey came when we approached the building used as a school.

Small kids, kindergarten through second, ran around in the bright sunlight, chasing each other in a fervent game of tag while a few of the boys, although much too short, still tried to toss the basketball through the hoop. We stopped at the fence surrounding their concrete-and-grass playground, watching them. A breeze blew my hair off my shoulders and sent it back around my face. Jensen looked at me with gentle eyes.

We only stopped for a couple of minutes before starting our walk again.

"I didn't see the fighting from the last war," I explained. "But I have seen the aftermath. It's why I originally wanted to make sure we could outpower the Gobel if it happens again. It's taken years for us to put everything back together and we'd won that war. It's also why I let Aric talk me into stopping the war so easily."

"It was bad?" he asked quietly.

Nodding, I told him, "Yeah. Things weren't good for a long time. My father has bore that sadness every day since. Then your parents died and everything got even worse. It's basically all my memories from when I started having memories."

"I'm sorry you went through that." He pulled me into him and held me tightly even though we were still walking.

After all the heavy stuff, I thought I should try to lighten the mood just a bit.

"Now, I might get to kick some Gobel ass and that's super fun."

It didn't work. He didn't break a smile. When we headed back for lunch, I hoped I hadn't scared the crap out of him.

The afternoon activities promised to be a lot more fun than "A Brief History of Gremalian/Gobel Strife That Includes the Death of Your Biological Family." At least for me. I wasn't sure what he'd think about it.

Aric spent the morning holed up in my dad's office, answering any and all questions he could about the Gobel government and people. I rescued him, saying he was imperative to my plan for Jensen. Which wasn't a lie. I knew Aric would be much more open to fighting me than Jensen would be. That way, we could show instead of tell.

Once we'd gotten changed into more comfortable clothes, I led them to the garage. It wasn't used for parking cars or working on machinery. It was clear of all clutter with wrestling mats covering the floor and four chairs off to one end. We used it for learning how to fight like a Gremalian and using our power properly.

"Welcome to the training room." I threw my arms out wide.

We told Jensen he'd just watch. I was getting pretty rusty from all the docile time in New York, which made me pretty antsy to punch something or someone. At first, Aric and I just stalked each other since our kinds were both taught not to attack unless absolutely necessary. It was always better to see what the other guy was gonna do first. At some point, I decided, *fuck that*; it was on.

"Don't go easy one me," I warned him. "It's the only way to get ready."

"Sure thing." But he didn't sound convincing.

Using my small size to my advantage, I launched. Aric never expected me to hit right at the waist. He hit the ground hard with a loud grunt. I'd knocked the wind out of him, but he was back on his feet before he could get a breath.

Then he charged.

Jumping out of the way, I didn't see his leg jut out, sweeping behind my knees. My butt hit the mat.

That would leave a mark. Time to get my energy out.

I threw a punch to his gut, hard and on target. He doubled over and took me with him, flipping my body across his back, twisting my arm, and pushing my face down to the floor.

Most of my punches hit their mark and, though Aric was strong, he groaned or stumbled with each punch. A right elbow—blocked, left punch—hit his jaw. A sweep of the leg behind his knee brought him to the ground.

He recovered quickly, flipping me over his back again. I landed on my ass again with a *thud*. With the number of times I met the wood, I thought that body part was numb.

Since Aric was Gobel and knew all the Gobel tricks, he never told me to stop no matter how many times I hit him. This training would be the only way I'd be able to anticipate every one of the Gobel moves when the time came for the big fight.

And we hadn't started to use our real powers yet.

I didn't cry uncle, either.

"You're going easy on me," I spat, though moisture speckled my forehead.

Aric snorted. "Glad you think so."

A right hook made contact just under my eye

and it stung the most out of all of the hits. A trickle of blood ran down my cheek. In the end, I was able to overpower him. His shoulders cracked against the floor and I landed on top of him.

Face to face, we came out of battle mode and started laughing so hard, we almost couldn't breathe.

I'd been in the zone during the fight and forgotten that Jensen had been leaning against the wall, hands clenched into fists and shoved in his pockets, watching us. We quickly hopped to our feet.

The look on Jensen's face was priceless. His eyes were wide, mouth gaped, muscles tight. Maybe having him watch Aric try to kick my ass hadn't been the best idea I'd ever had, but Jensen needed training even more than I did and this was just as important as learning the powers. We couldn't lean on those alone. It didn't always work out. He had to learn. It wasn't just a regular schoolyard fight. Gobel could be tricky.

"I think we broke him," I said in a poorly concealed whisper.

Aric coughed to cover the laugh and grabbed my shoulders to turn me toward him. Studying my face, his eyes homed in on the spot where his best punch had left its mark. With a gentle thumb, he wiped away any blood that remained. His eyes darkened with anger. He was mad at himself, probably for listening to me about the training in the first place.

When Jensen cleared his throat, Aric took a step back. The moment between us was too intimate.

Aric left the room without another word.

"So... " I said, smiling past the sharp pain in my cheekbone as I bounced over to Jensen. He was focused on the abrasion that Aric had wiped the blood from. "Don't worry, I'm a quick healer."

Before he could respond, my dad's voice caught my attention from just outside the training room. I pushed Jensen into the equipment closet behind us.

"What are you doing?" he asked.

"Shh." I put my finger over his lips, effectively cutting him off. "My dad," I mouthed.

"He knows I'm here."

I nodded. "And he's fine that, but if he sees you, he'll just want to watch us training or give us shit because you haven't done any yet. Or ask questions or be himself."

Once the voices were far enough away, we scurried back inside the house to the kitchen. We filled our arms with drinks and snacks, then tiredly climbed the stairs, heading back to my room. Well, *I* climbed tiredly. He just walked slowly so he could be next to me.

After dropping our goodies on the table by the window, I grabbed a bottle of water along with a small bag of chips and hoisted myself up onto my much-too-large bed. I hadn't realized how late Aric and I had trained or how much it'd taken out of me, so the firm comfort of my mattress felt good enough that I just about melted. Jensen did the same, flopping onto his stomach next to me. We snacked in silence... well, without talking. The crunch of our chips was actually quite loud.

"What's up with your dad?" he asked.

I shrugged. "I don't know. I guess it's like being the daughter of the president or something. He's never really had much spare time unless it came to training."

"You mean, like, you and Aric were just doing?" I nodded. "Your dad hit you?"

"Yeah, but it's not like that. There are some dangers that come with being Gremalian and even more if you're the kid of the head of The Assembly. It really was for my own good," I insisted. The look on his face said that hadn't made it any better. "If it helps, I totally kicked his ass when I was ten." Finally, he smiled. "Hey, I'm gonna hop in the shower really quick. I need to wash this sweat away."

"Okay." He pushed up off the bed like he was leaving.

"I don't want you to go. I mean, you can if you want, but I won't be long."

I had a feeling my eyes betrayed me. Jensen obviously knew my feelings and the look I gave him was a bit more pleading than I'd ever usually be.

"Then I'll stay." He lowered himself back down. I gave him a quick peck on his cheek and searched for some comfortable pajamas that didn't make me look like a bag lady. I found a set that I'd never worn before: pants made of thin pink cotton and a matching T-shirt in gray.

After starting the shower, I began to undress and noticed that I hadn't shut the door all the way. I knew Jensen; he wouldn't be anywhere near the bathroom, so I didn't bother closing it. I took the extra time to shave my legs—not that they needed it, but there was a man in my room. You just never knew. After quickly blow-dried my hair, it was still slightly damp when I was done.

Exactly as I thought, Jensen was still on my bed, arm behind his head, flipping through channels with the remote. I wondered if he'd noticed that his TV was bigger than mine. I had no idea why that was the thought that popped in my mind right then. Sexy guy sprawled on my bed... I thought of television?

Idiot.

"Man, sleep is gonna feel good tonight." I crawled under the thin blanket and cuddled up beside him. "So, tomorrow..."

He cut me off, knowing where I was headed. "I'm not doing that with you."

"What do you mean?" I bolted up. "You have to, Jensen. You can't be in the middle of all of this and be unprepared. You won't hurt me; I'm tougher than I look. The cut on my cheek is mostly healed. And we have to get whatever power is inside of you to come out, and that's not a euphemism." A lot of that was just a long ramble. That was something new since meeting him. *I didn't used to ramble so much.*

He smiled, then got serious again very quickly. "I know you're strong, Alyssum. It's not about that. But I can't, Alyssum."

"What about Aric? You could train with him for a while, then we could work on the other stuff." That seemed to be the best compromise, and I couldn't say the thought of seeing those two go toe to toe repulsed me.

He raised his eyebrow and tilted his head to the

side. "Somehow, I think punching him won't be an issue."

He patted his shoulder for me to lie back down and wrapped both arms around me, pulling me into his chest. I wasn't sure when I fell asleep or how long I was able to hold out before drifting off.

It was the comfort of being beside him that worked magic like no other.

Chapter Sixteen

Jensen was gone when I woke up.

It was still dark, twenty minutes before midnight, according to the clock next to my bed. He'd made sure I was comfortable, tucking me in snugly, before going back to his own room. I wished I knew how long he'd stayed and made a mental note to ask him later.

Since I hadn't had dinner last night, my stomach started demanding food. I took a little walk to the kitchen for a not-yet-midnight snack. I didn't turn any lights on as I grabbed a bowl, spoon, cereal, and milk. The energy-efficient lightbulb over the sink that we left on every night gave me enough light to move around without hurting myself.

"Hey," Jensen said, approaching me from behind where I sat at the island.

"Jensen!" My hand flew up to my heart and I dropped the spoon. "You scared me."

"Sorry." He leaned over, looking into my bowl. "That's the best you could do?"

"I... uh... can't cook and it's only a little bit before midnight," I said. He looked a little surprised. "Is that a deal-breaker?"

"Hardly." He scoffed. "Besides, I can, but you know making a sandwich isn't exactly cooking."

"True, but it's a whole lot more effort than I'm usually up for in the middle of the night." A low chuckle rumbled in his chest. "What has you up?"

"Water." He shook the bottle in my face as if he were stating the obvious.

"Ah, there's some in the fridge in your room," I pointed out. He eyed me and usually I could tell what was going on inside his head like they were a window to soul.

"I won't say I was kind of hoping you'd be up because of your insomnia. I won't say that." He cocked his head to the side, one corner of his mouth curling up.

"Ugh, always." I shook my head. My mom said I

was so high-strung, so tightly wound, that nothing seemed to help me sleep.

"How come you fall asleep so easily when I'm with you? Am I that boring?"

I laughed, shaking my head. "You make me really comfortable. Like my whole body just relaxes."

He liked that answer.

Even with the interruption to my sleep, I still woke back up much too early. Apparently, I wasn't the only early riser. Aric already had some eggs cooking on the stove. Newly toasted bread sat on a plate in the middle of the large island.

"Morning.Want some?" He tipped the pan my way.

"If you have extra."

He nodded while I took a seat on one of the barstools.

"We should talk about today," I said. He glanced over his shoulder. "I was talking to Jensen last night" —the muscles in his jaw tensed slightly—"and he won't train with me. He says he can't do to me what you did yesterday. I thought you could do it." He nodded. I hated it when he answered with body movements. "But at some point, we have to convince him. He has an 'I was raised not to hit ladies' thing that's driving me nuts. I'm strong. I can handle it."

Aric brought a plate of perfectly cooked eggs over and sat it in front of me, then tossed two slices of toast on top. "Yeah, Alyssum, that's what all the woman complain about." He changed his voice to sound feminine and said, "'*My boyfriend won't hit me!*'"

I threw a spoon in his general direction and missed, catching a small vase of flowers and leaving a snowflake-shaped crack on the front instead. Oops.

"Any sign of some power?" he asked, still chewing. I shook my head in response. "You better get on that, then."

My brows went down. "How can I make it happen?"

"There's a reason why our powers kick in just after puberty. Hasn't anyone ever told you that?" he asked. I shook my head because apparently, no one told me anything helpful in my life. "It has to do with hormones and whatever. Look, you're going to have to get him really... uh... frustrated."

I had no idea what he was talking about. In my defense, it was really early and I hadn't slept much.

"Like what? Give him really hard math problems? That always worked for me."

He shook his head and readjusted his position on the stool, showing he wasn't entirely comfortable with our conversation.

"No, Alyssum." His eyes narrowed and he drew out the next word. "Frustrated... "

I swore it took a full minute before his meaning sank in.

"Oh. *Oh.*" My breakfast suddenly got very interesting. "But why wouldn't it have kicked in before?"

Aric snickered and scratched his head roughly. "I've known him for a while now and uh... I don't get the impression he's ever had reason to be frustrated."

"Why's that?" I asked.

Aric shot me an evil grin. "I'm not saying he's a man-whore or anything, but he's known the pleasures of the flesh."

"Oh, god." I dropped my head into my hands.

Jensen and I haven't had that talk yet.

Aric dropped his plate in the sink, rubbed my head the way you would a little kid, and walked out.

"Jackass," I called down the hall with a smile.

I returned to my room to change out of my pajamas though the three of us had planned to meet at ten. My father had Gremalian business that would take him away for a few days, a truce talk with his Gobel equivalent that had been on the books for a while and likely wouldn't go well. Dad wasn't interested in giving up any of our land, an area that happened to be very rich in natural resources, and the Gobel weren't interested in anything else.

I heard his car pull out just after I'd gotten back to my room. No goodbye, no "See ya later, sport," no "Good luck training the savior of our society."

Aric and Jensen were already in the garage, sitting relaxed across from one another, when I got to them. No doubt, Jensen would have been at Aric's throat if he'd known about the conversation that had taken place just hours earlier.

"What?" I said, interrupting them. "No fighting yet?"

Their postures went stiff and their heads jerked toward me. I smiled at the way I'd taken them by surprise, then sat in my own seat, flinging my legs over one arm. I opened the entertainment magazine I'd brought with me. If I wasn't allowed to participate, then I was going to show that I didn't care when I cared a freaking ton.

Aric started by explaining the theory of Gobel fighting. I didn't listen to most of it. He said something about how mischievous Gobel could be, attacking out of nowhere when you least expect it. While they were strong, that wasn't the only thing to be on the lookout for. They all had powers, but not the same type or level of powers. It was more a hodgepodge of low-level powers that most of the time was just annoying. Since they bred like rabbits, they had the numbers to overcome their enemy.

Then it was time to fight.

They weren't overly aggressive right out of the gate. I pretended not to be watching until they got some of their pent-up energy or pent-up aggression out. In the beginning, Aric was able to avoid Jensen altogether. Jensen got frustrated when his third punch didn't land. My mind paused on the word *frustrated*. I tried to shake it out of my head altogether.

To cool down a little, Jensen pulled his T-shirt off and threw it toward the door. Watching his muscles flex and turn, I noticed how strong he was. I'd already known he had muscle definition from all the times I'd felt it just below his shirt, sometimes skin to skin. Watching him was mesmerizing.

"Alyssum?" Aric broke the spell.

"Draw," I said because they were actually pretty evenly matched.

They'd each gotten the other good enough to call it a tie. Apparently, my staring hadn't gone unnoticed by either of them. Neither had broken the skin though.

Honestly, it'd be helpful if they did. I could teach Jensen to call on his healing abilities or take him to the infirmary so he could get a sense of what copper could do.

"My turn." I got to my feet in one swift motion and joined them in the center of the room. "I know you're firmly against this, Jensen, but it's got to be done."

"I told you *no*." He started to walk away.

"What if it could save your life?" I called at his back.

He turned to me, his eyes on fire. "Do you think I care?" he yelled. "Do you think that matters if I hurt you?" His reasoning didn't deter me.

"What if it saves my life?" I yelled back. "Does it matter then?" His face scrunched up. I could see he didn't understand. "Look, I need practice too and I can't only use Aric because I'll get too used to him. Plus, you are here to save lives, mine included."

"Alyssum... I—"

"I know. I know you don't want to hurt me but trust when I tell you I can take it. I heal so quickly it'll be like it never happened."

He reluctantly gave in and came back toward me with a sigh.

His heart wasn't into it.

The first time he came at me, he missed on purpose. He threw a halfhearted punch that wasn't within a mile of my face. Over and over again he'd launch and miss.

It was time for a correction.

When he went left, I went right so his punch landed squarely on my jaw. Since he wasn't actually trying, it didn't have a lot behind it but he jumped back, horrified by what he'd done.

I just smiled and re-engaged.

Soon we were at half-speed and he was a natural. I only hoped that he'd noticed before we'd started that the small cut Aric had given me the day before was completely gone. He never said anything about it, though.

"Ow! Okay, enough. That really hurt," I cried after he landed a barely-felt kick to my stomach.

"I'm sorry." He had a horrified scowl on his face. "I told you I didn't want to do this."

He wrenched at his neck, then came over to help me up. I twisted my arm, gaining the advantage, and flipped him onto his back, landing an elbow to the chest.

"You can't fall for that," I said once we were on our feet.

He hunched over with his hands on his knees, gasping for air. "I think you broke a rib."

My face fell and I went to him to check it out. When I got within reach, he pulled me into his arms awkwardly and we stumbled back against the wall.

"I was told you couldn't fall for that."

Chapter Seventeen

My earlier conversation with Aric came back to mind when we broke for lunch, but I didn't have time to obsess about ways to get Jensen sexually frustrated because Dahlia found us—accidentally, of course.

I made the introductions, as she'd demanded, making sure to be very clear that Jensen was off-limits.

"So I never thought it'd be Alyssum who would bring a Gobel home to Mom and Dad." Daliah batted her eyes the way I knew guys tended to like. It took everything for me not to roll mine.

"You know it's not like that, Delilah. Or you should."

It was weird seeing two distinct parts of my life come together like oceans meeting.

"Do you want to go shopping?" she asked but it was a full thirty seconds before I realized she was talking to me.

"Where would we go shopping?" I asked because Delaware had nothing.

"There's a mall two hours away."

I groaned.

When I left Delaware, I'd hated shopping and only did it when I had to. Which was what happened in New York. I had to get clothes and things but I did grow to like it as a way to pass the time.

Two hours away though... Not so sure about that.

"I think I've enough of long car rides for a while." I glanced down at what I was wearing. "Besides, I'm sweaty and gross from training and it'd take forever to get me presentable."

"Fine. Fine. You win this time Alyssum." Then she shuffled away.

Daliah didn't need me to go shopping and would be just fine on her own.

The morning was for fighting and the afternoon was for trying to coax Jensen's power out. So, after eating, I took him back to my room.

This was the first time I'd ever been so nervous around him; I hadn't even been this nervous when we'd been alone in his apartment and his hands had started to wander, but that was because our passionate make-out sessions were never planned. They happened naturally. I'd never intentionally gotten a guy worked up just to say *no* in the end.

He dropped into one of the large chairs by the window, probably trying to avoid mucking up my beautiful, soft bedding with his sweaty body.

After announcing that I needed to shower, I headed toward the bathroom, yanking my shirt over my head, and threw it at his feet. He only got to see my bare back as I walked away but his eyes were on me. I could feel it as if it was an actual touch.

After I was clean, I wrapped the large, white bath towel I'd grabbed when getting out of the shower around me twice before I walked out to get some new clothes. The funny thing was, I hadn't even forgotten the clothes on purpose. I never took them into the bathroom with me. Never had reason to before then.

Jensen's breath caught as soon as I walked out in just the towel. "What are you doing?"

I turned a little sheepish. "I forgot my clothes."

"Are you trying to kill me?" His voice sounded

husky. He sighed a ragged sigh that made me giggle as he stalked over, brushed wet strands of hair off my shoulders, wrapped his hand around the back of my neck, and pulled me toward him.

His lips were soft and demanding against mine. His hot tongue slid over mine making me want to melt.

This was supposed to frustrate him but I'd never wanted sex with anyone more in my life. There was an ache that needed to be eased and he was the only one who could do it.

Moving us to the bed, his hands ran down my body, gentle at times, urgent at others, sometimes squeezing so tightly, his grip was deliciously painful. Jensen loosened my towel just enough to get his hands inside. His skin burned across mine. I wasn't even completely naked, but suddenly, I wanted to be.

Jensen's hand slid down as his continued distracting me with his kisses. Without realizing it, I spread my legs for him. His fingers teased around where I wanted them to be. Finally, after an agonizingly long moment, he put the pressure where I needed it. The sensitive nob sprung to life as Jensen began kissing down my neck.

I had to look ridiculous with a towel still

wrapped around my breasts, yet my legs spread wide to give him access.

This moment wasn't how I planned to lose my virginity but there wasn't anything that could stop me from letting it happen.

Jensen kissed and nibbled around my ear as the pressure built. Right at the moment that I thought I was going to propel off a cliff, his mouth covered mine again.

The world wonderfully exploded into a prism of beautiful colors.

That sounded so sappy even to me but there was no other way to explain what he'd done to me.

After I came back to earth, settling onto a soft cloud, his hand began to slowly climb. His hard erection pushed against my leg and this was going to happen.

Until there was a loud bang on my door causing us both to jump and Jensen to pull back while quickly covering me with my towel, and Aric called out, "Are we doing this or what?"

At least he didn't try to come in. That would have been even more awkward than when we'd been in Jensen's room when we'd first gotten back to Delaware.

"Or what." Jensen breathed into my now mostly dried hair, making me laugh.

"Be down soon," I yelled back, hoping he didn't hear my voice waver.

"We should probably go..."

It was the last thing I wanted and based on the bulge in his jeans, it was the last thing I wanted. But having sex right then would end his frustration and we couldn't have that right now.

I hopped up, holding the Egyptian cotton towel tightly to my flushed skin while I pulled out shorts and a tank top. I made the twirl motion with my index finger to tell him to turn around. He hadn't seen me naked yet and, while I was completely sure he would at some point, I had a job to do. His eyes on me right then would have me saying fuck training, fuck the Gobel, we weren't leaving that room.

Feeling a little devilish, I tossed my towel just in front of him once his back was to me so he'd know I was within arm's reach with nothing covering my body.

"Yup, you're trying to me kill me," he said play-fully, waving his arms behind him like he was trying to grab me.

"Nah, you'd be no good to me dead."

Once dressed, I ran to the bathroom to snag myself an elastic to pull my hair back into a ponytail. Then I got my shoes, grabbed his arm, and left my room.

The afternoon was fruitless. Jensen tried, he really did. Even though I gave a detailed tutorial on how I did what I did, nothing happened for him. It looked like he was going to have an aneurism or pull a muscle or something. We finally decided to call it a day.

Before Aric left the room, he leaned in and whispered just loud enough for me to hear, "Do better."

That pissed me off on two fronts. The first being that Aric shouldn't have been thinking of me frustrating Jensen, and second, our moment together after my shower should have left Jensen with raging hormones like it had me. He should already have been frustrated. I knew I was.

The moment Jensen and I parted ways, as it was his turn to shower and change clothes, I burst into Aric's room without knocking. Hearing the water in the bathroom, I headed that way. Again, I didn't knock, which was probably not the smartest choice because the room was filled with steam and he was naked in the shower

"What the hell?" I pounded the glass door once, just hard enough to grab his attention. He jumped pretty good, but I was too consumed with anger to notice his assets. Really, I didn't see a thing.

"Christ, Alyssum." Aric shut the water off, grabbed his towel, and followed me out into the main room. "So, privacy is just a concept for you, huh?"

I didn't look at his bare chest or the muscles rippling down. I didn't watch the bead of water tracing his body until it became inappropriate for me to see its destination... Or at least, I tried very hard not to. Some things were hard to ignore. Yes, I was with Jensen now, but I was still a woman.

"Privacy? You're kidding me, right?" I folded my arms under my breasts. He looked dumbfounded and confused. "Don't talk to me about... frustrating Jensen. Don't talk to me about any of that stuff."

"Do you think I want to?" His eyes blazed. "It isn't easy, but it's what needs to be done."

"What are you talking about?" Because either I really wasn't following or he was distracting me. It really could've been either.

"Just because I can accept that you're with him, just because I can stay friends with both of you, doesn't mean I want to be involved with... " He groaned loudly. "But what I said is the truth. I don't want my family to die." His voice softened just a notch. "And you're my family now, Alyssum."

Everything within me melted. I sometimes forgot that Aric had people he cared about on the other side, people he could very well lose.

"Sorry for bursting in here. I got your message, but you have to stop bringing it up, 'kay?"

"You know, if you want to see me naked in the future, you could just ask," he said as I turned the doorknob. "Anytime you want."

I threw a mid-wattage bolt to his shoulder. It singed against his wet skin, making him grind his teeth together.

"Mean," he spat playfully just as I closed the door.

That night, all hell had broken loose.

I heard it long before I saw it. As the first echo found its way upstairs, I ran out of my room and bumped right into Jensen and Aric.

"What the hell was that?" Jensen asked, holding me steady so I didn't face-plant onto the floor.

"Not sure. It's coming from the front room."

When we got close to the front room, I slowed down to peak around the corner and see what was happening. The hair on my arms stood up, like tiny wires poking out, and instead of the regular prickle up the back of my neck, much bigger electrical pulses punished the base of my skull. There was a hell of a lot of Gobel inside the house.

My father had someone by the throat while throwing instructions out at people I couldn't see.

"Gobel." I drew back against the wall. The guys followed my lead and pulled back to stay hidden as well.

"If you give us Aric, we'll leave." The heavy voice made my stomach drop.

I looked to Aric and saw his eyes on the ceiling, like a kid who'd gotten in trouble. "My dad."

"You two stay here," I said. Aric nodded. Only Jensen started to protest. "No, you need to stay here. They can't know you're here. They can't know you're you." I caught Aric's eyes and held them with mine. "Keep him here, no matter what." He nodded.

I took off in a run directly into the middle of the mayhem. I dove over a few guys fighting on the floor, taking out a woman at the shoulders. She hit the floor with a *crack*. Since the running had allowed me to pick up some static, I threw a bolt at the guy sneaking up behind my dad.

I took a deep breath, picked up all the energy I could, and sent a band of static across the room. People on both sides fell to the ground. The ring snapped against the wall. No one had ever seen me do that. Sometimes there were abilities a lady needed to keep to herself until she really needed to use them.

"Now that I have everyone's attention... Do you think there's a better way to handle this?" In the house, I couldn't pick up enough power to do any real damage to that large of a group, but that was fine. I just wanted to startle them out of fighting.

"I want my son," the man with the big voice declared. Aric's dad was a large man. He looked like he could be a linebacker on an human football team. He had dark hair cropped short and dark, flaming eyes. Maybe it was my imagination but it looked like flames peaked out at the edges of the abyss.

"Not gonna happen." I shook my head. He charged until I threw the biggest spark I could muster. I wasn't trying to hurt him, but no way in hell was he gonna hurt me.

"Kidnapping a Gobel is grounds for war in and of itself," he said, stalking toward me much slower, one small step after another.

"We didn't kidnap him."

I found Kale's pale face in the crowd. He refused to look me in the eye.

Aric's father was about to disagree when Aric showed himself from the hallway.

"They didn't, Dad."

"Aric!" The woman I assumed was his mother came forward. She was tall with the same dark hair and eyes that Aric had and he looked so much more like her than his dad. "You must come home, please."

"I can't, Mom. Not this time."

"Maybe some of you should wait outside," Aric's dad told some of the Gobel with him. "It seems this is a family matter."

With the fighting over, I ran back to where I'd left Jensen but he was no longer against the wall near the entryway. I searched the nearby rooms but when I didn't find anything, I decided to check the training room.

That's where he was. Alone.

Light from the moon crept in, giving me just enough to see him.

"There you are." I was slightly breathless from the search and the fear I might not find him, that somehow one of them had gotten to him. My stomach turned at the thought.

He jumped. "Yeah, I, uh... need to make..." He threw his hands up helplessly.

He was trying to throw energy. Something he hadn't done yet and would take time. Once he learned how to trigger it, it'd be easy but he wasn't there yet.

"Why the sudden rush for your powers?" I thought I knew and leaned with folded arms on the wall by the door. Some things I had to let him say, let him come to terms with on his own.

"You ran off into that"—he raised his hands in the general direction of the foyer—"and I had to stay back because I'm useless. You guys seem to think there's something inside me, so I need to get it out. What's the secret?"

I gave him a reassuring smile before walking toward him. "Well, Aric says the reason our powers kick in just after puberty is from the... frustration that comes with it." His brows furrowed in confusion before relaxing. What I meant must've struck. "He didn't seem to think you've been frustrated enough for it to kick in."

He winced, like he'd made a painful realization or was afraid that I had. I didn't care about his past and shouldn't either. How many women he'd been with was of no consequence to me.

"So, that's what you've been doing?" he asked.

"Yes." Three more steps brought me within reach of him. The intensity between us zipped through the air like a tiny electrical current yet he didn't seem to feel it.

"Did any of it mean anything?"

"All of it," I said quickly. "I wanted everything we've done to happen. More actually. I've wanted more and I think it would have in my room if Aric hadn't interrupted us. Am I wrong?"

He wet his bottom lip like he was remembering exactly what we'd done.

"But when I wasn't out of my mind with need for you, I did make sure we didn't go any further in hopes that it would spark something."

His hands ran over his face. "Ah. Well, you do a fine job."

"It really wasn't that hard," I said playfully.

"Speak for yourself," he threw back.

I snorted. A deep breath helped me work my courage into place so I could say what needed to be said. I hoped he wouldn't get angry and leave. "Maybe we've been going about this all wrong."

"How so?" Jensen got close enough that he could trail his fingers down my arms.

"Well, back in Putnam Valley, whenever Aric and I were together..." I jumped. A spark zapped my arm, like the static shock from a blanket. Not too painful. The important thing was that I hadn't done it. "Oh." A smile slowly formed. "So, when we were alone in his apartment..." A little bigger jolt caused me to take in a quick breath. "Aside from all the—"

The next shock was painful enough to interrupt me, like a hard, sharp pinch on each arm, or being snapped with the thinnest rubber band ever. The thin ones hurt more than the thick. I yelped.

"I'm sorry. Did that hurt?" Guilt dilated his pupils.

"Jensen, you did it!"

"I did? I did."

"Try again. Just this time not on me." I took a step back. If the voltage of his zaps continued to grow, I didn't want to be on the receiving end.

I pointed at the far wall. He closed his eyes, took a deep breath, and nothing happened. Aric came in, shirtless after the heat in the foyer, and when he stood beside me, I put a hand on his chest, then let it fall lightly toward his waistband.

Aric's abs tightened as his gaze dropped to me in surprise.

A shock of energy, big enough that it blew the hair off my shoulders, hit the chair, completely destroying it. Smoke smoldered and flames rose. The sprinklers rained water down to put the fire out, a little precaution my dad had put in throughout the house when I'd been a kid.

Jensen wasn't the only one to mistakenly set something on fire. Not that all Gremalians could set fire to things without something extremely powerful like direct lightning, but, somehow, Jensen had done it with just the natural static in the room.

I dropped my hands from Aric's waist. "Okay, you've got it," I said, getting pelted with water. "Now you know what you have to think about until it becomes second nature."

"Great. I get to torture myself."

His face fell. I had to admit, I kind of liked him being jealous. Before I'd officially become Jensen's girlfriend, we'd been all calm and grown-up about our situation. Maybe, back then, that had been an act and he'd always hated every minute I'd spent with Aric.

"Sorry." I patted his back with a chuckle. "Whatever it takes."

Aric seemed to put two and two together and figured out why I'd touched him in such an intimate way, though he didn't look mad about it. He was as committed to this as I was.

"How did he do that?" he asked.

"What?" I looked up at him once the downpour

had ended. I tried to squeeze as much water out of my hair as I could.

"Set that thing on fire using just the energy in the room?" Aric pointed to the chair.

"Maybe there was lightening nearby. It doesn't have to be that close."

"There's not lightening." he said.

I sighed. "It's something only the very powerful can do."

"What can Gobel do?" Jensen asked as he opened then closed his fists like he couldn't believe that had actually come from him.

Aric scratched the back of his head in a way that told me he wasn't the most comfortable talking about this. Hell, none of us were. Usually our full abilities were kept pretty secret within our own community. Aric telling us was yet another betrayal of his people. "We, uh, have some control over plants. Along with a few other parlor tricks. Nothing impressive."

"Plants?" Jensen asked.

"Yeah, plants," Aric confirmed.

So that Aric could give a demonstration for Jensen—I'd already seen Gobel control plants—I ran to the backyard, yanked down a hanging basket, and brought it back inside of the garage with me.

"Here." I set it down in front of Aric.

He sighed, rolled his eyes, and waved his hand at the basket. The flowers, wilted and on their deathbed from the oppressive heat we'd been having, bloomed and sprung to life in beautiful tints of purple and white. They kept sprouting until a small jungle of greens surrounded us. He dropped his hand.

"Impressive." I couldn't look away. It was so beautiful but I'd seen Gobel fight before and while it wasn't a war, I knew exactly how dangerous plants could become. "So, why do your people want the copper?"

"That's the thing. I didn't know until I talked to Kale. Mostly because I didn't pay attention to Gobel/Gremalian relations until recently, when tensions started to build again. It seems the copper allows us to heal too. Kale wasn't sure if it does anything else, like boost our power. I know copper can do that for Gremalians if they have enough of it."

"I get that you're saying copper helps Gobel and Gremalians heal, but why does copper do that? I mean, you'd think supernatural creatures would heal on their own," Jensen said.

"That'd be nice." Aric chuckled. "But no, apparently it's the copper that makes us heal quickly and The Gobel Assembly feels you guys have hogged the largest natural resource for too long."

The three of us headed out of the soaked garage to go change into dry clothes.

One the way, Dad stopped us. "The situation is handled. Aric will stay here with us but the rest of his family left."

My mouth opened in surprise. We were supposed to have other Gobel on our side. "But—"

"They're still with us, Alyssum," Aric assured me. "They'll be there when we need them."

This had to have been figured out before this happened. Before his family showed up here otherwise he couldn't have known that. Maybe he needed Kale there and that had been the plan all along.

I hated that I didn't know for sure and would just have to trust that Aric knew what he was doing.

After what Aric had told me, I decided that I didn't see the big deal over allowing the Gobel access to the minds. Sure, they could buy copper wiring in any home improvement store but it wasn't the same and it was hella expensive to outfit the entire community.

If compromised on the use of the mines or hell, just giving them a shit load of it would stop the war and keep Jensen from having to fight, I was all for it.

My new mission became trying to work a

compromise that neither side would actually go for. Everyone wanted to control the minds themselves.

In the beginning, when I'd first gone to see if Jensen was still alive, I'd had no qualms about thrusting him into danger if it meant putting an end to the many years of turmoil between the two sides. I'd thought ending the turmoil meant exerting our power and showing dominance by winning the war, but now I cared about him and didn't want to use him in that way, especially since he was only in Delaware because I'd asked him to come.

For the next couple of days, I left Aric to train Jensen so that I could have time to work on Dad so he'd agree to a compromise or figure out some other way to give the Gobel some of the copper.

Dad wouldn't even hear of me out but I'd keep at him.

This was now the best way out of the whole thing.

Chapter Eighteen

Dahlia had been hanging all over Aric since we
had our little "talk" in his room.

I could guess what he'd be doing with his time
and I didn't care. Daliah knew that Jensen was off
limits but I had no claim on Aric other than him
being important to me and I'd have to zap her ass if
she hurt him. Though I didn't think that was likely. It
was more likely that Aric would hurt Dahlia.

Jensen and I hadn't had much time alone since
the day I'd taken him on the tour of the town. It was
time to pause worrying about everything else. The
weather was warm and beautiful, a perfect day in
Michigan. I told him to dress comfortably; we were
leaving before lunch.

I drove us fifteen miles out of town, only stopping after we'd hit the Bête Gris Preserve. We'd walk from there. I pulled a picnic basket out of the trunk, which Jensen took from me right away, and we strolled, hand in hand, until we reached the water. A small canoe, pulled up on the shore for us to use, made crossing the water a snap.

I hadn't been absolutely sure that the canoe would still be there, but it was. He wouldn't even let me row. I'd done it a million times, alone even, although the way his muscles strained with the work was enjoyable to watch. Every time I offered to help, he'd brush me off. We made it to the other side just after the sun had crossed its midpoint in the sky.

"Are we bear hunting?" he asked as I kicked my shoes and socks off to dip my toes in the cool water. It was so refreshing. Our lakes remained pretty cold, even in the intense summer heat, so sometimes it was too cold to go in, but getting my feet wet offered just enough relief from the sun.

"Not bear hunting but this is somewhere I knew we could be alone for a while without anyone interrupting us."

"I do like the sound of that."

I ran my toes through the clear water.

"This is the Bête Gris Lighthouse. Your dad bought it for us a while back. We use it to light the way once in a while. It's run by remote now I guess. Anyway, I like it because no one ever comes here. It's quiet."

"It's beautiful," he mumbled from behind me.

He let the info about his dad go without asking questions, which was surprising. I'd expected he'd want to push me for more information as much as I wanted to, and often did, push my mom for more info. I lifted my eyes to him. He wasn't looking at the lighthouse.

"Hungry?" I asked. He nodded. "I thought you would be since you did all the rowing to get here and carried the food I packed and basically let me do nothing."

We laid out the oversized blanket from the basket, then set out lunch. I'd tried to bring every-thing: sandwiches, chips, drinks—anything we might need, yet things I could manage. We sat on the banks of an inlet that led to Lake Superior, the clearest water I'd ever seen. It was quiet except for the rush of waves and our voices. Isolated, we got to spend time together in a way we hadn't since leaving Putnam Valley.

"How's training going with Aric?" I asked before taking a bite of my sandwich.

"Fine. Somehow I don't have trouble hitting that guy."

I snorted. "You shouldn't have trouble hitting me either. In training that is. If you did it out of anger I'd have to mess you up."

He chuckled. "I wouldn't do that."

"I know. I'm teasing you."

"I haven't set anything else on fire."

After swallowing hard and taking a drink of water, I said, "I mean... that's not really the goal anyway. Yes, if you're in a fight, set the fucker on fire but we should practice that when we aren't in the house."

"Luckily you have the sprinklers."

I gave him a wide grin. "And why do you think my dad had those installed?"

He laughed and it was infectious. When we settled down, I asked, "Have you talked to your parents?"

"I have." He took a drink. "My mom keeps pushing for a return date."

"Should we tell her that we're keeping you?" I'd meant it to sound playful but it came out much too serious. "I'm kidding, of course."

"I know." He took a deep breath. "She told me I'd better not come back married."

Now I had to laugh. As if that was something we'd even discussed. "I can understand that, though. She's your mom. She'd want to be there when you get married." But then I let that topic fall.

Sometimes I got the impression he wanted to ask about his other parents, the people who'd actually created him but he never did. It was like the words were forming in his head and never made it to his mouth. Not that I could've told him much but I would've given him everything I had.

Instead of waiting, I said, "I don't know much about them" The way his jaw tightened told me he knew exactly who I talking about. "Since they died before I was born." I paused. "My dad knows every-thing, though."

His head snapped up. "What do you mean?"

"Our dads grew up together. He's never said much to me. I think it makes him too sad," I said softly. We'd finished eating long enough ago that I had no idea what time it was. "He'd answer any of your questions."

"I feel kind of selfish, you know?" he said. I shook my head, prompting him to explain. "Wanting to know anything. I have great parents. I didn't have a bad childhood, but here I am, wanting to know about people I've never met just because they're part of me somehow."

"I think that's natural. I'd want to know. Hell, I grew up with my parents and still have questions." That made him laugh. "Wanna see inside?"

We hopped onto our feet, packed the basket back up, and headed inside the keeper's house. I'd expected it to be dirtier. I hadn't been inside in years and while the air was a little stagnant, even that cleared with the breeze we'd let in through the door.

We wandered around and headed upstairs to the loft area. The view was spectacular from up there. We could see far out onto the water and, with the sun beginning its descent, we had about an hour before we really had to head back. He wrapped his arms around my waist from behind as a slight glow rose from the old lights that hadn't worked in decades.

"Hey," I said as I turned around, "did you do that?" He nodded. "Impressive."

"That would have been really handy in high school," he told me causing me to snicker and slap his chest. "You would have been handy to have around in about tenth grade."

I shook my head. "No, I wouldn't have."

He squeezed tighter. "I think you would have been."

I pushed my shoulders back so he could see my smirk. "I was in middle school."

He closed his eyes and groaned. Our age different wasn't huge now—just three years—but when he was sixteen, I was only thirteen.

"Right," he conceded. "That wouldn't have been great. I wouldn't have been able to have you then." When he realized how it sounded, he quickly added, "Nor would I have wanted to."

Jensen leaned down and kissed me gently at first but very quickly his mouth worked with a new intensity. He tilted my head back to take the kiss deeper and no matter how close we were, I always wanted him closer.

He dropped kissed over my cheek and down my neck to skitter across my collarbone.

My hands went up his shirt, feeling the muscles jump under my touch. With experienced fingers, he grabbed the hem of my orange tank top and lifted it over my head.

He held me tightly in his arms with a hand on the back of my head to keep me right where he wanted me as his lips met mine again.

Jensen tasted like a cool summer day. Like the

clearest water I'd ever swam in, and only released me so that he could pull his own shirt over his head.

I caressed over his chest slowly, taking my time to memorize the peaks and planes of his hard muscles. Then I flattened my hand over his heart where the fast beat matched my own.

He left me for a second to spread out the blanket we'd used for lunch then brought me to the ground with him.

Jensen hovered over me as I laid on my back, his fingers brushing a strand of hair out of my face. His lips burned my skin in all the right places while his hand trailed down the length of my body until he found the bend of my knee, which he hooked over his hip.

I closed my eyes and let him bring our bodies closer. We'd only taken our shirts off, but everything we were doing was sensual and intimate. Every move took my breath a way even more, every touch had me full of need.

I wanted him and he wanted me.

After he undid the button and zipper on my shorts, my muscles clenched when his hand slid inside. Fucking amateur.

I hadn't told him that I was a virgin yet, though

maybe I didn't need to. Maybe it didn't matter. Maybe he didn't need to know.

He circled my sensitive nub again, though unlike in my room, he didn't take his time. His expert fingers brought me to a climax almost before I knew I was headed for one.

Now, I wanted to touch him.

I'd barely gotten my hand into his jeans and brushed the top of his cock when his fingers wrapped around my wrist and pulled it back.

"Why—"

"Can't have you touch me," he said into the crook of my neck then dropped several kissed.

"You don't want me to?" That didn't make sense but what else could it have been.

He snorted and lifted his head to look me in the eye. "Trust me. I want you to but I'll make a mess pretty quickly right now. Wouldn't want to embarrass myself."

The thought of him coming undone by my hand was the least embarrassing thing I could've thought of then but if he was saying he didn't want it, I wouldn't push.

I wanted to stay there forever, in this moment, in the place where no one else existed. If we didn't leave soon, we'd have to stay the night and there were definitely worse things. But my dad wouldn't agree with me.

"We have to go," I said. My lips were slightly swollen from all the kissing.

"Have to?" He squeezed me even tighter.

"If we don't, it'll be too dark and we'll be stuck here."

He groaned, keeping his eyes closed. "Yeah."

At least he wanted to leave as little as I did. Reluctantly, I hopped up to put my shirt back on. "Don't be a baby."

"I'd really rather just stay here with you." His eyes focused on me, full of need.

"Me too, but they'll send out search parties and probably think the Gobel had something to do with us being missing." I looked down at his bare chest, mentally reminding myself we really did need to go. "We are pretty important, you know."

"I love you, Alyssum." The words spilled from his mouth and I couldn't be sure he meant them too.

One thing was clear. He may or may not have meant to have said it right then but he definitely meant what he said.

"I love you, too," I told him then laid back down beside him.

Jensen kissed me differently this time. It wasn't

full of need or desire it was full of love and reverence.

To think I could've gone my entire life not even meeting this man and now... I loved him.

We were slow getting home. Jensen wasn't trying too hard and I was happy for it. He rowed slower than a snail moved and watched me, smiling until my stomach went crazy with butterflies and I had to look away. We didn't talk much though, as if our glances said everything. Even in the car, which he drove home, we held hands but didn't need to talk. I did my best to get as close as I could by laying my head on his shoulder. It was perfect.

He rolled the ends of my hair between his finger and thumb as we stood outside the house. It was just past dark and things seemed pretty quiet. I wanted this moment without anyone else around and it seemed so did he.

People knew we were together, but intimate moments were better without an audience.

Our lips met, a gentle coming together of earlier declarations, then he pulled back to see my face, leaving me again wanting more. I was never ready for his mouth to leave mine or prepared for the way he turned me to complete mush with just a touch.

"I don't want to go in," I whispered, standing on

my toes with goose bumps covering my body, and not the kind Gobel gave me.

"Me, either. I'd rather stay with you."

I smiled up at him and hoped he knew I wanted that too. But father's house, father's rules.

After another few more stolen moments, we went in and up the stairs. I paused outside my door to watch him continue down the hall before gong inside.

The room became too big and empty. I decided to push ahead, tossing some pajamas on the bed, and as pulled my tank top over my head, the door swung open, then shut quietly. Jensen stood just inside.

I ran and jumped at him, wrapping my legs around his waist and arms around his neck, squeezing tightly with both. He moved us over to the bed then fell on top of me as soon as my back hit the mattress, his lips owning mine again.

A loud bang on the door reverberated through my room, breaking us apart but only enough to breathe.

"Yes," I called out, trying not to sound breathless, hoping whoever was on the other side wouldn't come in without being invited.

"Alyssum," my father called out, "please ask Jensen to meet me in my office." Our gazes found each other's, each wondering how my father knew he was in here. We listened until the dull thud of his footsteps was gone.

"He saw you come in here?" I whispered, even though I knew my dad was long gone. Jensen shook his head.

"There was no one around. I made sure." He pushed off to lie next to me and stare at the ceiling. "What does he want?"

"I don't know. I'll go with you."

"I think he wants me alone. Does he own any guns?" He cracked that half-grin that I'd come to adore.

"He doesn't need one." I wasn't being funny or flippant, either. If my dad wanted someone gone, he could make it happen without traditional weapons, though there were firearms in the compound. I didn't want Jensen to worry about that.

"I just wonder if it's *gremlin* stuff or *you* stuff."

Sitting up, I looked at him seriously. "Do not say 'gremlin' to my dad. You've got to stop calling us that."

With a quick kiss to my forehead, Jensen got up and headed for the door.

"Do you want me to walk you?" I asked. I wanted to give us a few more minutes together.

"I've been here long enough to find it."

Not what I meant but OK. "Come back when you're done."

He gave a slight nod before leaving me in my room, alone again. The man I loved was off to a private meeting with my father.

That was a totally normal thing to happen.

But we weren't totally normal.

Chapter Nineteen

Just after Jensen had left, there was another quick knock on the door before it opened and Dahlia poked her head through.

"Am I interrupting anything?"

"No."

"Too bad." She pranced over, plopping onto the end of my bed. "So, where'd you guys go?"

"Out to the lighthouse."

"Oh, I love that place. Romantic, if you want it to be." She giggled. I gave nothing away. "So, *did* you want it to be?"

In all our years of being friends, I'd never hidden anything from her until I left for New York. But I was finding now that I'd actually fallen in love, there were somethings I didn't want to share.

"It was great." That was all I wanted to stay on the subject but Dahlia didn't agree.

"Did you finally—"

"No. And I think too many people are concerned with that aspect of my life," I spat. Dahlia knew that I was a virgin—by choice—and I knew that she wasn't. We shared almost everything in our lives. With her raised eyebrow questioning me, I told her about the conversation with my mom and high-lighted the things Aric had said to me about Jensen. "So, he's got experience and I've got nothing."

"No, that means he's got *skills*. That's good. It won't be some bumbling ball of hormones like Sage," she said. I snorted, as if Sage had ever been an option for sex. "So, what's the holdup? Not ready yet?"

"Oh, no. I'm ready, but we're never alone with all this other stuff going on. And it was getting dark tonight, so we had to head back or, you know, deal with the wrath of my father who doesn't really trust all of this yet."

"Well, Aric and I—"

"Ahh." I clasped my hands over my ears. "I can't hear you. I'm not even listening."

She pried my hands back, then pulled the long, dark mane of hair over her shoulder. "Nothing has happened. Well, not nothing, but not that. Yet. And I do stress *yet*." She gave me a look that said she meant business. I swallowed hard and hoped she didn't notice. "When the time comes, we'll compare notes."

"I'd really rather not."

Jensen didn't come back, at least not when I was awake. I waited as long as I could, talking to Dahlia for a long time before falling asleep sometime after midnight.

I woke to her hogging my bed and covers, causing me to teeter on the edge.

I didn't see Jensen all morning, so I still had no idea what he'd talked to my dad about the night before.

There was a disturbance in the force. A commotion coming from downstairs with angry voices whose words I couldn't make out yet still knew what was being said wasn't good.

I hurried down the stairs, trying not to break my neck toward whatever was happening. Running toward a danger that I didn't know the extent of wasn't new for me and the air felt eerie like it did when the Gobel had shown up.

My dad had Sage, Aric, Jensen, and a lot of others with him. I came to a stop close to them yet no one spoke.

"There was another breach," Aric finally whispered. He wasn't the one who should've been telling me, hence the whisper.

"Sage?" I asked because getting an answer out of him was more likely than my father... Or Jensen apparently. When he didn't answer, I stepped closer. "Sage!"

He sighed then finally looked down at me. "An uninvited Gobel was on the property." As compared to the invited one standing in the entry room.

"That's not very smart to try to attack us inside the building. There's copped everywhere."

"Technically," Sage continued. "That means the Gobel would be able to heal quicker, too."

"Still a big risk." Then it occurred to me that healing may not have been the only reason they wanted the copper. "Unless it makes them stronger too." But I was looking at Aric. Watching to see anything that would give away that answer but he was a stone faced bastard right now, giving nothing away.

"Listen." Sage grabbed my arm to pull me away from the group causing Jensen to growl under his breath. I shook my head so Jensen wouldn't react. Whatever Sage was gong to say, I wanted to hear.

"Aric, Jensen, and I are heading out to bring Aric's brothers back. The ones that want to help us. I think the breach was because the Goble don't want that to happen. But there's only one way they could know it happened."

I shook my head emphatically. "Aric didn't tell them."

"I'm not going to argue that with you. Right now, the three of us are going. Only the three of us," he added when I opened my mouth to protest.

That was when I noticed my mother in the room, giving me the dusty eyeball. Who knew what feelings she was picking up on at this moment.

"You're not leaving me behind," I told him louder than I meant to. My inability to keep my voice down brought my dad's attention and that was the last thing I'd wanted.

"You're not going," Dad said loud enough for everyone to hear.

"Dad, I—"

"No," he bellowed bringing silence to the room. "For once in your damned life, you're going to listen to me Alyssum Bracken."

I snapped back like he'd slapped me, which caused him to soften his tone.

"Alyssum, the Gobel would love nothing more than to take you to make us bend to their will. If that happens, The Assembly will remove me from power and elect a new leader."

That didn't make sense. "Why would they do that."

"Because I'd be thinking like a father and not like their leader. So that I wouldn't be able to give into their demands to get my daughter back."

Aric and Jensen both moved much closer to us, though I didn't notice until Aric said, "He's right, Alyssum. My Assembly would love nothing more than to get you."

"And your Assembly would leave you to die," Jensen added.

He might've been new but clearly he understood more about the politics than I thought.

Sage cleared his throat. "I'm going to one more sweep of the building with my team and then we'll head out."

That gave me about ten minutes to pack a back-pack and get better shoes on so that I could follow them. Whether they liked it or not.

My father turned to walk away then thought better of is. "I forgot to wish you a happy birthday yesterday, Jensen."

My eyes widened in surprise and I gasped

quietly, recovering quickly when my dad's gaze homed in on me. How did my father know his birth—wait. He would've been there when he was born. But how would the Burkhardt's have known his birthday?

"Thanks, Mr.—"

My dad cut him off. "I told you, call me 'Ash.'" He clapped Jensen's shoulder the way a proud father would a son. So unfair. I never got that kind of attention from him. "It's not every day a man turns twenty-two."

"Thanks, Ash."

We weren't far apart, but I marched over to Jensen with a tense jaw. Aric turned away, smirking. He knew me well enough to understand that Jensen was in trouble. He'd been on the receiving end more than once.

"Why didn't you tell me yesterday was your birthday? Also, how does my father know it was your birthday?" My voice was quiet and angry.

"It's just a day. I assume he was there when I was born. There were some records in the car crash my mom said. Not much but a singed birth certificate. No names. Nothing they could trace family with but I guess it had my birthday." He smiled, touched my elbow, and said, "Good morning, by the way."

"It's your birthday, Jensen. I would have done something special."

He gave me a smug half-smile. "Do you really think I didn't thoroughly enjoy yesterday? I mean, sure, there's one thing I can think of that I'd have loved for my birthday, but I'd love that any day."

I fought off the blush rising from my chest at the mention of that. He pushed a lock of hair behind my ear, making my cheeks burn even hotter.

"I would have... " Then I pulled something out of the air. "Worn a sexier bra or something."

His body shook with laughter. "Your bra was sexy enough, trust me."

I gave him the look that said I was done joking and punched his shoulder. "You still should have told me."

Jensen moved in close and apologized. He didn't mean it.

"Well, I hope you had a good birthday, then." I turned to climb the stairs, taking two at a time.

"Best one yet," he called out to my back. I could only smile and shake my head with a sigh. "You're not mad, right?"

I turned slowly, narrowing my eyes to make him sweat it a little until I finally shrugged. "I can't be mad. I guess I haven't exactly told you everything, either."

Then I went back on my way. The next thing I knew, he was calling my name in a faux-whisper and yanking my arm to get me to stop.

"What haven't you told me?" His normally kind, gentle eyes had anger in them.

"Nothing. I was just kidding."

"No, you weren't." He searched my face, like he thought he'd see the answer there if he looked hard enough.

"It's nothing." I looked over my shoulder to see if anyone could hear us. "We'll talk later."

"We'll talk now."

He pulled me the rest of the way up to hide us away in my room then backed me into the wall with his palms flat beside me. I thought about finding someone who could build me a time machine so I could go back and unsay that stupid little comment. I didn't know what I'd been thinking. We hadn't talked about the more intimate nature of our lives before we'd met and I never intended to, not after Aric's comments about Jensen's experience.

"How do I ask this appropriately?" He sighed. "Have you ever done what we almost did last night?"

"No." I looked away, fidgeting with my fingers,

even though he completely surrounded me. Jensen closed his eyes, then put his lips to my forehead.

"You should've told me. That could've been bad."

"How so?" I swooped under one of his arms and plopped onto my bed. He followed.

"Your first time shouldn't be on the floor of some abandoned building."

"Hey, I love that abandoned building."

"But now I know," he whispered. His gaze scanned my face, covering every feature to the point that I couldn't take not looking at him. "Why didn't you just tell me?"

"We never talked about it."

"Why didn't we?" His hand wrapped around mine.

"I didn't want to." His face scrunched and somehow I knew it meant he wanted more of an answer than that. I rolled my eyes. "After everything Aric said about *frustrating* you... I didn't want to hear it and I didn't want my virginity to freak you out."

Jensen burst into laughter. "Freak me out? Please, you're not the first virgin I've ever met." I tensed, sitting with my back even straighter. "That's not what I meant," he added quickly. "I just meant, I wouldn't have cared. I don't care."

"Just to be clear... " I didn't want him to get the wrong impression. "It doesn't matter to me... I mean, about what you've done before. I just didn't want something built up in my head to make me self-conscious if we got to that point." He nodded and I could tell he was uncomfortable with where the conversation could lead so I playfully punched his shoulder. "I'm not asking you to tell me anything. I just wanted you to know what that was all about. I don't want to be compared to women who actually knew what they were doing."

"As if they could compare to you. Alyssum, I'd tell you everything if that's what you wanted. It isn't that," he said. My eyebrow-raising said, *"Then what?"* "Nobody else really mattered to me is all. I had sex with them. I'm in love with you. Those weren't just words."

Pulling him by the back of the neck, I gave him a kiss that was sure to make him know they weren't just words to me, either.

Once I'd pulled away, a little breathless, I asked, "What did you and my dad talk about last night?"

"Later," he whispered, looking me over before adding, "We have to get going."

"We?"

"Psh. Like I don't know you're coming whether

we want you to or not. Aric and I will just have to make sure we protect you."

I hurriedly put sneakers on and grabbed my backpack before rushing out the door.

On my way down the stairs, Dahlia stopped me wanting to talk but I didn't have time for that. I promised to text her later.

I was almost to the bottom of the stairs when I heard, "Alyssum, come back up here please."

This time, I took the stairs two at a time to get to her. "What's up?"

"You're going even though your father demanded you don't?" She eyed me.

"Yes. Because I'm part of this, Mom, whether he likes it or not."

"I know you are." She took me in with those knowing blue eyes, unlike any color I'd ever seen before. "Just... be careful, OK. I don't think your father could stand it if something happened to you. He'd never forgive himself."

"I'm always careful, Mom."

She snorted. "You are not." Her arms opened wide to pull me into a hug. "I'll have to trust that those young men who love you so much will make sure nothing happens to you."

"How do you know they love me?" I asked while she squeezed me tightly.

"A mother knows and we'll talk about all that when you get home."

Now I was my turn to laugh. "Sure thing, Mom. I love you."

"I love you, too."

She released me so that I could hurry back down the stairs. Tell my mother that I didn't want to talk about boys with her was useless. If she wanted to talk about it, we were going to and if I didn't participate, she'd still get her answers.

For now, I was going to do my part to bring our allies back to the house.

Except when I got to the entry room where the guys were supposed to meet up, there was no one there.

They'd gone and left me behind.

And I was fucking pissed.

Chapter Twenty

While the guys were off to get Aric's brothers, I spent the time in the garden, calming down and avoiding everyone else. There was too much anger inside me to have interactions with other people.

I did angrily text both Aric and Jensen, threatening them with bodily harm, not expecting to get an answer and I didn't. There were a lot of things that had the potential to piss me off, but just leaving me behind was so completely at the top, and at that moment, I couldn't remember all the other things on the list.

As I entered the house from the back, there was some yelling that I couldn't have heard outside coming from the entry room which was the complete opposite side of the house.

Shit. To hear it where I was it had to be intense. Right after an ear shattering shriek, something hit something hard. Like the floor.

If that was Aric and Jensen, they were getting a piece of my pissed-off mind.

After running through the house to get to the entry, I quickly saw it wasn't them.

What I saw overwhelmed all of my senses. I couldn't take it all in at once.

The bitter taste of acid rose in my throat as what was before me sank in.

There was a crumpled mess of fabric in the middle of the floor with oddly bent arms and legs. My nostrils flared as my bottom lip quivered.

My body understood what was happening before my brain did.

I ran to her.

My mother lay on the floor not moving. The sticky warmth that covered her body covered me as her blood soaked my hands. My hair fell in my face. I quickly put my hair back behind my ear and knew that I'd left a trail of blood across my cheek.

"Mom!" Tears began flowing like a river down my cheeks. "Mom, please, hang on. Somebody help me," I screamed.

Though if anyone could hear me, they would've

heard my mother and come to help then.

I pulled her body closer to mine. When I did, her head fell back in an unnatural way that should have told me she was already gone but I wouldn't accept it. There was copper everywhere. I just needed to get some to touch her skin to work faster.

But I couldn't remember where anything was.

I tore open her dress to try to find the source of the blood. If I could put pressure on it, I could give her more time. There was too much. Wherever it was coming from, I couldn't find it.

My body deflated into her. I set her gently onto the imported tile that she loved so much and dropped my head into my hands as a sob ripped through my body. Because of the blood, my hair stuck to my hands.

Then I curled over her like I used to when I was little and had a bad dream and let myself cry all of the tears I thought I had.

I was content to stay there with my mother and barely registered the voice that said, "What the fuck?" or the sounds of feet hurriedly coming toward me.

My body ached with the time that I'd been there with my mother and I didn't want to leave her.

A set of strong hands pulled me up but I refused

to let go, so my mother came with me. "Alyssum," Aric said. His voice sounded gentle and pained. "Alyssum, come on. Let go."

He pried my fingers open to release her and she hit her head, hard, on the hard floor. Not that it mattered, but it made me cry even harder. He wrapped his arms around me and carried me to my room, ignoring how hard I kicked and struggled. My heels battered his shins over and over yet he didn't flinch once or tell me to stop. I couldn't see anything through my blur of tears. I recognized shapes and colors inside my room when he threw the door open but nothing else.

If Aric was back, hours must've passed.

Where was everyone? Why hadn't anyone helped her? Or me?

He set me, gently, onto the bed. The familiar softness made it worse. I should've been down there; I should have somehow figured out that something like that would happen and stop it. Any energy I'd had was already gone when I collapsed against Aric's chest.

He stayed with me, allowing me to dampen his clothes with both the blood of my mother and the tears that were also stoking my fury.

Eventually, my eyes close because I didn't have it

in me to keep them open any longer. But I didn't sleep. Every sound in the room had me on high alert.

The door opened. Heavy footsteps came to the side of my bed and a gentle voice spoke barely above a whisper. "How is she?" Jensen asked. Aric shrugged against me. "What the hell happened down there?"

"I don't know," Aric replied, just as quietly as Jensen. "I've been up here with her. Didn't want to leave her alone."

"Right," Jensen said. "The house is locked down. They're trying to figure out what happened."

Aric held me up. When he stood, Jensen slid into his place and I pried my eyes open just enough to see him. Given how much of a mess I must have been, I shouldn't have been so relieved that he was close to me. My body relaxed almost completely when Jensen lowered it beside him.

I rested my head on his chest while he wrapped his arm around me, gently caressing my fingers which were covered in dried blood. A sound of concern got caught in the back of his throat and he pulled away to look at me.

"Is... Is any of this yours?"

I opened my eyes more widely. His face fell at whatever he saw in my eyes. Sadness, despair, and general horrific pain was what he found because that was what I coursed through me.

My voice wouldn't work so I shook my head. I wasn't hurt. I wasn't the one lying dead on the pale, ceramic tile that I'd spent hours picking out so that my husband and daughter would have a beautiful place to live. That'd been her.

"I'm gonna get you cleaned up, okay?"

I didn't care what he did. Right then, I didn't care what happened to me.

Jensen handled me like I was a newborn baby. He even carried me to the bathroom then set me on the edge of the bathtub and tried to use a wet cloth to wash my mother's remnants from my face and hands, glancing at my face as he went like he was watching a time bomb. It wasn't coming off. The blood had dried like cement in my hair.

"This isn't going to work," Jensen said. "Would you rather take a bath or a shower?"

I didn't answer right away. A bath might have been too tempting, too easy for me to get lost in the depths of the water.

"Shower," I muttered. The voice didn't belong to me. It came out incredibly hoarse and dry. Jensen turned the handles and the room filled with steam. He pulled my shirt over my head and told me to stand to remove my shorts then tossed my underwear and bra in a pile with the rest before helping me into the shower.

I knew I was in trouble when I didn't care that this was the first time he was actually seeing me naked.

The hot water felt so good that I wished it were even hotter, enough to burn the flesh off my bones. I must have given Aric all my tears because I didn't have any more left. I slid down the wall of the shower stall and wrapped my arms around my knees, dropping my head on top. While I was supposed to be using soap to clean my skin, Aric and Jensen were talking in the bedroom but couldn't make out what they were saying.

Then Jensen was back. When he stepped into the shower, I looked up to find him still fully dressed, minus his shoes and socks. His white T-shirt got soaked right away and his jeans started to get speckled, turning a deep indigo. With the softest hands, he brought me to my feet and took a soap filled cloth to wash me off. Then he used far too much shampoo to get the blood out of my hair. He made sure it was completely gone from my hands, face, and legs before cutting the water and wrapping a large towel around me.

Back in the bedroom, I watched him strip off his wet clothes, dry off at superhuman speed, and put on dry clothes that was almost identical to the ones he'd just taken off.

For a moment, I wondered how his clothes had gotten in my room and assumed Jensen must have asked Aric to grab some. I dressed myself in a comfortable pair of shorts and a T-shirt that Jensen had picked out, though he had to help fasten the clean bra he'd grabbed. I moved to my bed and slid under the heavy blanket with the man I loved tightly beside me.

He kissed my temple. "I'm so sorry. I should've been here."

I shook my head. "You had to go. I was so mad, too. At you and Aric for going without me. I was outside working off my anger when I should've been inside protecting my mother."

"I just wish you hadn't seen all of that."

"Me too. Thanks." I sat up, pretzeling my legs underneath me.

"For?" He looked confused. I nudged my head toward the shower. His face fell even more. "Well, I have always wanted to get you in the shower with me." He gave me a half-hearted smile.

I wanted to laugh yet could only muster up a

lame, fake-sounding chuckle. I knew I had to ask. "Does my dad know?"

He nodded. "He must. I could only think about you. I ran up here so fast that I really don't know."

The door opened. Aric peeked his head through, then came in with a tray full of pop, water, and a few snacks. He set the tray on the foot of my bed and climbed on beside it.

"I know it's a stupid question, but how are you doing?" His brows were knit together with concern.

"A little better now that I'm cleaned up." I leaned over and put my hand on his. "Thank you for staying with me." I looked at his fresh shirt. "Sorry about your shirt."

"That thing was ugly anyway." Aric grabbed a bottle of water and tossed it at me. "Drink it."

I took a big gulp and it was so cold that it almost burned going down my completely dry throat. "My dad? He's back, right? He wasn't here so I assumed he left after you guys."

I looked at the clock and was shocked that it'd already been eight hours since I'd found my mother. It was almost ten at night. Dahlia probably didn't know what had happened yet because she wasn't here. She wasn't even in Delaware and instead on a day trip with her parents.

"Yeah," Aric answered.

"And?"

"What do you think, Alyssum?" His voice wasn't harsh. It was sad. "He kicked into official mode to get the... cleaned up. Some people came for the... "

"Body," I said sadly and my voice cracked.

"Then he shut himself in his office and I'm not sure anyone's heard from him since." Aric played with his bottle a minute. "He asked about you first, though. I told him Jensen was with you. He seemed relieved."

At their insistence, I tried to choke down a bite of one of the peanut butter and jelly sandwiches he'd made for the three of us. The harder I tried, the sicker I felt. In the end, I spat it back onto the tray. "I think I'm gonna lie down for a bit."

"Good idea," Aric said, rolling off the bed. "I'll leave this over here." He put the drinks on the table by the window. "If you need anything, call my phone, send a smoke signal, whatever. Got it?" I nodded as he wrapped me into a bear hug, kissed the top of my head, then quietly left my room.

"Don't leave me tonight, okay?" I murmured, sliding farther down the mattress.

"Hadn't planned on it," Jensen replied. He pulled the blankets back and climbed in beside me.

"Yeah, you can't sleep next to me in jeans. I hate the feeling."

"I'll go get some pajamas."

"Sorry." I gave what I thought would be a big smile, but my cheeks barely moved. "I don't want to be alone. Even for a few minutes."

He thought for a minute before stripping off his shirt, jeans, and socks to climb next to me in just his boxer briefs. His body heat cocooned me, warmed, melted, and grounded me enough that I actually fell asleep.

Waking to him beside me, bathed in the white light of the moon, made me feel safer than anything could have at that moment. I moved up so that our faces were close enough to feel his breath on my mouth and kissed him. I knew how ridiculous it was to kiss a sleeping man, but I couldn't help it and it was a nothing of a kiss. Suddenly, his hand was on the back of my head, pulling me harder to him before breaking the kiss off.

"Can't sleep?" His lips barely moved when he spoke.

"I have been. A little." Then I kissed him again, opened my mouth to invite him in. He pulled back, taking me in with those sparkling blues before tucking me back in beside him even tighter.

He wasn't going to let me try to drown my pain in him tonight.

I woke up again, this time early, with Jensen's limbs completely woven with mine. Trying not to wake him, I pulled each one of mine out as if playing a game of Jenga. It didn't matter, though. Even with all of my hard work, his arm tightened around my waist and I groaned.

"I really have to get up," I said quietly. He grunted, not letting me go. "I have to find my father. There are things…"

The strong arm keeping me prisoner relented so I could move freely. At some point in the night, I'd put his T-shirt on but didn't remember doing it. I had a vague recollection of wanting to feel closer to him even though he was right there beside me. Why I'd take off my clothes to wear just his shirt, I had no idea. It hung just above my knees like a dress, held his smell, and was soft.

"That's a really good look for you," he murmured into the pillow. I glanced back, knowing my face reminded him of everything else that'd already happened and was about to. He got a smile out of me and, even with everything that had happened, I couldn't believe he was lying in my bed on his back with one hand under his head and the other on his stomach, looking all sexy the way he looked when he just woke up.

I started rummaging through the drawers to find something appropriate for the day. "I can't believe my dad hasn't come up."

"He did." Jensen pushed onto his elbows before sitting up completely with his back against the headboard. "He came in three times throughout the night, but you were asleep."

"Really?" Maybe he did remember he had a daughter, although I was fairly certain I wouldn't have cared either way and would've forgiven him due to his grief. "Did he say anything about you being in here?"

He nodded.

"Come here." He pat his shoulder to get me back on the bed, which was where I wanted to be anyway. I snuggled next to him. "He asked if I was staying the night in here. I told him I was and he nodded." Jensen paused and kissed the top of my head. "He asked how you were doing because the second time he came in, you were kind of... restless." He put a finger under my chin and pulled my face up to get a closer look. "How are you doing?"

"Numb, I think. I don't really know," I said. He

waited for me to continue. "I know I'm thankful that you're here, that Aric came in when he did."

"Me too. I wish I'd been here. I shouldn't have gone with your dad."

"My dad? You were supposed to be with Aric and Sage. Where were you two?"

He sat up straighter. "When we were coming back from Aric's family in Phoenix—who knew there was one in Michigan—we didn't get Aric's brothers, by the way—we saw someone run out the front door. It was weird. Ash and I took off after him. I didn't realize Aric had gone inside the house until later. It didn't occur to me that someone might have... "

"I'll need to talk to Aric this morning," I said. He nodded. "Alone."

"Whatever you need, Alyssum. I love you so much." His arms tightened even more around me and for the first time since we'd said those words not that long ago, I couldn't say them back. My throat and emotions were too raw from all the crying and what had happened the day before.

I didn't mean to fall back asleep. I really didn't have time for it, but Jensen was there and I felt safe and warm and I just lost myself.

Chapter Twenty-One

My bedroom door closed as I came out of a horribly restless sleep.

My father's presence still the air in the room and I realized that I was still curled up beside Jensen and now my father was there with us.

Then Dad cleared his throat loudly causing Jensen to wake. I hopped up so that Jensen wouldn't and stood before him. After all, I was covered but Jensen was in only his boxer briefs.

Not too long ago, my dad looked eternally youthful. Suddenly, there were bags under his eyes accented by the slightest cracks at the corner of his face. His hair seemed to have grayed. The gray might have been there before, but with the added stress of the previous twelve hours, it was definitely more noticeable.

"I—"

He raised his hand, cutting me off. "We need to meet in half an hour. Will that work for you?" I'd never heard such sadness come out of the mouth that had yelled at me more times than I cared to admit.

"Of course," I responded, just as quietly. Jensen watched us silently. I'd cried a lot the night before, leaving me without any tears first thing in the morning. Maybe, once I was rehydrated, there'd be more but I shivered at the thought.

Dad gave Jensen a little nod, then left.

"Half an hour?" Jensen's voice hadn't woken up yet.

"We have to bury her." I sounded much stronger than I felt as I started rummaging through my closet for something appropriate to wear.

"Already?" he asked. I nodded. "I'll go get dressed." He hopped up in just his boxers, looking for his pants.

"You can't... You can't come."

His brows furrowed as he rubbed a hand over the back of his head. "Why? I want to be there for you."

"It's how we do things, Jensen. When someone... Their immediate family and the head of The

Assembly are the only ones to attend the funeral. In this case, it's one and the same. Once in a while, an exception is made, but with everything going on... "

He took my hands in his, pulling me onto the bed so we were facing each other. "This doesn't feel right."

"Nothing does, but it's because you're still thinking like a human and about human protocol."

"I love you."

I could only nod and let him hold me for a few moments before it was time to get ready. Once I was dressed appropriately, there was a stop I had to make.

After knocking on Aric's door, I waited for permission to enter, hoping beyond anything else that he'd be alone. I couldn't deal with anyone else right now. Before I could obsess too much, he swung the door open and pulled me into his arms, squeezing tightly as he lifted me off the floor just to put me down inside.

"How are you? I've been going crazy wanting to know and didn't want to wake you in case you were sleeping."

"I'm holding up. Jensen stayed with me last night. That helped."

"I was hoping he would." Aric went to the table

next to the window and removed the magazines, books, and trash so we could sit at it.

"I need to know what you saw."

His entire body tensed. "The same thing you did."

"Aric..."

He sighed before answering me. I tried not to cry and was sort of successful, though tears filled my eyes a couple times. I had to squeeze them shut to keep the tears from falling. I'd cried throughout the night and now I was done.

"When Jensen and you dad took after whoever they saw, I didn't think about it. I needed to know you were OK. Once I was inside, I found you on the floor in the entry room slumped over your mother. There was so much blood that my heart turned cold thinking it was you. Then I heard you crying and I hate to say it, relief washed over me. Then I brought you up to your room." He took a breath and wet his lips before continuing. "I didn't see anything more than you.

"I already know all of that. I meant once Jensen got there and you left."

His face went a bit dark. Clearly, he didn't want me to know.

"Jensen's not going to tell me anything and you

know it." He was the only one I could trust to tell me everything without worrying about my feelings right now. "I need you to tell me.

"When I went down there after leaving you..." He pushed his hands aggressively through his hair. "There was so much blood. No one knew what had happened. The a couple of people took the body, and a group of women started to clean everything up in the entry room." He paused, watching me to gauge my reaction to which I wasn't giving him one. "Your people determined it was a deep cut to the jugular that was too much too heal without immediate access to copper."

"There's copper everywhere," I told him.

"I guess it wasn't enough."

Which I'd known. I needed a bunch of copper to make contact with her skin but couldn't make that happen in time. That was on me.

"They said it was quick. Like falling asleep," he added.

"It was a Gobel, right?" I asked. He nodded and looked completely guilty, even though I didn't even count him among them anymore. "Don't look like that. You didn't do anything. But why would they cut her throat and not use their powers?"

"Exactly," he said. I didn't understand. "If I

would've been here, maybe I could've stopped it, or if I would have just gone home when my parents first asked—"

"All that would mean is that I wouldn't have had my friend with me when I needed him most." Our eyes locked. If things had gone another way, we would have been much more than just friends. "I guess I have to go find my dad."

Pushing myself off his bed, my aching muscles and the pressure of what happened pushed down on me like I was about a million years old. Even though I'd slept the night before, I wasn't rested. It felt more like I'd been beaten with a baseball bat.

"He's in his office," Aric said. "He's been there since..."

I nodded, not wanting him to say the words. I knew she was gone. I wasn't delusional but hated even thinking those words and sure as hell didn't want to hear them.

"Hey, do you, um... know who it was?" I asked. Aric shook his head. "Do you have any ideas?"

"Maybe."

"Well, I hope it wasn't someone in your family because I'm going to end whoever k-killed my mother."

His jaw tensed. "I'll be right there next to you."

The fact that he was going to choose my side over his family said a lot. Though in this case, I'd do the same. It was one thing to attack, and even another to wage war, but it was completely unacceptable to break into someone's house and kill a person who wasn't part of any of it.

At least to me there was a difference.

"Oh." I opened the door, stopping short before leaving. "If you see Jensen, could you tell him to not wait up?"

"Sure. Where are you going?"

"I just need to be alone for a while."

Half an hour later, I stood, dressed and ready, in the entry room where I'd found my mother yesterday. Dad came out in his regular suit, the black tie just slightly off-center. I'd chosen a black skirt with a black button-down shirt because that would have made Mom happy.

She always loved it when I wore skirts or dresses.

My heels clacked against the path as we walked, alone, to our town cemetery. Security was all around, but they'd stay hidden unless they were needed. We didn't really talk. I mean, what could we say? Sorry, the person we loved the most was dead?

Silence was better.

Mom might have prioritized Dad my entire life

but I knew she loved me. She did spend time with me and we talked a lot. Relationships were complicated but I loved her.

After the short funeral service was over, and the plain, pine box—again, the Gremalian way—was lowered into the ground. We stood, looking at the fresh, brown dirt, staring as if somehow doing so would make this all become a nightmare that we could wake from.

But I didn't cry. This was the time for strength.

"I can't lose you, Alyssum." His sad voice surprised me in the quiet of the afternoon. "We need to be more careful with you. She'd never forgive me and you're all I've got left."

"Dad," I said, tears forming, "nothing's going to happen to me." Then tears finally fell.

My entire life, I'd been told that my dad loved me and he showed it in his own way. Of course he hadn't wanted something bad to happen to me but he'd never said it. Not like that. He was a man of action, not words, and hearing him say it shed a new light on everything I thought I knew growing up.

He was dedicated to the people of Delaware, but was that all just a way to protect Mom and me? If so, he now definitely would feel like he failed.

"You trust Jensen?" he asked. I nodded. "With your life?" I nodded again. "And Aric?"

"Yes, Dad. Both of them. They'd die before letting anything happen to me." I pulled Dad into my arms in a way I hadn't for far too long. I thought I heard him lose his composure when his body shuttered and what sounded like a sob hit my ear. I couldn't be sure because when he stood up, he had the same stone face he'd had before.

"You worry about everything else, Dad. I'm covered," I said.

And though it was the truth, Aric or Jensen would put my life before theirs, I didn't want them to.

The only person I wanted to suffer was the one who killed my mother.

Chapter Twenty-Two

Once Dad was back in his office, I decided to sneak away for a little while. To process without anyone watching me.

Was it a good idea?

Probably not.

Yet I did it anyway.

While sitting by Lake Superior, where I'd played as a kid, I thought about Mom or, more importantly, the various ways I would torture the person who'd killed her. I completely lost track of time.

Driving home in the dark, I understood that nighttime was the only time I could allow myself to wallow. In the morning, I'd have to be ready for battle and was certain I could muster up the anger I'd need to fight.

The house was completely dark when I pulled in the driveway though once inside, a golden line of light came from underneath the study door. Assuming it was my dad, and not wanting to bother him, I tiptoed up to my room, avoiding any creak in the floor that I could.

My room felt big and empty and I felt small inside of it.

When I found Jensen's T-shirt from the night before shoved under my pillow, I decided to put it on again.

But the mattress was wrong, my pillows too flat. In reality, I understood that everything was exactly the same, with the exception of me. It wasn't my stuff that had changed; in those twenty-four hours, I'd become a different person.

I was no longer the nineteen-year-old woman enjoying her first love and looking forward to putting some Gobel in their place. Instead, I was a grown-up mourning her mother and looking for some good, old-fashioned vengeance. I liked the other woman better.

After memorizing every pattern on the ceiling over my bed, it was clear sleep wasn't going to come. So I got out of bed and crept down the hallway with no destination in mind. My bare feet slapped against the tile down the far hall until I stood at Jensen's room. He'd be asleep so instead of knocking, I turned the knob slowly and the mechanism released quietly, letting me in unnoticed.

Jensen lay on his back, one hand on his stomach, the other out to the side. He looked peaceful, ridiculously content, exactly how I wished I could've been right then. Aric obviously told him not to wait up for me otherwise he would've been sitting in my room waiting when I got back.

I carefully climbed into his bed and lay next to him, barely making the bed dip. I wanted to get close to him, not to wake him. After pulling the covers back, I slipped inside.

Feeling his skin against mine warmed me up, even though I wasn't cold. My head fit right into that dip by his shoulder and I sighed as every muscle relaxed.

Then his arm was wrapped around me so tightly that I thought I'd woken him, but his breathing never changed and his eyelids didn't even flutter. Just as I was about to fall asleep, just as I'd rediscovered that beautiful tranquility where everything went quiet for a few hours, Jensen realized I was there.

"Hey." His head popped off the pillow in surprise. He rubbed his eyes, like he was trying to make sure I was really there.

"I couldn't fall asleep in my room. I hope you don't mind." My voice sounded tired, even to me, and I gave him my best innocent look.

"Mind? You're welcome in my bed anytime." He squeezed me gently to drive the 'anytime' home, bringing a small smile to my face. "I should've waited up for you."

"No. I didn't want that." I yawned. "I thought I wanted to be alone, but that sucked, so here I am."

"In my T-shirt." He raised an eyebrow.

"Yeah, it was on my bed and really comfortable last night, so... " I shrugged.

"Well, you can get a clean one whenever you want. Second drawer."

"Thanks."

"Don't thank me; it's for pretty selfish reasons." He looked back at the ceiling while I silently questioned him. "I can't help it if I find you wearing my clothes completely sexy."

I laughed quietly into his chest before reaching up to kiss his cheek. His fingertips brushed my midthigh. Something kicked in. Suddenly, all I wanted was to feel normal and better. I didn't want to think about anything but Jensen and me.

I crashed my lips into him so hard that he flinched in surprise but he didn't pull away. He slid his hands up the outside of my thigh while I let mine roam over the hard muscles of his chest and abdomen. He kept traveling higher until he stopped just shy of my bare breast.

"Alyssum..." he whispered against my face as if it was a warning.

My lips cut off anything else he had to say. Right then, I didn't want to talk about whether this was a good idea or have him put it to an end because of what had happened. No. For now, I just wanted to feel him and have him feel me. I wanted something normal. Something that would make me feel good.

Maybe it wasn't fair since I knew he was hesitant, but I leaned back and pulled the shirt over my head and tossed it to the floor. He flipped me over and settled between my legs and I laid almost naked beneath him.

An argument raged in his own head then evaporated all together.

His lips worked me over like they were being paid. They slid from my mouth, down my neck and chest until he was between my breasts. Then he lifted up and licked my already hard nipple making me grown.

When I threaded my hands into his hair, silently

asking for more, he pulled back and said, "Alyssum, we need to stop."

My heart clenched. "Why?"

"With everything going on... now isn't the time."

I furrowed my brows. "Now is the perfect time." The pain in my voice bothered me. "I just want something for me. Something for us that will make me feel better for a little while. I want to forget the last two days and be normal, even if only for a few minutes. And I want that with you." I bit into my bottom lip before adding, "Unless you don't want me."

A battle raged in his eyes as I waited to see which side won. He wanted me. I knew that already but he wouldn't want to take advantage of my pain. Jensen wasn't taking advantage of everything but I needed him to see that.

His decision was clear when he lowered himself against me, and kissed me softly at first and then more urgently.

He kissed and explored with his fingers as I dug my nails into his back. Every touch was like magic, bringing my body back to life in a time when my heart was hurting the worst it ever had.

Slowly, he slid my panties down and though we'd done a few things before now, this was the first time I was actually naked in front of him if you didn't count the shower when I was covered in blood.

This had to be better.

He groaned before dropping a kiss onto my lower belly and creating room for himself between my legs. He pushed me open wide then ran his tongue along my opening. My muscles clenched as did my fingers slicing into his shoulders so hard that it had to hurt.

Yet he didn't say a word.

He circled his tongue around the sensitive nub that was begging for attention.

My back arched off the bed as he worked, sending me closer and closer to euphoria. When the moment came, I let it take over. The pleasure washed over me like waves crashing into the beach, again and again until I thought I wasn't going to be able to take any more.

Jensen was gentle as he kissed the inside of my thigh before hovering over me again.

I cupped his cheeks and pulled his mouth to mine mostly because I was full of need for him but also, I didn't want him to tell me this was the end. That he wasn't going to go any further.

As his tongue pushed into my mouth, I took my hands to the waist of his boxer briefs and wasted exactly no time sliding under.

There was a hiss from between his teeth when I took his cock into my hand.

Jensen was about to pull away when I whispered, "Please let me touch you."

Every other time I'd tried this, he stopped me rather quickly. This time he nodded then dropped wet kisses down my neck.

His erection was hard and long, though I had nothing to compare it to nor did I want to. The skin was soft over the hardness. Softer than I would've thought and when I closed my hand around him, his muscles tightened and he groaned.

I only got to explore for a moment before he wrapped his hand around my wrist to stop what I was doing.

"Are you stopping this?" I asked quietly. He'd done it before so I was worried about it now.

"I have to," he whispered back causing my stomach to sink. "If I don't stop you now, it'll be over. I'd rather be inside you."

It took about thirty seconds for that to make sense in my head. Luckily, it was mostly dark in the room so he probably wouldn't see the wide grin that I now sported.

Jensen lifted off me then left the bed. I was about

to protest before he riffled around in a bag and came out with a condom.

Right. Safety first.

In one movement, he ripped the small package open then slid the latex over the length that was standing loud and proud.

Then he was back.

There was more kissing and more of him using his fingers to work me back up. Not that I wasn't already incredibly turned on but he wanted me at the peak again.

Slowly, Jensen pushed into me. It was an agonizing pace that I wanted to hurry but thought he was being careful since this was my first time.

It was foreign to have something inside me, stretching me to what I thought was my limit. His hand cupped my face as his mouth kept working against mine.

There were so many things I was feeling, so many things I was experiencing all at the same time.

With him moving inside me, it was like I realized just how much I loved him. How much I needed him in my life. Scratch that... wanted him in my life.

His breath came quickly while mine was almost non-existent.

It was him, it was me.

It was perfection.

Jensen kissed me one last time then said, "You should go use the bathroom."

Right. He was right but I was so lost in what we'd just done, I hadn't been thinking about anything else. I slid his T-shirt back down over me the hurried off to the bathroom. He'd just had his mouth on me yet I was more comfortable walking across the room clothed.

I shook my head at my own nonsense.

When I came back, Jensen pulled me into his chest. My back rested against his front an one of his arms wrapped tightly around my chest, the other around my waist, like he couldn't loosen his grip even a little or I'd disappear. Honestly, I didn't want him to.

With him was warm and safe, like I was exactly where I was supposed to be. Since I was more exhausted than I'd been when I'd started, he used his chin to move my hair out of the way so he could kiss along my neck and shoulder, keeping me awake with the electricity in his kisses pulsating through my body.

"I feel like a dick," he said. Not exactly the words I'd thought I'd hear. I'd expected whispers of love or even a few well-punned jokes.

"What? Why?" Wriggling out of his grasp, I sat up with my legs crossed. He was face down on the pillow. "Why would you say that?"

"Alyssum... " He turned just enough that our gazes locked. "You're sad and I took advantage of the situation. You came in here looking for comfort—"

"And I got it," I said. He didn't look convinced. I grabbed his face, pulling it as close as I could while still being able to see his eyes. "I'm serious. Jensen, I didn't come in here trolling for sex." He smiled at my description. "I needed to connect with something other than myself. I needed *you*." I thought I finally got through to him. "Besides, you know me and you know I wouldn't do anything I didn't want to. Please, don't ever, ever doubt that."

When his lips touched mine, my body melted even more.

"You okay?" he asked.

"I'm good. Better than I should be."

He pulled me back down beside him, wrapping me once again in the comfortable cocoon his arms had created.

"I called my mom," he said after a few minutes of silence.

"Good. It's easy to get wrapped up in this crap," I said, twirling my fingers around.

"The only thing I'm getting wrapped up in is you." He rested his hand underneath the shirt on my stomach, which made my heart threaten to run away. "Seriously, though. I didn't know what else to do today. You were gone. I thought I should tell them what's going on." My body tensed. "Calm down. I just told them that your mom died. Dad wanted to head out right away to do whatever he could for you."

"He adores me, you know." While I was being playful, his dad did seem to really like me.

"He's not the only one." Jensen's fingers absently trailed designs across my abdomen. "Obviously, I told him *no*, but they were going to be expecting me back soon. Because of this, they suggested I stay as long as needed."

"I'm glad we could help you out." The words came out more bitter than I'd meant them to.

His eyes sprang wide. "I didn't—"

I shook my head to stop him. "I know. I didn't mean it like that."

"Don't apologize to me. What I meant was that my mom won t charge up here to pull me home by my ear like she did in tenth grade."

"What happened in tenth grade?" I smirked at the idea of Jensen getting in trouble, especially with his mom, who worshipped the ground he walked on.

"I'm not sure—"

"Spill it. I need some Jensen gossip." I swore he blushed. It was slight. I almost hadn't seen it. That intrigued me.

"Well, I met the girl I was seeing at the football game. Things got... out of hand under the bleachers. Somehow, my mom got wind. She wasn't happy because the girl was older—"

"How old?" I had images of someone's mother in my mind, a whole *Mrs. Robinson* scenario.

"College," he admitted. My mouth dropped. "A freshman." He swallowed then continued. "Anyway, Mom showed up, bullied my friends, and found me under there with her. She grabbed my ear after screaming my name, of course, and dragged me out of there."

"Oh my god." I giggled at his story and the ease with which he'd told it. He was obviously trying to do anything he could think of to cheer me up.

"It gets worse." He sighed. "My friends were laughing so hard they couldn't breathe but then she threatened to call all of their parents."

"Oh, no."

"Yeah, well, they'd ratted me out so I wished that she would've called their parents."

The scene played out in my head making me giggle. Once I calmed down, I asked, "What were you doing under there that was so bad?"

Rubbing his fingers on each temple, he sighed again. "Let's just say, I was pretty disheveled and the girl didn't come out of there with me for a reason."

"Jensen! You had sex with a college girl under the bleachers when you were what? Fifteen?"

"I'd turned sixteen."

"'Cuz that makes it better?"

He chuckled quietly. "You asked."

"Tenth grade, though." I flipped to the side so I could watch his face. "Was that your first time?"

This was exactly the kind of thing I needed as a distraction.

"Do you really want to know?"

Probably not. "Yes." I poked his ribs hard enough to tell him I was serious.

"No."

"Man, I would have been in seventh grade. Weird." I thought about my own limited experiences for a minute before continuing. "The furthest I'd gone by sixteen—"

"Ahh, nope." He covered his ears. "I don't want to hear it."

"It's not that bad."

"Still, Alyssum." His hands cupped my face. "I can't have those images anywhere near my brain." I stayed quiet. "It used to kill me thinking about you with Aric. Like, literally keep me awake if I thought you two were out."

"Yeah. Funny thing about that was that I found myself thinking about you when I was with him, too. It's how I knew he and I would only be friends.." I yawned again.

"I'm glad," he said quietly. "I don't know what I would've done if it'd gone the other way because even if I didn't know it, I loved you then."

Tears prickled the corners of my eyes at his admission or over the sheer enormity of how my life had changed.

Either way, I could trust that he was with me and together, we wouldn't lose again.

Chapter Twenty-Three

Aric, Jensen, and Sage had been unsuccessful in retrieving Kale, though no one had told me since Aric found me in a heap over my mother's body.

Now it was back to business.

I spent the next week sitting through meetings where everyone else got to decide how we'd go about a second attempt to retrieve Aric's other brothers that wanted to be part of the solution.

Hearing what had gone wrong the last time and what we could do differently to make sure we were successful seemed like a waste to me. What no one on The Assembly wanted to acknowledge was that when you were out in the field on a mission, things went wrong and all the planning in the world wasn't going to be able to stop it. We'd all have to adapt and overcome any obstacles on the spot.

At least I got to spend those meetings with Jensen and Aric by my side so it wasn't a total waste.

Nights I spend with Jensen learning how to do all the things that I didn't know. Or some of them. I couldn't believe it was everything but every single time, he turned my bones to marshmallow. It was addicting. If not for this whole war thing, I would've been happy to spend my days in bed with him too.

Losing my mom didn't hurt any less but this gave me something else to focus on. Being busy was good and normal. The war wouldn't wait until I was done grieving and that would probably last a lifetime anyway.

This time, I wasn't letting them leave me behind.

Driving the ten miles with Jensen beside me, and Aric and Sage in the middle row of seats seemed like a terrible idea. I wanted to take two cars. Dad overruled, tossing me keys to the oversized tank—others would call it an "SUV"—he kept around for these types of situations. I could handle the black beast, no problem. What I didn't want was to be in such tight quarters with that group.

We would pulled over just outside of Phoenix, another tiny town in the upper peninsula of

Michigan that everyone's forgotten about, to get to the rendezvous point with Aric's brothers. They had to sneak away from their family and we had to get them inside my house without incident.

Not everyone was overjoyed to have Gobel on the inside.

Jensen's thumb stroked my hand as I drove with the other. Just feeling him beside me, his body heat bursting from his fingertips, made me relax and smile despite myself. With him, I felt at ease—grounded, even.

"You two?" Sage broke the cone of silence when he noticed our intertwined fingers.

"Perceptive," Aric said. "Is this why you're part of security?"

"What's that supposed to mean?" Sage sounded offended.

I saw Aric roll his eyes in the rearview. "It's obvious and you're just seeing it now. Not exactly sharp, you know?"

That shut him down and Sage didn't speak again until we were carefully pushing ourselves through the Michigan forest. Flanking each of my sides, Aric and Jensen both made comments I couldn't hear as we climbed over downed tree trunks, careful not to make too much noise. Only Sage kept off to the side.

"I don't even know why Ash sent him with us," Aric mumbled within hearing range. "Does he not trust us or something?"

"A good Gremalian leader would never fully trust a Gobel," Sage said.

"No one asked you, Sage," I countered, glancing over my shoulder at him.

"It's true. I don't even know why Ash is allowing this."

"To save your ass," Jensen growled.

"I've saved my ass plenty on my own." He thought for a minute. I could see him contemplating his next words as if he were already speaking out loud. "Actually, I think I recall saving your ass more than once." He pointed to me. "Or doing *something* with your ass anyway."

Jensen let the comment pass, leaving tension in their air around us. I ground my teeth almost to the point of pain. "Shut your mouth, Sage."

"I only take orders from your father."

"Really?" I stormed over to him. "I think there are a few details my father doesn't know. I could enlighten him."

"I don't even know what you're yapping about." Looking bored, he pretended to pick at his fingernails. "And if you had anything on me, you would've done it already."

"Your mother and sister have been through enough. That's why I haven't said anything." I took a deep breath to slow my heartbeat and calm myself. "But keep talking, asshole."

Aric and Jensen circled behind him, protecting me even when I didn't need it. I could easily take the guy. I'd done it before, but it felt good to know that I had people who'd do anything for me.

His face was full of disdain as if he was untouchable. "And what do you think you'd tell him? That I dumped you for someone else? I'm sure he'll be crying in his cornflakes."

Sage kicked a stick hard enough that it hit a tree and snapped in half. Jensen jolted forward. Aric threw out an arm to stop him and yanked him back a few steps.

I seethed, not believing he was going to make me say it. I could just let it go, let him continue being a jerk, say nothing. Who was I kidding? No, I couldn't.

"Well, *Sage*"—I spat his name—"what I could tell him is that you tried to pressure me into something I didn't want to do. He might not like that too much."

Jensen was in motion before my brain realized it

was happening. Luckily, Aric's reflexes were spot on and he grabbed the back of Jensen's shirt, yanking him back then whispered something urgent into his ear.

Sage's face drained of color. "I did not." I almost couldn't hear him.

"Yeah, ya did and you weren't even very creative about it. Now shut up, get moving, and leave the rest of us alone." I stalked away, not looking back.

Suddenly, Aric and Jensen were beside me much closer than they had been before, their stride matching mine, eyes boring into me. Just what I needed.

"Later," I muttered, picking up speed to put them behind me.

At least I'd been effective. Sage continued farther away from us without saying another word. I hoped he was pissing himself, wondering if I was really going to tell my dad what had happened all those months ago. I had no intention of doing it but found that I really liked watching him squirm.

After a short fifteen-minute walk into the area, three large shadows stood with the moonlight at their backs. They looked similar to Aric once I'd gotten up close, although they were all less attractive. Kale, and whom I'd later find out were Laken, Aric's younger brother who looked to be about fifteen, and Stone, another older brother, approached slowly. I swore I'd never be able keep the order right especially since they all looked so much alike. Dark hair, almost black with devastating dark eyes.

"Been a while, Brother." Laken gave Aric that sideways guy hug that must be taught in ninth-grade physical education. This kid was like a younger version of Aric. Almost as tall but with only part of the bulk. "When you took off, we thought maybe the aliens got you."

"No such luck, Lake." Aric mussed Laken's hair, then quickly introduced us.

Several female voices found us in the dark and were coming closer. Whoever the women were, they weren't trying to be quiet.

"Okay." I tossed the keys to Kale. "You and your brothers head back to my house. We'll distract whoever's coming and call for a ride when we're ready."

"Are you sure that's a good idea?" Stone asked. I figured he was referring to a bunch of Gobel arriving at the center of Gremalian government because if I were him, that would be my concern.

"Yeah, you'll have Sage. He'll *vouch for all of you*." I stressed my point for Sage's benefit. "There won't be any trouble." I said it with confidence because that was what I wanted them to hear. There could be flair-ups of tension, but I had to trust Sage and Dad would handle it.

When they started out, Aric hung back. "You have to go," I said.

"I'm not leaving you guys here. Let's find out who's headed this way." He climbed up a small embankment to get a better view, swearing under his breath before jumping back down. "My sisters."

"How many?" I asked, already formulating a plan.

"Just four."

"'Just' four?" Jensen said, shaking his head.

Aric headed out in front to try to diffuse the situation. Just from their stride and posture, he could tell they were pissed, he said. I stayed hidden behind a thick tree trunk and, across from me, Jensen did the same.

"We're not going home empty handed," one of them called out. "We're not disappointing our mother."

The leaves rustled as if caught in a breeze but there wasn't any right now.

The Brambles were using their powers. It was time to step in.

Following my lead, Jensen moved out and we

ran. I went right; he went left. I was too focused on what was in front of me to notice what the guys were doing.

Catching the tall, dark-haired Amazon by surprise, I knocked her to the ground. We both hopped up, throwing punches, which, for me, was the best way to pick up a lot of energy quickly. She threw a right hook to my jaw, then a knee to my ribs.

Choking for air, I flipped her over, back to the ground, and then threw my hands up to pick up more electricity. A small jolt hit her in the chest. I needed more. I threw my hands up again. So did she. Two branches pinned my wrists to my sides and wrapped around my waist.

I couldn't get loose no matter what I tried.

I was trapped.

She stalked at me slowly. "So, you're supposed to be uber-powerful, huh? Doesn't seem that way to me, not-so-scary-girl." She stood just outside my reach. No matter how hard I tried to kick my legs at her, nothing ever made contact. I was pretty sure I felt a bone in my wrist crack. Searing pain climbed to my elbow. I didn't make a sound, only gritted my teeth harder.

"You may have corrupted Aric with your 'talents,' but you're not getting the others. How long ago did you send them off?" she asked. I didn't answer, so she pulled a pocket knife out. "You want to answer, trust me." She pushed the blade to my throat as the branches tightened again.

The white pain in my stomach indicated that the pop I'd just felt had been at least one rib, maybe two. Still, I said nothing. The blade tore the skin on the side of my neck. A stream of blood hit my shirt. It hurt like a bitch, but my resolve was stronger.

This was what someone had done to my mother and I wasn't going to give the satisfaction of scream.

Then a shriek crossed the night sky, loud, afraid, and definitely female. Her eyes went from me to the direction of the noise, then back.

"I'll be back," she spat before running off. I wouldn't cry. I had to focus on getting out of her trap before she got back.

Jensen came out of nowhere and didn't see me until the last minute. "Alyssum, are you okay?" He pulled at the branches that wouldn't budge.

"Zap it," I said.

He took a step back, twirled his hands the way I'd taught him, and threw some energy at my bark-covered cage. Nothing happened.

"More," I whispered, feeling my consciousness slipping. The wound on my neck must have been worse than I'd thought. I'd lost blood before but had never felt lightheaded the way I did right then.

He picked up as much electricity as he could and I knew the outcome before it hit me. I screamed. My arms were on fire like the skin was melting off the bone, and I couldn't hold the tears back any longer. An acrid smell filled the air which told me that I was actually being burned.

He hit the branches with enough force that they began to break away, spilling out toward the ground. He caught me when I fell forward. Right away, we were on the move. I don't know how long it was before Aric and three of his sisters got to us. Jensen had just grabbed my hand when I felt a burst of energy flow through us. The lightheadedness was gone and I felt much stronger than before though the pain lingered.

We turned around, ready to fight.

Instead of finding the sisters on our tail, they were on the ground, writhing in pain. Aric bolted over to them and checked for a pulse. They were alive but down and it was our chance to get away.

"What the hell happened to you?" he asked me.

"One of your sisters." I left out that the burns had been from Jensen. I just didn't have the energy. "Tall, Amazon, mean."

"Cass. Alyssum—"

"Don't." I really didn't want him to apologize for the others.

We kept moving but I was slowing them down. After I tripped a second time, Jensen lifted me into his arms without breaking stride. It was a much more comfortable ride, although he didn't know to be careful of my ribs. I cringed with pain at every bump and possibly lost consciousness or drew blood through his shirt when I dug my nails into his shoulder.

Back at the main road, my dad's black monster sat waiting with Kale in the driver's seat. Carefully, I was placed in back, and as I got settled, the guys noticed all the blood. Kale had come back for us.

"Jesus," Jensen said along with a few expletives. With my eyes just barely open, I watched Jensen yank his shirt over his head, bunch it in a ball, and put pressure on my neck before climbing in beside me. Man, I must've been pretty bad off because nothing dirty came to mind when he'd taken his shirt off.

Aric and Kale whispered quietly in the front seats on the short drive back. I wasn't overly aware of what had happened once we were in my house.

There was a lot of commotion. My dad's voice

was angry and Fern, our healer called out a lot of instructions, which included telling Jensen to get me to my room.

Fern's hands were their usual gentle selves as she used a cool cloth to start cleaning me off. Her words weren't. She was a small redhead and had the temperament.

"Out," Fern growled at the guys. They started to protest, but she put an end to that. "I have to focus on her. I have to get her out of these clothes and check her over. You need to leave."

Dahlia pushed them toward the door. I didn't even know when she'd come in.

After Fern had finished cleaning everything and made sure the bones were set—which, let me just say, was not a pleasant experience—I started to heal. When I looked around, I found all of Mom's normal healing tricks around the room, including the copper ball that felt like it weighed a hundred pounds. It worked, though. By the time Fern had left and let the guys back in, the blood flow had slowed to a trickle and I could use my good hand to wipe it away.

"So, what's the verdict?" Aric sat at the foot of my bed and Jensen climbed on, very carefully, next to me.

"Fractured wrist, two broken ribs, a few burns on

my arms, and a not-small cut on my neck. That's pretty much it."

"Your ribs are broken?" Emotions, a cross between anger and empathy, flashed in Jensen's eyes. I nodded. "Guess I could have been more careful on the way back."

"You didn't know, and at least I wasn't left to die in the woods alone."

Wrong words, right sentiment. His eyes darkened and he didn't say much else.

Chapter Twenty-Four

For the next couple of days, no one would let me do anything, even though I had completely healed. It really picked on my nerves that Jensen and Aric were off doing who knew what because they wouldn't tell me.

I was fine. Not even a headache remained.

At least I could usually pick up some information in the halls though usually everyone grew quiet when they saw me.

There'd be a couple of more fights but nothing more than normal.

Well, if they weren't going to come to me with information, I was going to them. Him specifically. That day in the sitting room with my mom, she'd told me that Dad knew more about Jensen than he'd let on. Se didn't say those exact words but she'd said it just the same.

Now was the time to find out exactly what that was.

"Dad," I said. He looked up from the papers he'd been studying. "Did you hear about what happened in the woods?"

He nodded without looking up from his papers. "I thought I made it clear that you had to be more careful." His jaw tensed then he raised his said, almost-scared eyes to me so they could bore a new hole into my soul.

"I didn't mean that." I explained the moment when Jensen and I had turned around and found Aric's sisters writhing on the ground after that sudden powerful burst of energy tore through us. "So, what gives?"

He sighed heavily. "Years ago, Glen and I suspected something was different with us. We could... make things happen that we didn't mean to make happen. So, we hit the books, researched everything."

"What did you find?"

"We were both descended from a single, very powerful Gremalian who, due to a witch's spell, was cast off—"

"What does that mean?" I was really trying to follow him. It wasn't making any sense. I'd never met an actual witch but had heard that they existed.

"The witch's power was taken from him and sent to his descendants, but not all in one dose. Basically, through our ancestors, I ended up with half of the witches power, Glen got the other half. Together, we could draw the energy out of... well, anything. Sort of like completing an electrical circuit.

"During the war, we were able to incapacitate the Gobel by taking all their energy at once. They didn't stand a chance, really, once we'd figured out how to do it. That's also part of the reason he and I were hunted so maliciously. He had a kid, so your mother and I"—a hand fell on the framed photo of my mom on his desk—"sent the Sorrels away. I thought that would put the focus on me. I didn't realize the Gobel sent someone after them until it was too late."

"Wait, wait, wait." I rubbed my forehead. "So, Jensen and I are, like... related? Cousins?" I started to feel sick at the thought.

Dad laughed louder than I'd heard in years and certainly more than I'd heard the last couple of weeks. "Technically, yes, but it's far back enough that it doesn't really matter. I'm talking hundreds and hundreds of years. So, if you and Jensen were to have children, they'd be completely normal." My mouth fell open. Then he realized what he'd said. "But that's not something to think about now. I'm talking far, far, far down the road."

I chuckled at the way his words started to tumble out of his mouth. As if I'd even consider having kids in the middle of everything going on and I was way too young anyway. On the other hand, I was kind of taken aback. It was the first time he'd acknowledged the extent of our relationship.

"Yeah, you don't have to worry about me getting pregnant anytime soon."

I had to get to Jensen, tell him everything, and find a way to practice this new wonder twin power. Unfortunately, Aric would probably be our target. I hated that we had to use him so much, even though he never complained. It still sucked.

The next item on my to-do list involved Jensen. I understood that he'd been busy and yes, I figured he and Aric were trying to keep me in the dark because I'd just been injured. He felt guilty for burning me but there hadn't been a choice. If he hadn't I would have suffocated or been crushed to death before Aric's sisters even got to me.

I'd told him to do it but that didn't change the guilt.

Even with all that, I couldn't understand why Jensen didn't at least come to my room at night. Four days with nothing more than a quick *hello* or a peck on the cheek was enough. It was Friday night. There most likely wouldn't be any meetings on Saturday, unless something happened, meaning he should be free.

When I went inside his room, he was already asleep, so I took the opportunity to look him over. I knew he'd gotten hurt. One of Mom's healing coppers was on the nightstand which we used when someone needed the extra boost after a fight. When he rolled over there was a bruise shaped like the heel of a shoe on his left side.

That had to have been why he was staying away. He didn't want me to know that he'd gotten hurt.

Finally sensing something in the room, he quickly pushed himself up off the mattress. "Christ, Alyssum."

"Sorry. Haven't seen you around much. Figured this was the only way I could for sure get a moment with you." I brought my knee up to rest on the edge of the bed. "I mean, you are still my boyfriend, right?"

He didn't answer, not with words, anyway. Coming across the bed and taking my hands in his, he kissed me in a way that made my entire body come alive, toes curling and everything. Jensen was saying that I was still his with that kiss. My face flushed red hot the way his lips moved, the way he held my head and caressed my cheeks with his thumbs.

"I guess that's a *yes*," I said breathlessly once I was able to pull myself away.

"That's a *hell yes*."

Pushing him back, I climbed on top and felt a reaction right away. I wouldn't, couldn't, let his erection distract me, which was harder than I'd expected. I'd wanted the closeness with him these last nights but he wasn't there.

"What have you been doing with your time?" I asked.

"Things."

"Things with my dad? Aric? The Gobel? Things with hookers? Throw me a bone."

His body shook with laughter. "Where would I even find hookers around here?" Even though he was joking, I dug my fingers into the gnarly bruise on his side.

He growled as his face cringed at the touch. "Okay, okay. All of the above, except the hookers."

"How did you get this?" I traced my fingers over the wound again, gently that time.

"Aric." My eyebrows shot up. "We've been trying to see if I could do the energy-sucking thing on my own. He didn't have a good reaction to the feeling and kicked me. It's fine. It didn't work, though."

"Why alone? We can do it together." Watching him try to figure out what to say to me, probably choosing his words very carefully, it clicked. "So that you can leave me home. Is that it?" Again, his eyes answered. "No way." I threw myself off to allow him sit up. "I've worked on this for months. I'm not being left behind."

"We don't want you to get hurt." His voice was soft enough that I would have melted if he were saying anything else.

"'We'?"

"Your dad, me, Aric."

"Aric wants me to stay home? No way. He's never said—"

"Yeah, the wonderful, supportive friend you made doesn't want you dead. Imagine that." Jensen leaned back against the headboard.

"He *is* a friend—"

Jensen winced. "Look, I know he is. He also loves you." I tried to protest, but he wouldn't let me get anything out. "I didn't say you're in love with him or that he's in love with you, but he loves you. I've accepted that fact. I live with it every day. However, I will exploit it if it means never seeing you the way you were the other day." He paused. "Your mother... None of us want that for you."

"'Exploit it'?"

"Use it to get him on my side. Alyssum, I'm here because of you." He cupped my face, tracing my cheekbone slowly with his thumb. "You are the most important thing in my life. I didn't come here to help with some crazy, backwoods feud. I came here for you." Those blue eyes I could get lost in darkened and I thought I saw a little moisture popping at the corners. "If you're not in my world, there isn't much for me."

I couldn't let myself get lost in his magical words or swoony eyes. I had to focus because my parents hadn't raised me to sit home knitting when shit got real. His reluctance over me going with them came from somewhere other than the logical parts of his brain. It came from his heart.

"Jensen," I started. I dropped all the anger from my voice. Hearing his words had made me realize what he was going through. "What did you talk to my dad about on your birthday?"

"Lots of things." He sat up straighter.

"Like?"

"You. The whole normal, 'I'm watching you and you better not step out of line with my daughter' thing that all dads do." Picturing that conversation, I couldn't hold the laugh in. "And some gremlin stuff."

I closed my eyes. I took a deep breath before I opened them again and said, "Please tell me you did not use that word with him."

A cocky half-smile spread over his face. "No, I reserve that for you."

"Good. So, what stuff?" I asked. Again, with the choosing his words carefully. "I'm not delicate. Just spit it out."

"He said... He said that he wanted me to think about being the next in line."

That wasn't hard to believe.

Jensen's father, Glen, had been our leader. Had the Sorrels not run away to New York, Jensen would have taken over one day anyway. My dad had only stepped in because his best friend had asked him to and there was no way Ash Bracken would back down from something he saw as his responsibility. What I didn't understand was why Jensen hadn't told me before that Dad wanted him to take over eventually. He should have said something the next time we'd seen each other after their conversation.

"I didn't know how you'd feel about it. I mean, he's your dad. You're supposed to be next in line and I'm new to all this." He raked his fingers through his hair. "I'm not even sure I want to stay here once this stuff is done."

And there was my big fear spoken out loud. I wasn't afraid of the Gobel. I wasn't afraid of being hurt or killed.

I was afraid that when this ended, Jensen would leave and I wouldn't be able to go with him.

I'd lose him forever.

Chapter Twenty-Five

Someone had punched me in the gut. Or a sledgehammer had come out of nowhere and caught me right in the stomach.

Whatever it was, I wanted to throw up.

I'd kind of assumed that when Jensen agreed to come to Delaware with me, reunite with his people, he'd find that he belonged and stay. Stupid on my part. I'd thought that maybe one day we'd get married and pop out some Gremalian babies.

Now... I he probably still planned to go home.

But I couldn't live in the human world. Not long term. I wasn't sure how Aric's brother Kale did it but that wasn't me. I was made for that.

"You look sick." He sighed. "See why I didn't want to tell you?"

"You think this is about the next-in-line bull-shit?" I asked. He nodded. "I don't care about that. I don't want to be a leader and Ash would never pick me even if I did. I'm a woman and we've never had a woman leader. Now while I think that patriarchal bullshit should be shattered, I don't' want to be the one to do it because then I'd have to lead. I don't want that position. You know that. I've told you that."

"Yeah. You told me that but I thought deep down you'd be the one to shatter the ceiling."

"Look." I sighed and pinched the bridge of my nose to stave off an oncoming headache. "You were born for the job. Literally. Your dad did it, and your grandfather and his before him did it. Leading our people is in your blood."

"Then why do you look the way you do?"

Now my stomach turned for another reason. It was easier to tell him that I loved him than it was to speak my fears. "I never... I guess I've been pretty naïve. I didn't think that once you were here, you'd go back to your life in New York."

"My parents are there, Alyssum. My job. Dad wants to leave the garage to me when he retires. I have an apartment. Friends. Basically my life is there."

I nodded slowly, holding back some really girly tears. "I know. I just..." I wasn't going to let my own fears of him leaving make me cry. Not in front of him, anyway. I'd gotten a bit paranoid about people leaving me since my mom had died, but up to that point, I'd done a good job of hiding it. "I'm here."

The room stood still, neither of us knowing what else to say. There were problems with me going with him, if he even asked me to, because blending in the human world permanently could be tricky. If it didn't work, it wouldn't be because I didn't want it to.

"Okay, um..." I hopped off the bed and started for the door. "I'm going back to bed."

He was suddenly right beside me. "The discussion isn't over. Nothing's been decided. Let's just get through everything else first, okay?"

I nodded again but didn't turn to look at him because I didn't trust my voice or my eyes not to betray me.

"There's a dinner tomorrow," he said but I already knew about it. Dad's secretary had taken over planning important dinners which my mother used to do and she'd told me about the dinner. "Something about making sure there's support for his decision on the war."

"Yeah." I cleared my throat. "He doesn't need approval, but Dad likes to have it. He can't stand it if there's dissent within the community. At least not overwhelming descent."

"Right. He wants me for the day, but after dinner, I'm free."

I got up on my tiptoes to give him a quick kiss goodnight. It was all I had to give right then. "Maybe I'll see ya around."

He watched me until I'd turned the corner in the hallway. His eyes were heavy on my skin but I didn't look back. That little nugget of information about him going home had hit me hard and I really needed time to think.

Aric and Jensen were gone early again the next morning. I didn't see them when I woke up and instead found an envelope on the table with my name scribbled in what could only be Jensen's handwriting... or a serial killer's. I decided to chance it.

Alyssum, I thought, after last night, we could both use a reminder. See you tonight. I love you.

I dumped the rest of the envelope out and a small chain only big enough to be a bracelet fell out. The charm that hung down looked like my car. It was even copper-colored, as was the rest of the chain. It would go with the necklace my mother had given me. The necklace I'd taken off when I got home from New York and hadn't thought about again. Now... It was a reminder of my mother. As I put the bracelet on, I decided that I needed my mother close to me and added the necklace.

I spent the day helping Violet, the secretary, make sure everything was set for dinner. She wasn't used to organizing those types of events because Mom had always done them and this was the first dinner since she'd died. Dad was getting right back into the swing of things but that didn't mean he wasn't still sad. Maybe everyone else didn't see it but I definitely did.

Since only a few people had been invited to the dinner—Dad, me, Jensen, Aric, Dahlia, her dad, and the other three borough reps—everything got under control pretty quickly. The cook, along with the other help we'd brought in, was on top of everything.

The house smelled delicious. Better than any candle with the aroma of fresh bread and spices being infused into whatever was in the pots on the stove. While the dinner was being cooked, I got myself ready. Though dinner wasn't a formal event, I would still be expected to dress appropriately.

Rummaging through my closet, I found a bunch of summer dresses that I'd never worn before and decided on a nice pink dress with a halter top and a skirt that fell just above my knees. I went through ten different pairs of wedges before finding the perfect ones. They added a few inches of height. I styled my hair into soft waves to cover my shoulders and covered my face with just a dash of makeup.

Half an hour before our guests were to arrive, I was all put together and back in the kitchen to double-check everything. That place was a well-oiled machine and I was in the way. The kitchen people were great and they didn't need me looking over their shoulders.

Voices rose in the hallway leading to the Assembly room. By the time I'd gotten out there Dad called from his room upstairs. His voice sure did carry.

When I got to his room, I didn't go in. "Where are the guys?"

"Getting changed, he said as I peered through this open door. He was buttoning a shirt. "Everything ready, Alyssum?" I knew what his outfit would be and I figured Aric's and Jensen's outfits would be similar: dress pants and shoes with a button-down shirt that would have the top two buttons undone to keep it nice but casual. His cuffs would be rolled as well.

"Yup, and it smells great."

He turned, seeing me for the first time. Dad looked older than he had a few weeks ago, but there was a lot weighing on his mind. "You look beautiful, sweetheart, just like your mom."

"Thanks." That was the highest compliment a person could ever get from him, but I didn't know what else to say and was thankful when the doorbell rang.

Minutes later, everyone else had arrived except Aric and Jensen. The guests had drinks. Small talk was being made in the living room. I stood near the fireplace, which wasn't lit because it was far too hot and humid for that, gossiping with Dahlia with a few comments from Finch, the youngest of all the reps at only twenty-five, had dirty blonde hair and brown eyes. He was good looking to most people's standards and was tall. Or at least a lot taller than me. He was also always more comfortable with us than the much older people in the room.

Dahlia took my arm, leading me away with some excuse about the ladies' room, but all she wanted was some girl talk. She pulled me into the nearest bathroom which also happened to be the smallest.

"So, how's it going?" She had far too much perk to be around regular people.

"Ah, fine, I guess."

"Well, with all of our stupid rules, I couldn't be with you for your mom's funeral and my dad's suspiciously kept me busy since then." Dahlia primped her already perfectly put-together hair. "I guess Mom and I are going to Chicago to do some shopping, which is great, but you should come with us. Get away, new scenery, all that."

"Not a chance. I was recently attacked by Gobel, you know." I didn't want to do her caliber of shopping, and there was no way I was going to be left out of fighting. It was not happening. However, it was highly unlikely that she even knew how bad everything had gotten with the Gobel. She might not have even been told that a Gobel killed my mother thought she could've guessed.

Wait. Did they tell her my mother had been killed or that she died?

Though I did tell her what happened in the woods, I didn't tell her why.

Dahlia wasn't like me. Her dad kept her so in the dark, I never knew what I should say or not or if she'd have been able to handle it if I did.

"And Jensen?"

My eyes rolled involuntarily because of the

singsong quality her voice had taken on. "What about him?"

"You know, the good stuff. Come on."

I chewed the inside of my cheek for a second. "There's nothing to tell."

Before answering, I avoided her eyes, but she was watching every move I made, waiting for the smallest sign that I was trying not to give her.

"Oh, there's something. You wouldn't blush over nothing," she said. I still didn't answer and I didn't think I was blushing.

"I could tell you about the other night with Aric, which was ridiculously good."

"Please don't," I pled. Dahlia, my supposed best friend, wasn't letting me off the hook. "What do you want to know?"

"Have you, ya know, given the ultimate gift?"

"Keep talking like that and you'll be glad we're in a bathroom." I made choking sounds like I was going to vomit at what she was saying. When I giggled, she didn't see the humor. She raised an eyebrow and cocked her head, which said she'd wait forever for my answer if she had to. "Okay, fine. Yes, but that's all I'm saying."

She smiled an annoying, wide, almost-knowing smile that just made her look creepy. "That's all you need to say. I have a wonderful imagination to fill in the rest."

I hurried out of that bathroom before she had a chance to elaborate on her imaginative skills. No doubt she had something far kinkier in mind than what actually happened between Jensen and me. I went back to the front room to wait for everyone else and took pity on poor Finch, who'd been left with only the older men.

The minute the guys came in, Dad hijacked them to his group of people to introduce Aric. The reps had already met Jensen what with all the time he'd been spending in The Assembly room. Handshakes were exchanged all around, which was surprising.

That was what surprised me most about the entire situation. Many of our people embraced Aric fully, not even caring that he was supposed to be the mortal enemy. It wasn't clear if that was a tribute to their trust in Dad, their belief in me, or just how awesome Aric was.

Jensen's eyes stayed on me with the corners of his mouth turned up in a Cheshire grin. When Dad brought Aric over to meet Finch, Jensen came too. Aric leaned over to whisper something in Dahlia's ear which caused her to giggle. Jensen placed his hand on my bare back. His soft fingertips traced my spine, forcing me to control a full-body shiver.

"Can I talk to you?" I whispered.

He nodded, leading me from the room, never moving his hand from my skin, to the hallway that ran behind the living room, where no one would see us.

"You're beautiful."

"Thanks. And thanks for this." I shook the charm on my wrist at him. "It looks like my car."

"Yeah, that's how we met. You sabotaging your car," he said. A pink shade of embarrassment covered my face. He knew I'd been the one to let the antifreeze out? How embarrassing. "Are we okay?"

"We're okay. I don't like being left out and I'm not going to be, but I have to remember that those decisions are official ones and not personal. And you have to separate being a leader if that's what you're going to be, and being my boyfriend." I stopped. That wasn't where I'd meant to take the conversation. "We'll get to that stuff later. Sorry. And I love it. It matches my necklace."

"I know."

Jensen leaned over to kiss me and immediately I lost me senses, never hearing the others leave the room. Not until my dad called my name.

Then we had to go to the dining room.

We sat next to each other with Aric and Dahlia across the table, Dad at the head to my right, and the four reps next to him, two on each side. Salads came first. I picked at the leafy greens, half-listening to Dahlia ramble on about the shopping trip and half-listening to Dad and the reps. I wasn't sure Aric even knew she was talking. If he did, he was paying zero attention.

Jensen didn't seem to care what anyone was talking about. He was more concerned with his hand on my knee, which began inching its way up my thigh and under my skirt as soon as the salads were cleared. Turkey, roasted potatoes, a wonderful noodle dish that I could never remember the name of, and three separate vegetable dishes did nothing to distract his fingertips from teasing the sensitive skin on my leg.

The worst part was that he was talking to Aric as if he wasn't even doing anything, whereas I got distracted and held my breath to the point of light-headedness more than once. Even when I moved his hand down, he always put it right back. His finger traced circles around my inner thigh.

At least no one could see what he was doing.

"Excuse me," I said suddenly, placing my napkin

on the table next to my plate and stook up when I couldn't take another minute of teasing. Jensen's cocky grin followed me out the door and simultaneously made me want to punch him in the face and take him back to my room.

Neither was acceptable right then, so I went to the bathroom instead. A quick splash of cool water to the back of my neck cooled me down pretty well and, when I returned, everyone else had already retired to the living room for coffee.

That night, Jensen came to my room after changing to spend the majority of the night talking about everything that had happened, from my mom to practicing our newfound energy-sucking power.

"So, what was that at dinner?"

"Payback," he answered quietly, caressing one cheek while the other lay on his chest.

"For?"

"Like you have to ask, Alyssum. You tortured me for quite a while. Did it work?"

"Nope," I answered, my voice giving me away.

"So even better than I planned, huh?"

I playfully punched his ribs, adding a touch of oomph. He felt it. Then I filled him in on everything my dad said about us having an ancestor in common to our babies turning out normal.

He ignored the babies comment but was ready to practice.

Aric was less-than-thrilled to play guinea pig to our mad scientists later the next morning. The way his muscles tensed when I told him what we needed was slight, imperceptible to someone who didn't know him as well, but he agreed without hesitation. We just had to let him know when we wanted him in the training room but I wanted to try connecting with Jensen alone first.

Recreating the scene in the woods proved harder than expected. We'd been scared back then, even if Jensen wouldn't admit it. Everything had been so chaotic that making it happen again on purpose... I didn't know how to do it.

Jensen and I met in the training room and sat for hours, legs folded beneath us, facing each other. We held hands, closed our eyes, and focused. Nothing happened. Not even the tinies zap of electricity. Well, I definitely felt *something*, but not the power surge that had happened in the woods.

He caressed my hands with his thumb, which had the opposite effect than what we were trying for.

"Stop it," I whispered and slapped his hand

away. He only chuckled which wasn't the focus I was looking for.

We tried again, but he ended up taking it in a whole other direction every time. This time, I ended on my back with him on top, settled between my legs, pushing his erection against me.

He wasn't making this easy.

Once I could force myself to break free of him I went to get every piece of copper I could hold to boost our power. Then we tried again. Even that didn't work.

Soon, I was starving. We took a break to grab a quick sandwich, then found Aric and brought him back with us. He and Jensen tried fighting, but they didn't put in much effort. Nobody even drew blood. I started to think we'd all become too close of friends to even bother training and said as much, but that just started an argument.

"I could always go get Sage," I told them when their *fighting* turned into laughter and a slap fest. They both groaned. None of us wanted to do that. We were comfortable just the three of us.

Out of nowhere, Aric grabbed my wrist, pulling my body against his tightly right before covering my mouth with his. I pushed away, but he was actually a lot stronger than me and too soon I was brought back to the kisses in New York. In that moment, every-thing else faded away.

I didn't want this. I was with Jensen. Yet at the same time, I didn't want it to end.

There was something wrong with me.

I couldn't even hear Jensen in the background but Aric squeezed me with one hand on the small of my back and the other clenching my hair. His lips were now my focus. The touching, the tasting... no. It needed to end. I was in love with Jensen. That didn't stop my stomach from dropping like I was going down stairs and missed a step.

I was lost. My fingers drifted up, stopping just as they'd skimmed his hairline.

Then he was gone.

Trying to catch my breath, I watched as Jensen got himself to his feet. He must've lunged and taken Aric with him.

Jensen jumped back to me, grabbed my hand, and turned to say something.

The unfamiliar surge of energy, just different enough to be noticeable from what normally happened when we used our power, snapped through us.

He'd taken Aric down, but when Jensen grabbed my hand, we connected. It was the same thing that had happened in the woods when we faced Aric's sister.

But Aric... he was still on the floor, his face drooped in sadness. No. Sadness wasn't the right work it was like looking at a voice.

I yanked my hand out of Jensen's and watched as Aric slowly began to recover.

Obviously, something happened when Jensen grabbed my hand. We were connected and energy more powerful than I'd ever felt before had come from us and done something to Aric.

I just didn't know what or why or how it had happened.

Aric pushed his long body up, moving in a haze, like he'd just woken up from a dream. He made his way toward us, angry. Very angry. *Pissed off* was more like it. When he leaned in close, came through clenched teeth with more venom than I'd ever heard from him.

"Don't ever do that again," Aric spat. "Whatever just happened while I was on the floor. Don't do it again."

"I could say the same to you," Jensen said. "Maybe you should keep your lips her."

"I did it to piss you off," Aric insisted. Jensen's jaw only tightened more. "It worked, then."

Aric's eyes searched mine like he was looking for an answer that I didn't have to give. Whatever we'd done to him in those few seconds on the floor must have been hell because his eyes had darkened and the kindness that was usually there was gone. He stalked away, slamming the door on his way out with such force, the entire floor vibrated. I didn't like what I'd seen in those few seconds he'd looked at me.

I shook it off. "What the—"

"Don't." Jensen put his hand up.

"What are you mad about?"

"You have to ask?"

"Come on, Jensen. He only did it to get us angry enough to make this happen."

"Yeah, I *do* know that's why *he* kissed you," he snapped. I gave him the *what* look. "What I don't understand is why you kissed him back."

My heart clenched. He was right. I had some explaining to do. But I had no explanation. "I—"

Jensen shook his head and said, "There's no excuse, Alyssum. There's nothing you could say to make this better right now."

Then he stormed out of the room, punching the wall near the door on the way out.

Kissing me was Aric's fault but he had good

intentions. I thought Jensen would get over that once the sting wore off. It would. They'd be friends again.

But me kissing Aric... I wasn't sure that was something he could ever forgive.

I'd fucked up royally and now had to fix it.

Chapter Twenty-Six

After Jensen left the training room, I grabbed my phone and sent Aric a text asking him to meet me in the library we never used. No one would look for us there so there couldn't be any assumptions.

The dark-green room had been one my mom had spent most of her time in. She'd loved it. I hated the room, but, ever since she'd died, I could feel her in there and it had quickly become my favorite room as well. After my bedroom, that was. Nothing could compare to that.

I would have gone to Aric's room. Actually, before his little demonstration, I wouldn't have given it a second thought, but I certainly didn't want to be seen coming or going or, in some way, be "caught" in there.

But before I delt with him, I needed to talk to Jensen.

He'd been so angry when he stormed out of the training room that leaving him to stew overnight seemed like a bad idea.

After lurking outside his bedroom door for at least a full minute, I took a deep breath and knocked. He didn't answer. Trying to listen carefully, I didn't even hear him moving around inside. I knocked again, then tried the doorknob.

He'd locked it. I slowly pulled my hand back as this heavy feeling settled in my chest. He never locked the door that I knew of unless I was inside with him.

Now he was locking me out.

"Jensen," I called out, my forehead against the wood. "Come on, we need to talk." He still didn't answer. Maybe he wasn't in there. I couldn't be sure but where else would he have gone? "OK," I said quietly.

While the idea of him ignoring me made my blood boil, I decided to be mature about it and concede that he just needed some time. Instead, I'd figure things out with Aric.

After sending Jensen a text asking if we could talk, I headed to the library to see if either was in there and found Aric with only a small lamp beside him.

"Hey," I said, coming around the couch to sit down gently. He was in a chair, his long legs stretched out toward the fireplace. "So..." His eyes left the empty fireplace to find mine. "Okay, so that was unexpected. What were you thinking?" He smirked. "You know what I mean."

"Look, kicking the crap out of each other wasn't working. I hit him where I knew he'd get the most pissed. I had to work his greatest fear."

I shook my head. "You guys were barely even trying. What do you mean greatest fear?"

"Losing you. In general, but specifically to me." He was right and his scheme to piss Jensen off had worked. In the process, Aric had shocked the hell out of me, as had my reaction, but that was something I wanted to bury deep inside and ignore. My maturity only went so far.

"Okay, but why were you angry?"

Aric rubbed his chin where several days of whiskers had grown in. "That's a little harder to explain." The expectant look on my face kept him talking. "That was just about the worst thing I've ever experienced."

"The energy-sucking thing?"

"Yeah, it was horrible. It didn't just take my energy or leave me incapacitated. That would have been manageable. It actually sapped my will to live."

"What do you mean?"

I really wasn't getting it and the sadness that took over him as he remembered what he'd felt made me want to cry or hold him, but that would probably be bad because I was sure the minute I made any gesture of affection, Jensen would somehow burst through the door and I'd be even more screwed.

Anyone could've seen us and while that wouldn't have been out of the ordinary before, if someone told Jensen, it'd sign the death warrant on my relationship. That much was sure.

If Dahlia heard what happened then saw us, that could've caused Aric problems. Though I don't know how much he'd care.

Though he and Dahlia spent time together, neither had defined their relationship. But Dahlia would have been hurt if she found me and Aric together and knew he'd just kissed me.

"You could have killed me and I would have thanked you, Alyssum. The world meant nothing to me in those few moments."

"Wow," I said. He nodded. "That's terrible."

"You're telling me."

Now I felt somewhat guilty for doing that to his sisters, but, in my defense, we didn't do it on purpose and they had been trying to kill me. Jensen and I would have to reserve it for very extreme circumstances only.

"I need a drink." I slapped my thighs. He grunted. "I meant to quench my thirst, like water, but I know my dad keeps beer in the fridge and you're welcome to that."

Together, we went to the kitchen, falling back into the easy way we usually were with each other. As we left, me with a bottle of water, him with an open beer he was actively drinking, and another for later in his room, we turned toward the stairs in time to see that Jensen had just come back in from outside and was headed upstairs too. The anger on his face hadn't dissipated and those blue eyes that normally sparkled at me were cold steel shooting daggers my way.

Awesome.

"No, wait." I hurried over and grabbed Jensen's arm to stop him from climbing away from us. Aric didn't say anything. Instead, he took the stairs two at a time to leave us alone while throwing me an *"I'm glad I'm not you"* look. "I know you're mad. At me, at

Aric. But come on, Jensen, we can't ignore this. Can we please talk?"

His shoulders slumped and he allowed himself to sit down onto one of the steps. I followed suit leaving just enough space between us that we wouldn't be touching but close enough that he could reach out to me at any moment.

"I'm annoyed with Aric, not mad." Jensen's voice remained low, yet what he was feeling was clear and it wasn't good. My heart raced like it was running for its life and my hands shook. "He had his reasons and, as much as I don't want to admit it, it probably was the best way to get things moving."

"Okay..."

"But you, Alyssum? I'm pissed. You didn't even try to fight him off. As a matter of fact, you were totally into it." He swallowed down his anger. "I had to sit there and watch you enjoy kissing another man. It'd be different if you protested at all but you fucking didn't."

I sighed. He wasn't wrong. Though I felt like I tried to pull away when Aric's lips first touched mine, I don't know that I did and even so, I wouldn't die on that hill because he was right. I didn't push him away. "I'm sorry. I wish I could explain what happened."

"Try."

"Have you ever… Hasn't your body just taken over before?" I asked. His face remained still. "When he… did that, obviously, I had a reaction, but it's because some kisses can't be ignored. I just… I reacted. Or didn't react. I don't really know what happened."

His jaw clenched so tightly, I was expecting some teeth to start breaking.

"I'm with you, which is exactly where I want to be." I didn't like or appreciate the pleading tone that had crept into my voice, but there wasn't much I could do about it. This right her might've been the thing to break us up and it was the very last thing that I wanted. "Plus, you've felt what happens around Gobel. Hell, you even thought you might be bi-curious because of it. It's the same for me."

The corner of his mouth twitched as he contemplated what I'd I said. Then he sighed. Jensen stood to his full height, said, "I'm going to bed," and took off up the stairs before calling back, "You coming?"

Yes… Yes, I was.

Sleeping in Jensen's arms was my idea of perfection but this night, it was even more so. Number one, I actually got to sleep right away, something that had eluded me since I'd been a kid. Number two, I knew he wasn't too mad if he allowed me in his arms. And at that moment, with his face close to mine, I didn't care what Aric had done or that we were on the brink of war with the Gobel or that everyone I cared about might die. It all just fell away, even if only for those few perfect seconds, and that felt good.

"Mmmm." Jensen moaned as he stretched while pulling me closer. "Any chance of a day off?"

"You can answer that better than I can. I haven't seen or talked to my dad in, like, a week." I eyed him carefully, trying to guess what was going on inside his head, but he was getting really good at keeping me in the dark when he wanted to.

He groaned in frustration, which meant I had to ask.

"Is that a *no* then?"

"Probably not the best idea, but I feel like we haven't been able to just have fun," he said. My eyebrow cocked up suggestively, which caused him to chuckle. "I mean, like, a normal couple—a date, a movie."

That made me smile. He was still the same Jensen I'd found in Putnam Valley.

"Meet me after lunch?" he asked.

If my smile had been any bigger, my face

would've split in two. "Thank you, thank you, thank you." I squealed then covered his face in kisses.

'Course, I spent the few minutes it took me to get to my bedroom kicking my own ass for being such a kid, but if yesterday had taught me anything, it was that I was his completely and I didn't want anything to screw that up. Time off together was the gift I hadn't thought to ask for before now. I knew two things for sure: I was going to look hot and I really couldn't care less where we were going.

After lunch the next day, I was out in the front yard waiting for Jensen, but it was Aric I saw first.

"Heading out to pillage the village?" Aric asked as he came toward me.

"Something like that," I replied. He stopped a foot away, leaning on his arm against the porch railing. "You?"

He shrugged. Okay, things were kind of weird now and I didn't want them to be.

"Why don't you come with us?" I offered.

"Yeah, I'm not into that sort of thing, but who knew you were such a freak?" He tapped his chin like he was thinking about it. "Then again, it could be interesting."

Giving him a playful but hard shove, I said, "You wish. Seriously, I think we might go see a movie and you should come. Weirdness isn't allowed, remember?"

He relented with the condition that he could bring Dahlia. I could deal with that, especially since it was probably more so he wouldn't feel like a third wheel than anything else.

But I'd singlehandedly killed the idea of Jensen and me alone. No I had to hope he wouldn't be upset.

We walked into town as four friends on a double date, like nothing else existed in the world. As any one of us could have predicted, the film playing was about eight months past being a new release, but we didn't care. Three out of the four of us were used to it. Jensen might have gotten movies the day they came out in Putnam Valley, but this far in the boon-docks, we had to wait.

The theater was jampacked. With war on every-one's minds, I guessed they were looking for an escape. After we'd gotten popcorn and drinks and found seats, Dahlia and I noticed some women we'd gone to school with. I wouldn't exactly call them friends, but we didn't hate them, either.

Dahlia took a handful of popcorn and flung, one after another, at the group of three, who immediately spun to see the culprit. After seeing it was Dahlia, they laughed, came over to talk for a few minutes, and then headed back. For the first time in a while, I felt like we were normal young adult. It was nice.

When the movie started, there was no semblance of order inside the theater. People spoke in fake whispers and several couples started making out in the corners. Dear god, I hoped they were just making out because there were sounds coming from them that I had to block out. Complete denial was how I preferred to operate.

"Go to the restroom with me," Dahlia whispered in my ear.

"Why?"

"We're women. It's what we do. Come on." She yanked my hand hard enough that I had no choice but to stand.

"Apparently, I have to use the restroom," I whispered at Jensen. I tried my best not to step on Aric's toes as I passed by.

"What?" I asked as she washed her hands. I leaned a shoulder against the wall since I hadn't been the one who'd needed to come there in the first place.

"Nothing," she said too quickly.

My eyebrow shot up, letting her know I didn't believe her.

"We have to keep mysterious for the guys," she

said but I snorted. Mysterious was one thing I'd never been. "I feel tension in the air between you two? What happened?"

Two freshmen stopped to look at us, eyes wide. Dahlia dismissed them. "Move along, Bambi."

"You guys, who?" I asked once the other girls had made their escape.

"Jensen. Unless there's someone else I don't know about," she said. I shrugged. "Why are you so tight-lipped about things? I'm your best friend. Like with Sage, you never said—"

"I didn't have sex with Sage. That's nasty."

"Bet you wouldn't have thought it was nasty then." She moved on to applying a fresh layer of lip gloss. "What about Aric?"

"What about him?"

"Was there anything between you two?"

Uncomfortable. That was the only way to describe that particular moment. Aric and I hadn't discussed what he'd told her or what we should say, but, in the grand scheme of things, not much had happened.

"What'd he say?" I countered.

"Not much." Dahlia glanced at me from the corner of her eye. "Just that you went out a couple of times, but you weren't his type."

"Oh, I'm not, huh?" Two things told me she was lying. First, I knew her well enough to know that she would say something like that just to see how I'd respond. Second, Aric would never tell her anything.

She pondered a moment. "No, he didn't. I just wanted to see your reaction."

"You're mean, but nothing really happened between us."

"Yeah, I figured. You're totally meant to be with Jensen but why the tension."

There was no way I was going to tell her that Aric kissed me and pissed off Jensen. No good would come from that so, I said, "It's just training stuff."

Dahlia rolled her eyes then stood up strait to give her gloss work a second look. "I'm really glad my dad never wanted me to train in anything but using my powers for the good of the people. No fighting for Daddy's Little Girl."

That was exactly what happened. When we were kids, I'd leave school and go to train for hours. Dahlia went home and did whatever she wanted. Her dad wanted her to be able to defend herself so he taught her all about her powers, of course, but he swore no daughter of his would ever fight in Gobel war.

She wasn't cut out for it anyway.

I gave her a smile as we left the restroom to return to the movie and our dates. Bedlam had broken loose to the point that Aric and Jensen had begun to participate. Aric tossed chocolate-covered raisins into Alera's shirt, eliciting a round of giggles from the group of cheerleaders. The woman had the goods and wasn't afraid to give everyone a little peek. Aric and Jensen were smiling and laughing in a way I hadn't seen in quite a while.

It was good to see them at ease again.

As with everything, the fun eventually had to end. After the movie had ended, we grabbed a quick bite and headed home, relaxed and stress-free.

That too couldn't last

Chapter Twenty-Seven

THE NEXT DAY, it was back to business, as usual. My father caught me early, just as I was leaving the kitchen after breakfast, to tell me that Aric, Jensen, and I needed to do a little spying on the Gobel. There were some rumors going around that Gobel were recruiting non-Gobel, humans I assumed, and he wanted some firsthand intelligence.

He and Elliot, the head of the Gobel Assembly, weren't even on speaking terms anymore. It had never gotten that bad before. There'd always been some kind of dialogue between the two. War was closer than I'd wanted.

I headed to my room and changed into jeans—we'd be in the woods, after all—a T-shirt, and hiking boots. I was locked and loaded, so to speak. Only one thing was missing.

"Hey, where's Aric?" I asked as Jensen came up beside me in the entryway.

"I don't know. He wasn't in his room, either."

"Well, we need you to head out," Dad ordered. "You shouldn't have to engage, so just the two of you should be fine."

"Yeah, but it's weird he's not here, right?"

"Alyssum, I don't know where he is. Just go."

Official Ash, a voice I hadn't heard since my mother had died, had given the order and it had to be followed.

We piled into the monster to head toward Phoenix. At first, we didn't talk. Once we were off the property, Jensen didn't hit the gas the way I would have.

"Hey, Grandpa, the speed limit is higher than thirty-five these days."

"Ha ha." He sped up just a bit. "Since we're without our third wheel, does it mean this counts as a date?"

"You wish. I'm a little harder to impress than that."

"Don't I know it."

I slapped his arm playfully and let my mind

wander to the regular life we'd lead after the Gobel issue got settled. That only caused me to think about him leaving, but I had to force it out of my head. We hadn't revisited the issue and I still had no idea what he wanted to do after everything was over. He could leave. I knew that he wanted to go home yet still hoped he'd stay with me. Living in the human world would likely be impossible for me.

A hard break brought me out of myself, letting me know we'd arrived.

"Hey, you okay?" Jensen asked as I came around the back of the SUV.

"Sure." I headed toward the forest.

"Wait up." His fingers circled my wrist and he pulled me into his chest. Oh, how I loved being safely wrapped in his arms. He kissed the top of my head. "What are you thinking about? You got quiet all of a sudden."

"You leaving." Turning away from him, I took a few steps into the woods, toward the Gobel compound. "Going home. I want this over because I don't want any of us to be constantly looking over our shoulders. At the same time, you might just leave. And, as much of a stupid, needy girlfriend as it makes me sound, I don't want you to go."

He scoffed and I was glad that I couldn't see his

face as I walked slowly in front of him. "Do you really think I'm just gonna run out the minute this is over? What kind of man do you think I am?"

"A good one. You'll want to go home. You have a job, an apartment, your parents, and a woman your mom would love you to marry. There's a lot there for you."

His laugh bounced off the trees and seemed louder in the solitude of the forest. "Yes, my life to this point his there though I'd point out that my mother can marry Ashley if she loves her so much because I won't. But Alyssum." He yanked me to a stop and moved in front of me so that I'd look up at him. "You're here," he said. "I'm not saying I won't go home at some point. It's something we"—he gestured between the two of us—"need to figure out. I love you, Alyssum. I can't just ditch you. And I promise you that I'm fairly certain my future wife isn't in Putnam Valley."

My heart thudded against my chest. Was that him saying he'd thought about marrying me? Considered it? I wanted that to be true.

"Maybe in New York City then? Is that where you'll find her?"

Jensen snorted and wrapped his arms around me,

holding me tightly to his chest, and kissed the top of my head. "Not a chance."

It wasn't long before we hit the outskirts of Phoenix and started to feel the race of goosebumps up our arms and over our bodies. I reminded Jensen that we had to keep our distance because as much as we could feel them, they could feel us, too.

We climbed a little higher on the hill to overlook central Phoenix and the Gobel headquarters. Aric had told us once that if we ever wanted to observe his people, this was where we should do it from. We'd be far enough away that the Gobel below shouldn't be able to sense us, but we could still hear them.

Jensen and I watched a dozen or more Gobel training in hand-to-hand combat as if they'd get that close in battle. Okay, maybe I could be a little cocky, but I liked to think of myself as confident. We sat there for hours, until the sun started to set, watching their every move, listening to every word we could, and not talking to each other.

There were times I'd catch Jensen watching me and times I'd watch him when he wasn't looking. Maybe it was lame, but I liked looking at him and there was something very intimate about only being able to communicate with a look, wrinkle of the nose, or a smile. It also started a slow burn somewhere deep inside me. Those kinds of feelings needed to be repressed, given the fact that we were mere feet from our mortal enemy.

Once we were convinced that we'd gotten all the information there was to get, we headed back, dirty, sweaty, and stiff-muscled from being in the same position most of the day.

As we got closer to my room, I stretched, elongating my body as far as it would go, and rubbed the back of my neck.

"I'm going to hop in the shower before I do anything else. I think there might be a full lawn's worth of grass in my hair."

"Sounds good to me," Jensen said, acting as if he were going to follow me into my room.

"That would be nice." I pushed against his chest. "But my dad is roaming around, so…"

"Fine, fine."

Laughing, I watched him walk, shoulders slumped as if someone had just killed his dog, showing his dislike of showering alone. When I could no longer see him, I headed in. The water felt good running down my body, washing away all the dirt and sweat. With only a towel wrapped around my body, I headed into my room for some clothes.

"Jesus Christ." My body jolted hard.

"Nope, just me." Jensen smiled as he lay comfortably on my bed.

"You scared the hell out of me."

"Sorry, I like to see you mostly naked, so I couldn't resist." A coy smile played with his lips.

"Ha ha. I have to get dressed. We need to go see my dad."

He didn't budge, but his eyes followed my every move as I pulled out a comfy pair of jeans, a T-shirt, bra, and fresh panties and took them to the bathroom.

"You're mean," he called in with a playful tone. He waited long enough to hear the sound of my blow dryer to come in and take a seat on the edge of the tub. Obviously, the earlier outing had the same effect on him that it had on me.

After I'd tied my sneakers tightly, Jensen and I left my room. We'd just made the turn toward the stairs when we heard voices. We couldn't make out what they were saying. When I tried to charge ahead, Jensen pulled me back. Before we could make our move, Aric came bounding up the stairs.

"Hey," I said once he'd seen us. "What's going on down there?"

"Brought someone to your dad," Aric said casually. I couldn't imagine what he was talking about.

"Who?"

Something about him looked off. I couldn't put my finger on it right away, but I knew him well enough to know when there was something going on. He sighed, struggling with the words. "Got a message from Kale earlier. It wasn't my family, Alyssum."

I knew he was talking about my mom. Her death had weighed on his mind a lot like it did mine. Maybe it was because he was my best friend or because he'd found me down there on the floor, covered in her blood, unable to tear myself away from her body.

"I didn't think it would be." Not when I was in a rational mind at least.

"But Kale did some digging and found out it was a guy named Wes. So I went and got him."

My eyes started to fill. I felt consumed by anger, though a small part of me felt fear. Jensen wrapped his arms around me and pulled me into his chest.

"He's... here." Ice traveled through my veins and my whole body started to vibrate.

"Yes," said Aric, as if reading my mind. "But don't worry about it. He can't hurt anyone anymore."

That was what was off in Aric's eyes. It took a full sixty seconds for his meaning to sink in. After wiggling loose from Jensen's embraced, I jumped into Aric's arms, surprising him, but he grabbed me just the same.

"Thank you," I whispered, hoping that he'd get all that I wasn't saying.

He held on to me and he breath skittered across my neck as he buried his face in my hair. I didn't have time or the desire at that moment to remind myself that Jensen was standing right there, watching our exchange.

There was no way Jensen could mistake this for anything more than it was. Gratitude.

Once Aric had put me back down, he said, "It wasn't right. That was murder, not war, and he had to answer for it."

Jensen leaned against the wall, waiting for our moment to pass.

"But you can't—" My heart was breaking for him. The magnitude of what he'd done for me was overwhelming.

"I know," he whispered.

Our eyes locked and a couple of the tears that had filled my eyes escaped, running down my cheek. Aric wiped them away quickly with his thumb before remembering that Jensen was there. He snapped his hand back and shoved it in a pocket.

"Right, um, Ash wanted me back as soon as possible. I just had to tell you first." Then he stalked away, leaving me speechless.

"So, what was that about?" Jensen asked once Aric was out of earshot.

"Aric killed the person who murdered my mother."

"I got that part."

Blinking several times on my way back to him, I took a deep breath to clear my thoughts and calm my nerves. "He can't go home again."

His eyebrows slammed down. "What do you mean?"

"He can't go home again, Jensen," I said, a bit louder than I'd meant to. "It was iffy before. Right now, if he were caught, they'd try him for treason and their punishment is harsh, trust me. But now... he was a murdering traitor and he'd be put to death for sure. He can't go home. Ever."

Chapter Twenty-Eight

ONLY ALLOWING ourselves a couple of minutes to let Aric's situation ruminate, Jensen and I headed off to my dad, whom we found in the office. Large and imposing, he stared out the window. His girth almost spanned the entire frame. While I noticed he was staring in the direction of Mom's grave, I didn't mention it. The office looked different, smelled different even than it had throughout my childhood. The touches missing were hers and its absence made me miss her even more.

"Dad."

He jumped at the sound of my voice. "Ah, right." He sounded distracted. "What's the word on the Gobel?"

Dad made his way across the room to his chair.

Back in official mode, any memories that had been in his head a minute before were now gone.

"Not much, actually." Jensen took one of the chairs on the other side of the desk. He looked very comfortable, like he completely fit in. "We were out there most of the day and nothing seemed unusual." He paused. "Then again, I guess I wouldn't know if something was out of place."

They both looked at me expectantly.

"Yeah, everything looked normal. Just a bunch of training, hand to hand—"

"That's different. Gobel don't usually like to get up close and personal."

I sat in the other open chair. "I know, right? But I didn't pick up any humans or anything unusual. Although from what we overheard, I think an attack may be coming soon." Waiting for his response, I contemplated what else I wanted to tell him.

"Well, we're ready. Right, Jensen?" Dad asked.

Jensen nodded.

"Dad, we heard something about Aric while we were there. Let's just say he doesn't have many sympathizers for fraternizing with us. And now..."

"He's a good man," he said. I'd known that already, so it didn't allay any of my fears. "And he's proven himself as a friend of the Gremalian people, so Aric will always have a home here."

I wondered if "here" meant here, as in our house, or if he just meant among our people. I wasn't going to ask right then. Maybe when I got my dad alone.

"That should make Dahlia quite happy," my dad added.

Yup, it would and now I knew that Dad felt, no matter what, my place was with Jensen, which was fine by me, but that little part of me that didn't like following the rules resented the implication that I needed permission to be there. However, part of what I'd learned since I'd left Delaware to find Jensen was that sometimes you had to pick your battles so I let it go.

"Hey, where is she anyway?" I asked about Dahlia. "I haven't seen her around."

"She and her mom left for Chicago."

"Oh, right." I shrugged. She'd told me that and had even offered to take me along.

"They went to Chicago *now*?" Jensen asked.

"Her parents wanted her and Blossom out of town when the shit hits the fan," I said. I smiled at Dad's disapproving look. "That way, she'll be safe. I wouldn't know what that's like."

Dad cared a lot about my safety. He'd said mom

and I were the reason he did anything, but his idea of keeping someone protected meant keeping them close, not sending them away.

"As if I could send you away, Alyssum. You two weren't raised the same. Those who can fight do. Those who can't go shopping."

The three of us laughed. Even with his more limited exposure to Dahlia, Jensen knew enough how coddled and sheltered Dahlia was from all of this.

Then Dad added, "Besides, the last time I tried to keep you safe, you ran off on your own hundreds of miles away."

"True, but it was for a good cause." He was talking about New York and even he couldn't argue that was a bad idea now.

We decided we had to go on the offensive, that it was time to take the war by the collar and show the Gobel what we're made of. My dad put the call out, kind of an alarm of sorts, that we were all to be in the meeting room in two hours.

Our meeting room, where we held town meetings, aired grievances publicly, and had trials, was connected to the east side of the house, like a large reception hall. Soon, the room would be filled, standing-room-only, with Dad, his advisors, and now

Jensen sitting at a table that stretched almost the width of the room. There was a sound system with speakers in front of each of their seats so everyone could hear and another tall mic between two sections of chairs for anyone who needed to be heard.

My chair was in the front row, where I'd always sat with my mom. It would be the first time I'd attended one of these without her. It made me sad. One of the other members' wives would occupy the seat next to me now. Jensen and I walked, hands clinging together, slowly toward the room. At the end of the hall, Dad and his Assembly waited, talking quietly until everyone else had gotten seated.

"Well, this is it, huh?" Jensen said before letting me go in.

"Guess so. Some people are going to be pissed."

"I trust your dad."

"Me too." I wrapped my hand around the back of his neck and pulled him down to me so that I could give him a kiss. I didn't care that some of the more conservative assemblymen *tsked* at the public display. I only wanted Jensen to know I was behind him no matter what happened.

Jensen walked away and I took my usual seat and bent my legs into a pretzel. One of my knees shook nervously as I glanced around, taking a mental attendance. Security was in their place along the side-walls, ready to step in if things got out of hand. The rest of the chairs were full, with others squeezing in wherever there was room. The meeting quickly became a "standing room only" situation.

We Gremalians sure were a loyal bunch. Not one person able to fight for our people wanted to be left out.

Then they came in. Even the old guys looked strong and determined as The Assembly took their seats—Dad right in the middle, his second-in-command to his right, Jensen to his left. Jensen found me right away and gave a little smile.

"It has been decided," Dad started once everyone had quieted. "We will embark on an offensive battle plan. We can no longer sit and wait to be attacked. Given the latest intel, I do not feel it's prudent to only act in defense." That was Dad taking the blame in case anything went wrong.

A small pocket of the audience erupted. Dad let them. It was their opportunity to get some of their frustration out. Within seconds, a spokesman for that group, the second borough, stood in front of the microphone.

"We will support you, Ash," Skye Parker began. He was around thirty years old and looked like he could be a model with his perfectly coiffed hair and sparkling blue eyes. Not my type and too old but he was a good fighter. "You've never led us wrong. However, we would prefer waiting it out. The Gobel have threatened before and not acted. We can't be sure they will this time. Is it really worth the lives of our people?"

He turned back to his group to be slapped on the back for having the guts to speak up. *Really, people*, I thought, *you say the same thing every time. "Let's wait"* wasn't going to work anymore. I didn't understand how Skye couldn't see the fact that the Gobel had already acted. There had been several breaches and my freaking mother was dead. What more did they need?

"I understand that concern, Skye." Dad took a deep breath before continuing. "I know that some of us may not come back and I do urge you to secure your wives and children."

He paused again and I watched as he chose his next words precisely before saying them. Only a few women ever participated in defense or security, mostly because they had small children to care for, and if their husbands were lost in battle, those kids needed someone to be there.

That was when I finally saw Aric. He leaned

against the wall in the corner by the door. Most of the time when Aric wasn't with Jensen and me, he was with his brothers. They were being kept away from the rest of us and I assumed, Aric was making sure they were up to speed on their training. But there was only one Gobel allowed in the room. Our eyes locked for what seemed like a long time.

He and I had failed to stop the war.

"My own daughter will be with us and, as a father, that makes me proud. As a father, it puts a fear inside of me that I've never known before."

The silence of the room was deafening. It wasn't their leader talking and he never let them see anyone but their leader. He cleared his throat.

"We will be outside, ready to go at four tomorrow morning. Those of you who do not wish to stand with us don't have to. But be sure, however many or few of us there are, we will do everything we can to ensure the safety of our people."

With that, he stood and left the room. The others followed suit.

It was seven in the evening. We had nine hours before we started a war.

Chapter Twenty-Nine

It was like I was in high school, waiting in the hall outside of class for a boy I liked. I'd only done that once or twice with Sage. Even when we'd been dating, I hadn't been so attached that I'd have gone out of my way to see him, yet there I was, my back against the wall, waiting for Dad to let my boyfriend go.

The meeting room cleared out. I was alone and couldn't help laughing at myself a little. Just months before, I'd wanted nothing more than to fight the Gobel, show them we weren't backing down against their perceived infringement on our community. But that was before Jensen. Before my mom had died. Before I'd become best friends with a Gobel who'd given up his family and his ability to ever go home, for me. Even with Jensen's and my "superpower," I knew that all could be lost. Now I just wished peaceful negotiation would have worked.

Thinking about all that and more, I slid to the floor and brought my knees up to lay my head on top. Someone dropped beside me. Jensen nudged my shoulder with his, like I hadn't already known he was there.

"Hungry?" he asked softly. I shrugged. "Why don't I go get us something and we'll meet in your room?"

I nodded quickly before he kissed the top of my head and left me alone again.

A while later, he came in without knocking, carrying a pizza with Aric right behind him.

I smiled widely. The three of us sitting on my bed, TV on, munching on pizza like we'd done before all of this was the best way I could've thought to spend the night.

But Aric was preoccupied with his phone.

"Dahlia?" I asked as I nudge Aric with my toes after he'd sent yet another text. He nodded. "Aww," I teased.

"It's not like that."

"Then how is it?"

"I don't know. We hang out. Even now, all she talks about is shopping." He shook his head.

"She doesn't know much about what's going on," I explained. He knew that, yet I felt like I had to say it, to defend her in some way. We all fell silent. "My dad will keep his word, you know." Aric's eyebrows shot up. "About having a place for you here."

"I know," he answered, barely above a whisper.

"But can I ask you something?"

He nodded.

"When we met, you were set on stopping the war. I mean, you even converted me. But now it's happening and a lot your family is on the other side."

"So, what's the question?"

"You know the question."

Jensen cleared his throat, which made me glance over at him. He used his eyes to plead with me to shut up. I didn't listen.

"You want to know why I'm going to stay and fight against my family?" he asked, which was exactly what I wanted to know. I nodded. "Alyssum, I don't know. I don't know how it's going to be if I come face to face with one of my siblings or my dad. Kale's sneaking back there tonight to get some things that could help and then we have Laken and Stone already here but... I just don't know. All I can do is hope it doesn't happen."

The pizza started to sit in my stomach like a brick. I tossed the half piece I held back into the box. Aric did the same and I noticed Jensen had already finished. He shifted his weight on the bed uncomfortably.

"Well, I'm going to bed," I said. "Need my beauty rest for tomorrow."

There were still so many questions left but they weren't getting answered tonight.

With that, Aric left the room and I shut the box of pizza and placed it on the table by the window. When I turned back around, Jensen was pulling my sheets back. He sat down and removed his shoes. After he'd yanked off his shirt and started unbuttoning his jeans, he looked up to see my questioning face.

"What?" he asked.

"What're you doing?"

"Undressing." He smirked.

"I can clearly see that, but you don't usually sleep in here in case my dad comes in. Unless something tragic happened, that is. And I think we should both be well rested for the morning."

"I told your dad I'm staying with you tonight."

"What?"

He came around the bed, jeans undone and hanging sexily low on his hips. "I always want you, but tonight I want to stay with you. We don't know what tomorrow's going to bring and I don't want to leave tonight. I told your dad because I didn't want him to be surprised if he came up here."

"And he didn't care?"

"It's like those first nights after your mom. He seemed kind of relieved, like knowing you're taken care of means he can do what he needs to."

When he looked at me, I was trying to picture the conversation between him and my dad, so the look on my face may have been less-than-inviting.

"Um..." Jensen started refastening his pants. "Unless, of course, you don't want me to stay."

"What?" I shouted loud enough to startle both him and me. "I do. Of course I do."

"Then let's go to bed."

We climbed into bed and hit the off button on the TV remote. We snuggled together and my body relaxed right away. One day, I'd have to figure out what that was all about, but not that day. I needed all the sleep I could get.

. . .

The alarm buzzed early, so early that all I wanted to do was slam the damn thing against the wall, roll over, curl my body around Jensen's, and go back to sleep. But that wasn't in the cards. We had one hour to get dressed, eat—it was completely important not to have a case of low blood sugar going into battle—and be on the other side of the meeting room.

Jensen and I dressed in silence. Jeans, a T-shirt, and a hoodie, since it'd be chilly that early in the morning. We both put on hiking boots. The last thing to do was pull my hair back into a braid so it couldn't block my line of sight.

Just as we were about to leave my room and head to the kitchen, there was a light knock on the door. Jensen opened it to find Aric, also dressed, and three of us headed downstairs. We sat in the kitchen, eating eggs and bacon and my dad joined us. I couldn't think of anything to say. No one else could, either, I guess. We spent a painful ten minutes just listening to the sound of each other's chewing.

"Alyssum." Official Ash called me back as we started toward the meeting room. The guys kept going to give Dad a moment alone with me. "I know you, but I'm asking that you hang back as much as possible."

"Yeah, right, Dad." I rolled my eyes without meaning to.

"I'm serious. The only reason I'm letting you go is the power you and Jensen have together. Otherwise, stay back and let us handle things. I couldn't take it if... " He swallowed hard. "I'm asking, not telling. As your father."

Emotion annoyingly formed with the lump in my throat, but I pushed all that down to nod. "I'll do my best," I answered, and really, that was all I could promise.

Jenson stood in the foyer, staring out the window.

"Ready?" I asked him. He nodded. "You've trained really well, better than anyone I've seen in a long time, so you'll do fine." He nodded slowly. "And our super badass wonder twin power doesn't hurt."

I wanted to give him one last kiss, for luck, for reassurance, for goodbye in case something happened to one of us, but Sage burst through the front door before I had the chance.

"Everybody needs to get out here." His voice was breathless, like he'd been running miles.

"What happened?" I asked, running the short distance to him.

"They found out we were coming to Phoenix today. I don't know how. The Gobel have attacked first."

My eyes just about jumped out of my head, then Jensen and I were on the move.

Chapter Thirty

Outside, we found Kale and Aric getting into an SUV with Dad and several others. They tore out, throwing gravel in their wake. We ran until the forest came into view. It was dark, but with the full moon and lighting sky, I could see the mayhem. It was a true battle—fists flying, electricity being wielded like a sword. Tree roots shot out of the ground into some of our people like the tentacles of an octopus.

We hadn't wanted this fight to be in Delaware. It had been the best way to keep those of us who weren't fighting, safe.

"Fuck," Jensen muttered under his breath before taking off running.

It was too much to take in all at once, so I focused on one thing at a time. Sage was being overtaken. I ran to him, throwing sparks as quickly as I could pick up the energy. It was enough to distract the Gobel man. Sage threw an uppercut. The guy fell.

I hit another two with higher wattage. They didn't get back up. I kept going until a tree branch hit me in the back. Dull pain radiated down my legs as I hit the ground like a sack of potatoes.

It took too much effort to try to get back up.

While I ignored the pain, Dad, Aric, and Kale were calling out to me and running for me on the other side. It was nature versus nature. I pushed up, found my footing and continued into battle.

I tried to find Laken and Stone, but it was still too dark. We had electricity. They had the entire freaking forest. A strong hand grabbed my arm, yanking me back to my feet.

"You okay?" Aric's eyes went everywhere but mine.

"I think so."

He pulled me close, then we were off to help the others.

As I fought, both with my body and my power, I kept an eye out for Jensen. If we had stayed together, we could've ended it before it had begun. Our power together only worked against the Gobel. We didn't know the range, but any would have been better than none.

I slipped into autopilot, hitting anything that got close. Finally, I got a glimpse of Jensen about a football field away. I had to get to him.

The beast appeared in front of me. Aric's sister, the one I'd had a run-in with before, slammed into me, hard enough that I hit a tree trunk and fell to the ground. She pulled me back up before I could shake it off. She knew what she was doing too, because her meat hooks wrapped around my wrists immediately, making it impossible for me to pick up electricity.

"What did you do to me?" She hissed. I didn't answer. "You know what I'm talking about. You took everything from me. How did you do that?"

"I... don't... "

She squeezed harder, making my eyes water and the pressure on my wrists threatening to snap the bones. Just then, a large branch grew behind her and came down on her head. Her eyes bugged and her breath caught. She dropped my hands and fell into a heap on the ground. I looked from her to Aric as I struggled to get going.

Forcing my legs to move, I climbed over her and through some brush until I could get over to Jensen. The minute his hand grabbed mine, the energy coursed through us both, almost until I couldn't take it anymore. The Gobel around us fell like Aric had when we'd practiced on him. We knew they'd recover as soon as we disconnected, but the longer we held them under, the longer it would take for them to recover. We moved as one through the crowds, dropping the Gobel as only we could.

"Let them go." Elliot, the Gobel leader, made his way toward us with his hand outstretched. Dad was there in an instant.

Elliot matched my father in size only he hand long brown hair that was pulled back into a ponytail, a style Dad would never choose. His eyes were dark, disturbingly dark.

"Stay back," Official Ash's voice boomed. The sun started to rise, making me realize how long we'd been out there.

"How are you standing? Why aren't you on the ground with the rest of them?" I asked myself more than anyone else. I was incredibly confused.

Elliot's beady, black eyes focused on me. "We all have secrets, Alyssum."

Stunned that he'd used my name, I watched Aric behind him trying to break through our power. I felt terrible. When I'd grabbed Jensen's hand, I hadn't even thought about the fact that Aric would be going down with the rest of his people and I knew just how much he hated this feeling. But we couldn't stop, not yet. Dad called for all the Gremalians to gather together, then told me to get back to the house.

I wanted to protest. No matter what, whatever peace was negotiated, we couldn't risk Jensen and I being in the same place once we'd broke the hold we had on the Gobel. They'd be angry like Aric was when it had first happened and some would likely lash out. I thought he was just trying to protect me but this time, I followed orders.

Waiting in my father's office, which faced the clearing where the fight happened, was horrible. I hated being able to see Dad and Elliot but not hear what they were saying. Their arms flailed, big gestures that showed they really meant whatever they were saying. Dad got close to grabbing Elliot by the throat and then the Gobel started backing away. They were leaving but we had so much more to do.

First, we needed to find the casualties. Any from their side, would be returned to them as had been the way since the first Gremalian.

With things dying down, my back and cheek suddenly felt like they were on fire and my muscles stiffened. I touched my cheek softly and came back with a little blood then hurried over to the mirror on the way. There were some scrapes and some bruising but it didn't look too serious.

Time to find out the terms of the truce. I hauled ass out of the office and down the hall to the foyer just as Dad, Jensen, Sage, Kale, Laken, Stone, and a few others came through the door.

"Is everybody okay?" I got to Jensen first and saw a few nicks and scratches. Otherwise, he seemed fine. His thumb gently caressed whatever scratch was on my cheek. "It's fine," I said, continuing to ignore the pain in my back.

"Where's Aric?" I asked. Nobody answered. I yanked the door open, running out onto the porch, but he wasn't there, either. The area was too quiet.

"Where is he?" I asked louder. When no one offered an explanation, I put it together myself. There was only one reason I could think of that would make Kale look ashen and ready to puke while Laken already looked like he'd been crying.

Without thinking, I took off back out the door and toward the woods. I'd run all the way to Phoenix if I had to. I wanted revenge for the death of my friend. Since Jensen had run out right after me, I didn't get too far before he caught my arm, yanking me back. Physically, he was stronger, so when he started to move, I did too. Even dragging my heels against the dirt did nothing against his bigger body and better muscles.

"What are you doing?" I screamed. As I twisted to try to get away, I stumbled, but he never let go. I did succeed in causing a couple of friction burns on my arms from his grasp.

"Stop fighting me," Jensen spat, squeezing my arm even harder. I thought if I stopped, he'd let me go, so I did. I stopped everything, put my feet flat on the ground, and even took a couple of regular steps. When he knew I was cooperating, he released his hold on me. "He isn't dead," he yelled bringing me to a stop. "He isn't dead but they took him back with them."

Relief over the fact that Aric was alive washed over me and if he was alive, then I wasn't too late. Sweet relief washed over me. If Aric was alive, then I wasn't too late. Jensen and I, along with Aric's brothers, could leave right away to intercept Aric and bring him back. I didn't say any of this to Jensen until we were inside the foyer with the battle-weary others.

"What's going on? They've got Aric. Why are we not going after him?" I demanded. No way would I have left that battleground and let them take Aric away.

"It was the only option they'd agree to." Dad wouldn't look me in the eyes.

"He went willingly." Kale barely got the words out and Laken turned away to hide tears.

"What the hell does that mean?"

"He went to save us." Kale swept his hand toward his brothers. "I told him we'd all go, but he insisted."

"Why was he so important?"

"Because they know about Wes, on top of working with you guys and what they called 'brainwashing us' into this. Apparently, we're not really welcome back, either."

"So let's go get him."

"We need a plan first." Jensen sounded calmer than I felt he should have.

"A plan? The plan is to go get our friend back—now." We didn't have time to fuck around. We needed to act.

"Alyssum—"

"No, Jensen." Anger grew out of fear of what would happen to Aric. "They'll kill him. You know that," I yelled, my voice bouncing off the walls, bringing everyone's attention to us.

"We can't go half-cocked. We're not doing that. We need to think this through," he yelled back, the vein in his neck popping out. His anger was directed to the wrong place. It should've have been me he was yelling at.

"Half-cocked? I'd say you're fully cocked right now."

His face tensing in anger said I was pushing all the right buttons… or all the wrong ones.

"He'll be dead before you and my dad get around to a decision. I'm going and you"—my finger hit his chest—"should come with me. If this were reversed and it was you who had been taken, I'd have to run after *him* to catch up. He wouldn't be standing here arguing."

Taking a breath, I decided to come at him another way. I was going, no question, but I would prefer to have some backup. "Jensen, he's our friend." The gentleness in my voice worked on him, at least a little because his face softened, as did his voice. "Come with me."

"We aren't going today." He pushed the point home as if he thought I'd just fall in line.

My jaw clenched. "Don't tell me what I am or am not going to do. You're not my father. You're not my leader. I'm going and you should be, too!"

His face remained hard and his jaw tightened more. His decision was made, as was mine. I'd crossed his line in the sand, though I'd never thought we'd be standing on opposite sides.

Taking several steps away from him, ignoring Dad's words, I let the venom loose from my mouth. "You're not coming? I guess you're not the man I thought you were." His eyes drilled into me harder, finding their way to my core. "If this is some leftover jealousy, don't worry about it. I'm done."

Anger exploded over his face. I didn't care about that. It was the hurt behind it that almost made me compromise. *Screw that.* Turning on my heel, I blew through the door. It slammed behind me and shattered the frame.

Walking out, two sets of feet closed in behind me. Kale and Stone followed me to the car. We climbed in and started it. Without hesitating, I sped out into the burgeoning summer day to get my best friend back.

I'd have help: brothers who would give their lives for Aric, brothers who didn't think twice about coming with me.

The three of us just had to get there before they killed him.

Right after Book

Thank you for reading the first book in The Empowered Series.

The war is coming!
If you would like to see more from Alyssum and Jensen stay tuned for **The Goblin War** and what I have in store for you. I hope you're ready to see what happens next. **PREORDER NOW!**

War is coming.

There's no stopping the war between the Gremlins and Goblins but Alyssum's first priority is getting her best friend back after his people took him as a traitor.

Unfortunately, the prodigal son and current ex-boyfriend, Jensen Burkhardt, isn't there with her. All of his words swearing to protect her apparently didn't mean a thing.

She'll deal with all of that later. For now, it's get Aric back or die trying.

Preorder The Goblin Prince now!

Do you love rock stars?

FOREVER GRAYSON

Forever 18 Book 1

One night changed everything.

One night with Lilah three years ago and I can't stop thinking about her. I didn't even know her last name. I've enjoyed the constant women on the road but not one of them made a mark like she did. She'd wanted me when I was nobody and now, women only want me because I'm somebody.

When our stylist quits right before we're about to head out on tour, our manager hires a new one.

Magically, Lilah walks back into my life.

Except she wants to keep things professional while all I can think about it getting her naked again.

Until I see something that I can't unsee and I know she's been lying to me for three years.
This lie could cost her everything but for me, it could change my life.

Get Forever Grayson now!

Love your rock stars? Check out...

Daisy

Pushing Daisies Book 1

Daisy's too young for Lawson. But that's not going to stop her.

Being in a band with my brothers isn't always easy but we just got our big break. Somehow, our manager snagged us the opening spot for Courting Chaos. Even with having to live on a bus for months with my four brothers, this is an opportunity of a lifetime.

Their manager, Lawson, is stupid hot but after witnessing me in an embarrassing situation, I know there's no hope of anything between us.

Grab Daisy today!

Still want more?

Cross

Courting Chaos Book 1

A sexy drummer and a rock god's daughter…what could possibly go wrong?

All I want is to spend a nice summer with my rock
star father.

But then some random guy assumes I'm a groupie
and tries to kick me out of the venue.

That's never happened before. Imagine my surprise

when I find out that the random guy is actually Cross Rhodes, the smoking hot drummer for Courting Chaos, Dad's opener.
I don't fall for rock stars—ever. Yet Cross quickly has me wanting to break *all* the rules.

Grab Cross Today!

THE HARBOR POINT SERIES

A new adult contemporary romance series

Meet Gio and Sal.

Two damaged men who meet the woman who can
set them right.

Then there's Cash.

He's not damaged but he's ready to do the healing
when he meets Gemma.

Check out the Harbor Point Series today!

THE FALLOUT SERIES

A new adult romance series

Coming home is hard.
Finding out the boy you loved had a baby with your
former best friend... heartbreaking.

Check out The Fallout Series today!

GAMBLING ON LOVE

A new adult romance series

Desperate times call for desperate measures so Flannery Tate is selling her virginity.

Check out Gambling on Love today!

I you'd like to just keep up with my sales and new releases, you can follow me on BookBub!

Bookbub: https://www.bookbub.com/authors/heather-young-nichols

About the Author

Heather Young-Nichols is a USA Today Bestselling author of contemporary and paranormal romance. A native of the great and often very cold state of Michigan, she is better known at home and to her friends as the Snarker-in-Chief. A job she excels at beyond anything she could have imagined. She loves many things, but especially cold coffee, hot books, and baseball. But not necessarily in that order.

Find Heather on Social Media or by visiting her website.

heatheryoungnichols.com

facebook.com/heatheryoungnicholsauthor
instagram.com/heatheryoungnichols
amazon.com/Heather-Young-Nichols/e/B00KKTM54A
bookbub.com/authors/heather-young-nichols
tiktok.com/@heatheryoungnichols

www.ingramcontent.com/pod-product-compliance
Lightning Source LLC
Chambersburg PA
CBHW030913300726

48970CB00001B/143